Instigati

Kiki Archer

Title: Instigations
ID: 21428134
ISBN: 978-0-244-63185-7

K.A Books *Publishers*

www.kikiarcherbooks.com

Twitter: @kikiarcherbooks

Published by K.A Books 2012

Copyright © 2012 Kiki Archer

Kiki Archer asserts the moral rights
to be identified as the author of this work.
All rights reserved.
Author photograph: **Ian France** www.ianfrance.com
ISBN: 978-0-244-63185-7

*For Angela King.
Thank you x*

Instigations.
The sequel to Kiki Archer's best-selling lesbian fiction novel
But She Is My Student.

CHAPTER ONE

There was a wail, a gasp, and a dramatic fall to the knees. Results day; and tensions were high. The students on the outer edges of the main school hall were silently waiting, wide eyed and nervous. The ones in the middle were squealing and shouting and gasping with joy. The ones making a quick exit out of the fire doors were cursing their own stupidity for failing to revise and believing they wouldn't be bothered when their awful results were finally confirmed.

Kat was sitting at one of the tables at the front of the school hall, flicking through her allocated box of remaining brown envelopes. She smiled as she found the name she had been searching for and gently lifted it into the trembling hands of her student. She gave the pale girl a reassuring nod and genuine wish of good luck - even though nothing at this point could change the results displayed on the shaking piece of paper. Kat watched as the girl hurried back to her small group of friends and peeped at her results. Initial trepidation quickly turning to brazen pride.

Kat smiled to herself. This was turning out to be a very rewarding day. A day where everyone's hard work was finally paying off. Teaching was Kat's lifetime vocation and she relished every moment of the job, viewing each challenge as a personal mission where nothing but the best would do. She didn't like to admit it, but she was universally liked and respected by the students at Coldfield Comprehensive School. She had even managed to win over the infamous cast of trouble makers who seemed to wreak havoc in all other lessons, but offered her their very best, if still slightly underwhelming, behaviour.

Kat glanced up from her table and saw one such troublemaker. A very sunburnt Chianne Granger was pushing her way past the older students. She looked like she had put on a good stone in weight since the end of the summer term and was thumping forwards in some tight wedge heels that made her feet look like trotters - coincidentally matching the rest of her piggy appearance.

Chianne arrived at the table with a huff and stuck out her big buck teeth. "Where was you last week, Miss Spicer?"

The smell of potent perfume hit Kat immediately, but she managed to mask her shock with a warm smile. "Hello Chianne, how are you? We're handing out the A-Level results today. Your GCSE results were last Tuesday." Kat always tried to be calm and kind no matter the situation.

Chianne blew an exaggerated puff of warm air up towards her solid black quiff and put her hands on her hips. It had cost her £1.20 for the bus over from the Peachell's Estate and she was going to get her money's worth. "Huh, you make it sound like I don't know nothing." She batted her eyes, looked at Kat, and tried to wink - something that was very difficult given the amount of mascara clogging up her tiny eyelashes. "Well, I do! One A star, seven As and a B. The A star was in history." Chianne puffed up and pouted.

Kat coughed unexpectedly and ran her fingers through her thick blonde hair. "Wow."

Chianne leaned over the desk, trying to put her cleavage on show. The fact that she was a 44 double A didn't seem to matter. "So you, Miss Spicer, have got *moi*, for A-Level history in September." She winked again and tried to jiggle her chest. Nothing moved. "I bet I've just made your wildest dreams come true! Me and you for two years." She sucked her teeth and glared at the table to the left, suddenly lowering her voice two octaves and addressing the other teacher. "You told me you were gunna ring her."

Janet Louza, the Head of History, piped up from the table next to Kat's. "Yes, sorry, Miss Spicer, I must have forgotten to mention Chianne's wonderful news when you phoned in about the GCSE results last week." She lowered her voice to a whisper. "I didn't want to spoil the last bit of your holiday abroad."

"I heard that," growled Chianne, slowly turning back around and putting her prettiest voice back on. "Anyway, see you in September, Spicer. Only two weeks to go." She winked again and gave a little wave of her fat fingers. "That's all I came in to say."

"Well thank you, Chianne. I'm honoured that you came in to tell me that piece of good news." Kat paused and fixed her blue eyes on the heavily dolled up student. "Seriously though, Chianne, you should be really proud of those results. Well done."

Chianne almost gave a genuine smile but instead she sucked her buck teeth and spun to leave, deliberately adding a wiggle to her bottom that was wobbling naturally on its own; Miss Spicer's crush was clearly as strong as ever and she was going to enjoy teasing her for the next two years.

Janet Louza jumped into the plastic seat next to Kat. Both watched in disbelief as Chianne clumped heavily out of the hall, offering insults to the Sixth Form students she passed. "Don't ask me how she did it, she was barely predicted a pass in most subjects!" Janet placed her hand on Kat's shoulder and offered a squeeze of encouragement. "I have faith that you'll work wonders with her." She believed it as well. Miss Katherine Spicer had been the best thing to ever happen to her failing history department at Coldfield Comprehensive. Kat was fiercely intelligent, always professional, and had managed to secure a one hundred percent pass rate for the classes she taught last year. This had, in turn, nudged Coldfield ahead of their rivals, John Taylor's.

The Head Teacher, Kirsty Spaulding, had called Janet in for a congratulatory meeting since history was now the top performing subject across the school. Both knew that this wasn't down to Janet and the same system she'd been following for the past twenty five years. The success was Kat's. It was Kat's belief that every single child who crossed her path would reach their potential, and they did. Most never even realised what their potential was until their favourite Miss Spicer opened their eyes wide enough to see it, and tuned their brains in deep enough to achieve it. She was great, and all at Coldfield knew it. All except the jealous English department women, that was.

Kat accepted Janet's prolonged look of earnest as her first challenge for the term ahead. Janet accepted Kat's look of slight worry as nothing more than shock. If anyone could turn the hulk of Chianne Granger into a mewing pussy cat, Miss Katherine Spicer could.

Kat sighed and shrugged her shoulders, turning back towards the large hall and the groups of students that had started to thin out. Her eyes were immediately drawn to Diane Pity and Fiona Mews who were walking through the glass double doors that were encrusted with the school's shield. They were heading from the staffroom, through the hall, and towards the open fire escape. Staff presence on results day was optional and they were the last pair Kat had expected to see giving up a day of their summer break to congratulate, or commiserate, the nervous Sixth Form students.

Kat watched as Kirsty Spaulding clattered through the glass doors, clapped her hands sharply, and wolf whistled at the pair of English teachers. Kirsty then waited with crossed arms for them to arrive in front of her. There was a wagging of fingers before she quick-marched both teachers towards her office. Kat wondered if the poor English results were top of the agenda.

"I read a good Joanna Trollop book on holiday actually," said Janet with her eyebrows raised, tracking their path.

"Don't be rude, Janet," laughed Kat, pleased that her old fashioned Head of Department was finally managing the odd joke here and there.

Janet shook her head, causing the ruffles on her high-necked shirt to flap. "Well look at them! I know it's not a school day, but what on earth do they look like?"

Kat had often thought that Fiona Mews looked like an air hostess from a low budget airline with her long black hair scraped back into a permanent plait, known to whip you if you stood too close when she turned. Diane on the other hand, could pass for a bleach blonde, low grade, Julia Roberts from any of the hooking scenes in Pretty Woman. Both had tried their hardest to intimidate her in her first year at Coldfield, using her sexuality as their main bit of fodder. They hadn't succeeded, and Kat only had one last hurdle to overcome - to disclose to her Head of Department the identity of her new girlfriend. Janet had tried so hard to be all 'new age' as she had put it, and support her protégé's lifestyle choice, but she didn't like to ask too many questions, or get too involved.

Janet still found it rather peculiar that a woman, especially one as naturally beautiful as Kat, could be attracted to another woman - 'I mean what goes where?' - she had asked after one too many sherries at the Christmas bash. Kat had tried to describe it as cuddling and Janet had appeared somewhat appeased and relieved, but both realised it was not a topic of conversation either would like to repeatedly frequent. So they maintained their acceptance, but ignored the details.

There was however, one detail that Janet did need to know. Kat checked that no students were approaching their table and began. "I've had such a wonderful summer and I've actually started to see someone new." She looked at Janet with sincerity. "I'm really happy."

Janet blushed immediately. "Oh, right."

Kat just had to go for it. She kept the eye contact. "Actually, you know her..."

The noise of Poppy Jones wailing in glee and flapping her freshly opened results sheets above her head filled the hall. "Three As!! Oxford, here I come!"

Kat paused as a lump caught in her throat. The morning really had been a mix of emotions for students and teachers alike. She watched as Poppy's mum and dad raced into the hall and proudly threw their arms around their daughter, disobeying her request for them to wait in the car. Kat focused her attention back on Janet, who was now fiddling with her necklace and starting to perspire. "Janet, my new girlfriend's Freya. Freya Elton."

"Ah yes, very good," came the quick response. The Head Teacher, Kirsty Spaulding, had already briefed Janet on the likely news and advised her on how best to react. Freya had been a pupil in the Upper Sixth last year and the star of Kat's history class; but the relationship only started once she had signed off from the school in July. The Head Teacher had told Janet that the relationship was all legal and above board and Janet, after her shock, had told herself that that was all she needed to know.

"Isn't it a bit odd?" Janet couldn't help herself.

"Which bit?" Kat was now equally as embarrassed as both were once again in the position with the other, discussing things they would rather not discuss.

"Well, the fact that she was your student." Janet ran her fingers through her curly grey cloud and tried to come to grips with it. "How are you equals?"

Kat really didn't want to get into this now, but needed Janet on board. She checked the hall once more. No one with a surname from D-G seemed to be approaching their desk. "It's only a three year age gap and most of our friends think she's the older one of us."

Janet paused, *our friends*, how peculiar for Kat and her ex-pupil to have *friends*. There was so much to this whole lesbianism thing that she would never understand, but she realised she had to be all 'equal opportunities' so decided to go with - "Thumbs up for girl power then!"

Kat wasn't sure which was more awkward, the thumbs up gesture, or the slight hug that followed. What she was pleased about though was the lack of importance it seemed to hold. Janet had acknowledged, questioned slightly, and then accepted with a strange hug and quick dash off to the ladies. What more could she ask for? Kat smiled to herself as she saw Janet passing through the double doors, and watched as another Sixth Former tore open their small brown envelope and collapsed to the floor in tears of joy.

Kat smiled. This had been the best summer of her life. She was head over heels in love and happier than she had ever been before. Freya was her world and today their future would be decided. Suddenly she felt the butterflies. Freya was approaching her desk. It still got her every time. The way her shoulder length chestnut hair would sway gently as she walked. The way her mischievous green eyes glistened with passion, and the way her pretty face lit up every time she smiled. Kat stood up, leaned over her desk and kissed Freya on the cheek. "Hello."

"I wasn't expecting that," whispered Freya, feeling her heart swell inside her chest. She realised that small gesture would have taken a lot for Kat, and in that instance loved her a little bit more.

"How else should I greet my girlfriend?" Kat whispered in return.

Freya smiled, mesmerised by the piercing blue eyes. She broke the connection and coughed in announcement. "Ahem, Freya Elton, please."

Kat flicked through the remaining small brown envelopes. Her desk had a large white sign on with the black letters D-G clearly displayed. Students had a three hour window to come in and claim their results. Some chose to open them there and then, others hid them away in deep pockets, waiting for their nerve to arrive, and the ones who didn't want the limelight had them posted to their home address instead. Freya already had her plan.

Kat held onto Freya's fingers as she passed the envelope over. "Here you go. Good luck." She didn't know who was more nervous.

Freya grinned cheekily. "See you at the sand dune in an hour?" *Freya's* sand dune had quickly become *their* sand dune, and was in fact nothing at all like a sand dune apart from its sunken appearance. It was a private hollow on Coldfield Park that Freya had found years ago and subsequently spent many an afternoon sheltered by its private nesting of heather and bracken, lying on the soft grass, revising, or sunbathing, or more recently, making love.

"Sounds great," said Kat, remembering their last outing.

The charged connection was abruptly broken by the noisy sound of cheap high heels steadily increasing in volume. The clipping stopped abruptly. "You two look like you've got the same suntan," sneered Diane Pity, sliding up closer to Freya's side.

"Yes definitely," flared Fiona Mews, trotting up to the desk and peering down through two large nostrils at Kat's brown arms.

Kat stood up and her elegant height instantly took away some of their power. "We have the same suntan because we've been away on the same holiday." Kat was never intentionally mean but she wanted to kill the conversation so added, "How were the English results?"

Diane ignored the question. "Together?"

"Yes, we went on holiday together." It was all very matter of fact and it felt good that she had nothing to hide. Their faces were a picture so she continued. "It was beautiful. We went to Sorrento. Sun, sea..." She was going to leave it there; there was getting your own back and there was childishness. "...staffroom calls, I need a drink." She nodded as she passed Janet who was making her way back to the table.

Freya watched as Kat walked confidently across the hall. She couldn't resist adding to Pity and Mews's horror. "...and so much sex it was beyond belief!"

Diane and Fiona simultaneously leaned against the desk for support and watched in disbelief as Freya almost skipped out of the open fire exit.

Kat stood still in the staffroom. She needed a moment to compose herself. Diane and Fiona still had it in them; the ability to intimidate and make her question herself. She pulled a small plastic cup from the dispenser, trying very hard not to crack it, as so often happened to the stressed out staff members just trying to get a drink from the temperamental water cooler. The plastic crinkled but didn't split, so she pressed the button on the gurgling machine, glancing around at the staffroom that would once again become her home in a couple of weeks. The room always seemed to have a musty feel to it, with odds and sods lying around for literally months on end, like the bicycle wheel she was now staring at. It had appeared last December and remained shoved between two of the low chairs in the geography department's area, even though none of them claimed to know anything about it. She looked back towards the door - yep, the discarded computer hard drive was still serving as a reliable door stop. She sipped her water slowly and looked up at the main notice board. Nothing had been updated and there were still posters advertising the staff end of term beer bus and the inter-form sports tournament that was inevitably rained off. She jumped at the sudden movement.

"Come here big girl," shouted the Head Teacher Kirsty Spaulding, shooting out from behind the pigeon holes and grabbing Kat tightly around the waist. Kirsty knocked the plastic cup onto the floor. "I told you that you'd do it!"

Kat bent down to pick up the cup but Kirsty pulled her up, shoving a small hip flask into her hand instead. "Here, have a swig of this. You deserve it! I hope I didn't scare you! I was just doing a routine bit of surveillance." She tapped her nose. "You know how I like to."

Kat nodded with a slight smile.

"Anyway, Katherine, your results have transformed this school. We are the top performers in the county for the very first time." She unscrewed the lid of her hip flask and tried once again to give it to Kat. "You have no idea what this means. I've been asked to conference on *leading edge schools*. I mean leading edge! John Taylor's have never been leading edge." She took a swig herself. "You, Missy, are a superb teacher!" She stood on tiptoes and reached up to squeeze Kat's cheeks. "Just keep it up, big girl." She turned to leave but shuffled back for one last hug. "And for your information, Miss Pity and Miss Mews are on their last warning. I know how dreadful they were to you last year and I have the Governors' full support that this school would be better off without them." She pushed her moon shaped glasses back up her nose. "But it is so hard to get rid of teachers, even the god damn awful ones like them."

Kat was about to reply, but Kirsty had turned once again to leave and was shuffling quickly out of the staffroom towards the hall; the hall where she had little idea of who any of the celebrating students actually were.

Kat breathed a sigh of relief as the staffroom door slammed shut. Kirsty was a fantastic Head, but completely cuckoo and every encounter she'd experienced with her had been unbelievably bizarre. Her support meant a lot though and Kat remembered the way Kirsty had instructed her to go and claim Freya on signing off day last term. Two months ago, she thought, *was that all?* It felt like she'd been with Freya for a lifetime. Kat smiled and reached back down for her cup, filling it once again with some much needed ice cold water. The summer had been hot and the staffroom was stuffy. She checked her watch and thought about Freya waiting patiently in the sand dune, wondering whether she would indeed be able to keep her word and refrain from opening the brown envelope until she arrived.

CHAPTER TWO

Freya lay on her back, basking in the warm afternoon sun. She had everything she'd ever wanted, and at eighteen thought that was pretty good going. She was with Kat, and that was all that mattered. She thought back to her behaviour last year and felt a deep sense of shame, just thankful that Kat had been so knowing and so right. Right in her course of action and knowing in her perception of events. Her insight making all of this now possible. Both were so glad that they'd waited.

The loud *OO-OO-OO* of a couple of swans flying overhead caused Freya to jump. She watched them descend slowly and knew they'd be making their way to the large Coldfield Lake, joining the families of moorhens and giggling couples in wooden boats trying desperately to row in a straight line. She rolled onto her front on the rug and pulled the brown envelope out of her pocket.

"I hope you weren't thinking of opening that, madam?" teased Kat, gently stepping down the grassy slope and lowering herself to straddle Freya on the red checkered rug. She rolled her over and kissed her with passion. They were still at the stage where every encounter was heated, raw, intense and impossible to stop. Neither could ever imagine it not being like this. Every inch of their being wanted the other, and they wanted it now.

Freya gasped in between the intense searching kisses. "You looked so sexy sitting behind that desk in the hall." She gasped again. "And when you kissed me on the cheek..." It was getting too much, Kat was so arousing, so consuming. "...I just wanted to pin you to the table." She moaned as Kat kissed deeper. "Take me, please. Take me now."

Kat loved the way Freya could be so demanding, so naughty, and so explicit in exactly what she wanted. She was the more experienced of the pair, but Freya was definitely the more adventurous. Kat continued to explore with her mouth but managed to whisper. "How about I tell you your results as I take you?" She could be naughty too if she wanted.

"Yes," moaned Freya as she felt her breasts being cupped under her white t-shirt and her nipples being stroked. The private nesting was secluded enough for neither to hesitate, worry, or think twice.

Kat pulled the loose v-neck down below Freya's breast and replaced her fingers with her mouth, using her hands to open the brown envelope, relying on touch to feel inside for the important piece of white paper. She gently bit Freya's nipple as she pulled out the paper and laid it on the ground, causing a groan of delight. "It's out, it's open and I can see it." She returned her hands to Freya's breasts and gently kissed her on the mouth, double checking once more the results that lay on the soft grass. She slowly undid the buttons on Freya's jeans and walked her fingers across the top of Freya's black pants that were already wet with desire. "In English, you got an..." She pulled the pants to one side and pushed two fingers deep inside.

"Ahhh!" shouted Freya in pleasure.

"Yes, that's right, you got an A." She smiled and teased Freya's earlobe with her teeth, gently moving her long fingers slowly in and out of the warm tight opening. "In biology, you got..." She quickly added a circular motion with her thumb to Freya's throbbing pulse.

"Ahhh!"

"Correct again, you got an A." She lifted up the loose white t-shirt exposing Freya's perfectly bronzed stomach and began to kiss down the smooth abs towards her belly button. "In general studies, you got..." She continued her journey and took Freya completely in her mouth.

"Ahhh, Kat, yes!"

"Mm hmm."

Freya moaned, she felt completely disorientated. "An A?"

"Mm hmm." Kat continued her rhythmic kissing and thrusting.

Freya was so close now it was excruciating. "History?" She gasped deeply. "What ... about ... history?"

Kat ignored the question and instead kissed so hard that her fingers were squeezed like never before in a massive tightening that in turn caused her to gasp out in surprise.

"Ahhhhhh!" Freya felt her body shake as the intense waves of pleasure took her to a place of deep satisfaction.

Kat rested her head on the quivering bronzed stomach and smiled. "You said it."

Freya hardly knew where she was, let alone the outcome of her history A-Level exam. "An A?" she managed.

"Yes an A. Four As." Kat pulled herself up to Freya's eye line and hugged her with such pride. "You got four As. I love you so much."

Freya threw her head back down onto the rug and took a long breath of satisfaction. "How incredible."

Kat immediately knew she wasn't talking about her magnificent exam results.

CHAPTER THREE

Jess and Lucy maintained their crouched position behind the large black kitchen table, mostly hidden by the draping red tablecloth. They watched as Kat and Freya entered the spacious apartment hand in hand. They were the sweetest, yet sexiest couple they both knew, and were thrilled with the way Freya had fitted in so easily. She was mature, smart, funny and loving, and it was the loving that mattered to them. Their very best friend had finally found her perfect partner, someone who adored her, just like they did.

Lucy jumped up first. *"Congratulations and celebrations, and du du du du du du du du du du durrrrrrrrrr.* Does anyone apart from Cliff Richard actually know the rest of the words?" She was giggly and overcome with excitement.

Jess was still not fully standing and used the table to haul herself and her bump the final distance. "Surprise. We laid on a buffet and wine to celebrate." She paused catching her breath. "We are celebrating, aren't we?"

Freya flicked her shoes onto the rack by the door and pulled the crumpled piece of white paper out of her jeans pocket. She dashed over the polished laminate floor and skidded to a stop in front of the extravagant buffet table. She lifted the sheet to their eye line.

Lucy stared open mouthed at the exemplary results. "Bloody hell!" She looked at Freya and then at Kat. "You two are a match made in heaven." She shook her blunt black fringe and peered even closer at the results. "I dread to think what your pillow talk's like. All quadratic equations I bet!"

Jess giggled and spanked Lucy's firm bottom. "Why on earth would it be all quadratic equations? Neither of them did Maths!" She reached out her arms and pushed out her bottom; she needed to create a space for a hug. "Come here, Freya. Those are incredible results. Well done."

"Boffs the pair of you!" joked Lucy, pulling Freya from Jess and lifting her up for a full bodied hug, forgetting just how powerful she was, then suddenly remembering when Freya let out a small '*ouch*.'

Kat had stayed in her position at the door, watching with pride as her two best friends showered the love of her life with deserving praise and congratulations. All three were glowing and she realised it was a mental snap shot that she would remember for a very long time. Jess, five months pregnant, excusably chubby, throwing her curly auburn hair back in laughter. Lucy, more muscular than ever from her well suited job as an aerobics instructor, giggling and shaking her fringe in mock outrage. And Freya ... Freya shining in the middle with her wide smile radiating and her green eyes twinkling. A small, unanticipated tear slid slowly down Kat's cheek.

Lucy hollered. "What are you doing standing by the door, you divvy? Come here!"

"Oh you have such a way with words," said Jess, reaching for her twelfth party sausage of the afternoon.

Lucy put her hands on her hips. "I know! Listen to this: Birdie birdie in the sky laid a turdie in my eye. If cows could fly I'd have a cow pie in my eye."

"What on earth are you talking about?" mumbled Jess in between bites.

"It's a limerick. My Auntie's got a book of them in her toilet. I read once that practicing limericks will tighten the muscles in your tongue. Hey you should practice them, Freya. I'm sure Kat would appreciate it!" She nudged Freya gently, sending her completely off balance. "You might have four As but I bet you don't know what an upper topper titty flopper stopper is?"

"A what?" spat Jess.

"An upper topper titty flopper stopper."

"A bra?" offered Freya, regaining her stance.

Lucy felt genuinely miffed, was there anything that Eagar Elton and Super Spicer didn't know? "Okay, what do you call a Japanese drummer boy whose father has diarrhoea?"

Kat joined the giggling group. "Lucy, you're priceless."

"You don't know do you?! Yes! You pair don't know!" She puffed up with pride, shook her black bobbed hair and announced: "A slap happy Jappy, with a crap happy pappy!"

Jess almost choked on her mouthful of peanuts and grapes. Her cravings had really opened her eyes to a whole new world of food choices. "I'm going to miss you, Lucy Lovett."

"It'll be Auntie Lucy soon, and please can we have one day that doesn't end up with emotional wailing?"

"Suits me fine," said Jess, already wiping a tear from her rosy plump cheek. She had one week left in the flat and was as devastated as she was excited. Her year to date had been a rollercoaster of emotions, but she was relieved to finally be starting the life that she had always dreamed of. Gary had sold his bachelor pad and her parents had helped them place a hefty deposit on one of the new starter homes near The Chase. It was only a forty minute drive and she realised the gang would still come and visit, but she knew deep down that their paths were separating, slowly growing apart. She sniffed back another tear.

"I know what you're thinking, and you're wrong," smiled Kat, enveloping Jess in a soft hug. "How many times do I need to tell you? You're not getting rid of us that easily."

Jess started to sob. "But you and Freya, and Lucy and Ben, are at such an exciting time in your lives with the parties and fun days out and holidays and..." She smiled and sniffed in a wet tear. "...great sex; and what will I be doing? Probably the ironing and moaning about my stretch marks, or the mortgage rates, and Gary won't want to touch me after little miss has popped out and widened my passage to the size of the channel tunnel." She giggled realising she was being ridiculous, but at the same time she knew she was in mourning; in mourning for the wonderful life that she had shared for the past few years with her very best friends.

Kat took both of Jess's slightly plump hands and spoke with passion. "What you'll have is a little baby girl who will grow up knowing she is the luckiest little lady in the world, blessed with a beautiful mummy like you."

Jess looked deep into her kind blue eyes. "Thank you, Kat."

Lucy shouted from the kitchen. "And you can always have surgery to tighten your foo foo!"

"My what?" giggled Jess, squeezing Kat's hands and returning to the buffet table.

Lucy wobbled back into the lounge and handed out the four glasses of sparkly. "Cheers girls!" She took a large gulp and looked at Jess. "Your foo foo. Why, what does Gary call it?" She turned to Kat and Freya who were now cuddled up on the black leather sofa in the modern, but cosy, lounge area. "I bet you two use all the correct terminology. Especially you and your A grade in biology." She teased Freya playfully. "What do they call it? A vagina-glorifica-clitoria or something?"

Jess swallowed a mini scotch egg and wiped the escaping breadcrumbs from her chin back up into her mouth. "Gary calls mine a kitty."

Lucy wailed with laughter. "Here kitty kitty kitty kitty. Does poor poor pussy need a stroke?!"

"I think it is just called a vagina." Freya was still getting used to Lucy's crazy sense of humour, but realised, as Kat had warned her, that she never meant any harm. She smiled at Kat. "We're still at that polite stage where we just say *'touch me here or kiss me there,'* aren't we Kat."

Kat reddened and took a gulp of the sweet tasting sparkly. "Alright! Those two are always saying I'm a bit of a prude. I don't want you thinking that too."

Freya thought back to all of the raunchy escapades they had got themselves into over the summer. "Trust me, I don't!" she laughed.

"SPILL!!!" squealed Lucy, already refilling her glass. She caught Kat's stare and dutifully changed the subject. "Actually before you do, there was one thing that I was wondering. Seeing as it's results day, does anyone know how…" She decided to mouth out the spelling of the name to soften the blow. "...how B." But then realised it made no difference. "...how Bea got on?"

Bea had been a fellow Sixth Former at Coldfield Comp and had tried her hardest to make Freya her own, and in some respects she had succeeded. She had suckered her in and they had become the school's popular lesbian power couple, even winning joint prom queen at the end of term. It had never been love though, and was in fact an emotionally controlling and embarrassing experience that Freya just wanted to bury. She spoke quietly. "She's moved to France with her family. Her mother has opened a permanent gallery somewhere in the Loire Valley and she's enrolled in the local college studying extended psychology."

Lucy coughed up some of the fizzy bubbles. "Appropriate then."

Kat hesitantly joined the conversation. "I heard she got straight As." She was relieved to have found out from Kirsty Spaulding that Bea's results were being posted to a foreign address and that she wouldn't be turning up at school to claim them; or trying to claim her ex-girlfriend as well. She reached for Freya's hand. No matter how hard she tried, she could never fully quash her own inbuilt insecurity and it was the one thing that infuriated her best friends.

Jess saw it in Kat's eyes. "Bea might be intelligent, but she's not a patch on you, Kat." She eyed her best friend's shoulder length blonde hair, stunningly beautiful features and awe inspiring figure, thinking once again how she would be more at home on the front cover of a top class fashion magazine, or on the red carpet at the Oscars receiving a prestigious award, not holed up in some bog standard comprehensive school in front of a load of whiney students. She caught Kat eye. "Not a patch."

"Look she was a psychotic bitch. We all know it." Lucy paused. "Sorry Freya."

"Don't apologise to me. I'm the one who should be apologising"

No one spoke.

"Right, end of conversation," said Kat, killing the awkward silence.

Freya gently squeezed Kat's knee. "Come on, it's nearly time for us to break the news to my parents."

Jess gave her glass of sparkly to Lucy, a sip had been plenty. "Your results?"

"Yes." Freya grinned and her green eyes twinkled cheekily. "And the big news."

"Bloody hell!" Lucy necked the glass. "You two are the bravest bitches I know!"

CHAPTER FOUR

Freya pulled her pale blue Clio onto the block paving drive and stared at the house. It was identical to the six others that curved around the neat little cul-de-sac. Tar flecked orange bricks, four pvc windows and a red door. Her parents placed great importance on the value of fitting in, even trying to ensure that their pot plants complimented the neighbours'. Neither had quite managed to get their heads around her - as they put it - desire to be different.

Freya noticed the missing Volvo. "They're not back yet." She stroked Kat's little finger with her own. "I did say four and we are slightly early."

Kat took the hand and kissed it gently. "You do realise you'll have driven them crazy by telling them they had to wait until now to hear their beloved, precious, only daughter's results."

"Yes, why do you think I did it?!" Freya made a backing off gesture with her right hand. "Patrick and Sue need to loosen their control."

Kat laughed. "You love them really."

"I know I do." She grinned cheekily. "But do you know what I'd love right now?"

"What?"

Freya smiled.

Kat raised her eyebrows. "In your car, on your drive? No way." She glanced out of the window. "Look! Mrs Smith's curtains just twitched!"

"Hmm, maybe Jess and Lucy were right. Maybe you are a bit of a prude." Freya knew that would do it.

Kat exaggerated a pout. "You really want me to go there?"

"Yes," said Freya with a straight face.

Kat composed herself. If Freya wanted raunchy then she could give her raunchy. She unclipped her seatbelt and slung it back over her shoulder, pushing her boobs out and reaching for Freya's upper thigh. "Right, you sexy little bitch. Take me inside and fuck me over your mother's kitchen counter."

Freya didn't know whether to laugh or run for her life. "I was only teasing."

Kat maintained her serious stare. "I'm not. I need to be fucked and I need it now."

Freya giggled nervously. The piercing blue eyes were actually a turn on, so she slid out of the car, ran around to Kat's side and dragged her by the hand to the red front door.

Kat leaned against the coarse bricked wall in the open porch way and teasingly opened the top button of her shirt. "I want you to be hard and fast."

Freya fumbled with her keys, eventually dropping them to the flecked carpet as the door swung open. "Come here." She kicked the door closed and pushed Kat against the floral wallpaper, kissing her roughly.

Kat broke it off, took Freya's hand and walked her past the numerous school photos of Freya through the ages, and into the kitchen. "I want you to fuck me from behind against this counter." She signalled to Sue Elton's prized worktop which no one was allowed to use in case they scratched the sparkling marble surface.

Freya was in a state of excited shock. "You never swear!"

"You insinuated I was a prude ... I'm just showing you I'm not. Now fuck me."

Freya gulped and stood behind her, slowly undoing her white shirt button by button, kissing her neck and exposing her black lace bra. She pulled down at the cups with both hands and Kat's large pert breasts popped forwards. She gently leaned her over and heard Kat gasp when her nipples brushed against the cold marble. Freya unzipped Kat's black trousers and kissed the curve of her back, pulling them down enough to enable her to slide her tongue between the cheeks of her firm bottom. She pulled Kat's legs apart and used both hands to reveal her target. Everything was exposed.

Kat rested her head on her hands which were flat on the marble surface, arms bent at the elbow. She felt so exposed and vulnerable, but yet so free and in control. She very rarely swore and had never in her whole life spoken dirty, but this was a thrill and the atmosphere was intense. She closed her eyes to avoid them being drawn to the trinkets scattered around Sue Elton's homely kitchen. There was a never ending display of ceramic signs that read statements such as *'Mum's kitchen. Heart of the home,'* or *'Dinner choices. 1 = Take it. 2 = Leave it.'* She suddenly felt Freya's tongue slowly slide down her back, through her cheeks, stopping just above her bottom. She realised that Freya didn't know where to go.

Kat couldn't resist it. "Just how rude do you want me to be?"

Freya grinned. "O.M.G! I love this side of you."

"Really?" said Kat, momentarily lifting her head from the marble surface.

"Yes! Now tell me what you want."

Kat teased. "Well, I think we should save *that* for another day." She returned her head to her arms and closed her eyes once more. "I want you to use your fingers to fuck my pussy."

"O.M. Bloody. G!" She stood up behind Kat, reached round for her breast and teased her nipple. "Say it again, but dirtier."

Kat smiled. "Screw my foo foo." Freya started to giggle, so Kat increased her volume. "Split my kitty, you bitch."

Freya was trying not to wet herself. "Be serious!"

"Me?!"

"Yes, you!" Freya composed herself and ran her two fingers between Kat's legs. "I'm going to fuck you hard and fast with my fingers."

The electric touch instantly took away Kat's laughter and she moaned with satisfaction. "Yes do it. Fuck me hard and fast."

Patrick and Sue Elton pulled into the drive and noticed that the red front door was slightly ajar. Patrick had been told to go and investigate while Sue protected the Volvo. What if the burglars had

Freya tied up and then proceeded to tie her and Patrick up and make off with the car. No, Sue had declared, it was best for Patrick to go and check. The fact that nothing as exciting as a stolen hanging basket had ever happened on the cul-de-sac in the past twenty five years had failed to quash Sue's fear of the dangers in this life.

Patrick opened the front door and gave an immediate thumbs up. Sue could be ridiculous at times but he knew it best to entertain her demanding behaviour.

Silly man hasn't even checked yet, thought Sue, seeing the signal and undoing her seatbelt.

The shout was loud and clear.

"Fuck my wet pussy, Freya. Fuck it. Harder. Yesssss! I want my pussy fucked hard and fast. That's it. Yes! Fuck my pussy."

Patrick dashed back towards his fast approaching wife. "Wait a minute, darling. Kat and Freya are just in the kitchen."

Sue bustled past him. "Great! I can't believe it's four o'clock and we still don't know how she got on. Utterly ridiculous telling us so late in the afternoon."

"Wait, Sue, wait."

Sue pushed the red door back open. "Freya? Freya sweetheart! Come on!" She bent to take off her shoes, reaching for her latest pair of warm slippers.

Freya lifted her head. "Oh shit. Quick." She shoved Kat by the bottom, sending her hopping, with her trousers around her ankles, towards the bathroom. She raced quickly to stall her parents in the hall.

"Freya, darling! Come here." Sue walked forwards and took Freya's hands. "So come on then!" She released her grip and wiped her fingers on her grey woollen skirt. "Your hands are wet. Have you been chopping the veg?"

Freya tried to hide her panic. "Something like that."

"Well you better not have been using my marble counter, young lady. I don't care how well you've got on!"

"She's only teasing," said Patrick, not quite able to look at his bright eyed daughter.

Sue bustled past Freya and peered into the kitchen. "Where's Katherine?"

"Mum, I've told you, it's Kat." She also peeped back around into the kitchen. "She must be in the bathroom. You two go and sit in the lounge and we'll bring in a tray of tea and I'll show you how I did."

"Oh for goodness sake, Freya. Just tell us."

"Not in the hall, Sue. Come on, let's do as she says. It is *her day* after all." Patrick raised his eyebrows and tried to gently remind his wife of their earlier conversation.

Freya ushered them into the pristine lounge and quickly returned to the kitchen, closing the door as she entered. Kat peeped her head out of the bathroom and both raced towards the other with mouths aghast in horror and excitement; but instead of the cries of worry or giggles of nerves, they found themselves back in a passionate embrace. "You're just too much," whispered Kat, finally breaking free.

"Me?" Freya widened her eyes. "I think it was you who was doing all of the shouting!"

Kat smiled and whispered into her ear. "Well at least you don't have to tell me to just touch *down there* anymore."

"Well I certainly won't be shouting for you to fuck my wet pussy when we go and see your mum and dad!" The giggles had begun.

"Do you think they heard?" asked Kat as she made the final adjustments to her trouser zip.

"Do you think we'd be standing here like this if they did?" Freya made a halo sign above her head and pointed at her girlfriend. "Don't worry, my mother will still think you're the second coming. I wonder what compliment she'll pay you today?"

Kat smiled, the reaction from Mrs Elton on their first introduction had indeed been a surprise. It was as if Sue viewed her as the chair of the parish council, or the head of the women's institute. She behaved like one of those women who wanted to befriend you in order to improve their perceived social standing. Kat couldn't work out if it was the fact she was a teacher, or the belief Sue held about her wonderful education, or possibly the detail that her father was a doctor and the information that she grew up in one of the idyllic Cotswold villages. Whatever it was, Sue Elton had been overwhelmingly appreciative of Kat's desire to *'take on her daughter'* as she had embarrassingly put it.

After some hasty preparation, Freya carefully walked back into the lounge with the four steaming mugs of tea balanced on the worn floral tray. Her parents were perched on the edge of the cream corduroy sofa, anxiously waiting. For a moment she felt bad. They had been so desperate to accompany her to the school and had promised to stay in the car while she collected the results, but she had said that wasn't an option. They had begged for a phone call from the hall instead, but when that was rejected they had to settle for this. Patrick smiled encouragingly. His daughter had always been rather temperamental and neither he nor his wife fully believed her fiery nature to be completely extinguished. So when it came to something like this, they did as they were told. Or at least Patrick did.

"Freya, this really has been rather ridiculous you making us wait this long." Sue couldn't help it. "I mean who do you think has nurtured your education for these past eighteen years? Who brought you all of your books? Who paid for your laptop?"

"I did?" said Patrick.

"Oh Patrick, stop it!" She shook her head at her daughter. "Freya, I just want it noted that this was not the way I envisioned it."

Freya placed the tray on the glass table. "Well there's a lot about my life that you probably never envisioned, Mother." She took a deep breath and took Kat's hand, guiding her to the matching cream sofa seat. "There's a reason I wanted to wait until now." She paused and looked at Kat, reassured by the warmth radiating from her encouraging blue eyes. "I wanted to wait until we were all here at home," she coughed, "because there might be some more great news to hopefully follow this." She quickly pulled the piece of crumpled white paper from her pocket and was about to announce her results when her mother cut in.

"Oh for goodness sake. Now I'm worrying about the news after this bit of news. Why is everything so dramatic with you? Why can't you just do things the easy way?" She tutted and tried to engage Kat in acknowledging and seconding the tut, but Kat kept her eyes firmly on Freya.

"I got straight As," whooped Freya, flinging the piece of paper towards her parents and jumping into the air. "I did it, Dad," she whispered as Patrick shot up and surrounded her with the proudest hug of his life.

Sue retrieved the piece of paper from the floral tray and shook a couple of drips of tea from its corner. "Can you see where you came nationally?"

"Mum, I got four As! That's the best you can get." She was still trapped in her father's warm arms and looked over his shoulder. "I've got my pick of the universities."

Patrick immediately stepped back. "But I thought your first choice was Birmingham. Oh please, please don't tell me you want to move miles away."

"I don't. I accepted Birmingham this morning."

"Oh you tease." The hug was back. "You don't have to spend your trust money on halls. You're close enough to stay here and we can check your work and help you with your coursework." He glanced at Kat. "But we'll give you girls the space you need." It was the first time he'd actually managed to look at Kat since they had arrived home. She had seemed like such a professional, mature, clever woman. Always composed and together. The thought that she liked to talk dirty was just too hard to believe. He sighed and hugged his daughter again, realising it wasn't disgust or abhorrence he felt, but pride and slight jealousy. The closest he ever got to a wet pussy was when he found the neighbour's cat stuck in his gutter last winter.

"So Katherine, what do all of these scores mean?" Sue patted the corduroy seat recently vacated by her husband.

Kat edged over and took the paper. "These just show how she got on in each module, but all that really matters is that she got straight As. It really is quite a feat."

"You did it as well, didn't you?"

"Yes, but contrary to what the papers say, exams are actually getting harder." Kat smiled and took Sue's hand. "What Freya's achieved is outstanding."

Sue felt a buzz of importance and looked up at her daughter still giggling with her father. She had to admit it, Freya may have caused no end of conflict for the past eighteen years, but this, this she had got right. "Yes it is, isn't it. Come here, clever clogs." She stood from the sofa and stretched out her arms. "I'm very proud of you."

Freya squeezed her mother quickly and added, "Well don't get too comfortable, everybody. There's some more news."

Here we go again thought Sue, my daughter's about to ruin this moment as well. It was always the same; beautiful dresses deliberately muddied with the climbing of trees, family photos spoilt with an outstretched tongue, childhood tantrums in the most embarrassing of places. Yes, it was all a long time ago, but it was still very hard to forget.

Freya's mischievous green eyes twinkled. "I'm moving into Kat's apartment on Friday."

"Kat's apartment?"

"Yes Mum. I'm taking Jess's room in Kat's apartment."

"Oh no you're not, young lady."

"Oh yes I am, Mother."

And we're off, thought Patrick, taking a seat on the sofa, lifting his mug of tea, and wondering if he should tell Kat his wet pussy story.

CHAPTER FIVE

Lucy tapped loudly on Freya's bedroom door. She pushed it open quickly and popped her head around the corner. "Caught you!" She gave an elongated wolf whistle. "You two just can't get enough can you?"

Kat and Freya placed their weighty history books down on the double bed and looked up.

"Is this as hot as it's going to get in here?" asked Lucy, looking around at Jess's old shelves, now full of novels, reference books, and miniature models of the human skeleton and muscular systems. There wasn't a pink trinket or tarot card in sight.

The move had been quick and easy. It wasn't that Jess had been forgotten, more that Freya had fitted in with ease. Two weeks in and she'd not caught them once. Her and Ben were constantly being found in some adventurous position in some inappropriate location around the apartment. It was as if Mr Long was their fifth housemate. In reality, Ben wasn't even their fourth housemate, but he was rarely out of the place. No one seemed to mind though, and he more than paid his way, always insisting the takeouts, DVDs and booze were on him.

The move in day had been bizarre with Freya's mother fawning over Kat and her framed certificates, reminding Kat to keep her daughter on the straight and narrow. Kat had tried to crack a joke about the straight, but backtracked quickly when it became obvious that Sue wasn't following. Lucy pondered for a second at the memory. "You know, I'm sure your mother thinks you two are just friends. Or that Kat is like your education guardian or something!"

She walked into the bedroom and picked one of the boring history novels off the bed. "Looks like she was right."

"My mother knows that this is the best all round. I get to take that step away from home, to grow in my own confidence as an individual, without having the horrific conditions of university halls and temptations of all night parties." Freya grabbed Kat's waist with a tickle. "That's how Kat sold it anyway."

"She just needed a nudge in the right direction," smiled Kat.

Lucy mused with intent. "I might be climbing up the wrong tree and barking here, but it seems to me like you could nudge Mrs Susan Elton in whichever direction you wanted, Kat!"

"Don't! That is just wrong!" wailed Freya.

Kat reached out from the bed and grabbed an article from the new IKEA desk that Freya had recently added to the room. She thumbed the numerous pages and paused for a second to find her place. "Well, interestingly I was reading this earlier and it's a new study by," she flicked back to the front page, "by the Journal of Personality and Social Psychology, which found that a suppressed same sex attraction and a strict upbringing can lead to homophobia."

Lucy had switched off at the words *interesting* and *study*, but wanted to contribute so added, "Perez Hilton tweeted today that homophobes are secret gays."

"I think it's the same story," offered Kat, kindly.

Freya sat bolt upright and flicked her long wavy hair. "Are you two trying to suggest that my mother has suppressed her desire for women because my grandmother was strict and now she's opposed to me and my same sex partner?"

"No, I just think she is a secret gash gobbler." Lucy always managed to deliver her lines with such a straight face.

Freya had to giggle. "Could you imagine?"

Lucy plonked herself on the end of the bed which creaked under the weight of her muscular frame. "Right, Kat, would you rather Freya's mother gobbled your gash, or Freya's father fingered your foof?"

Freya grabbed the article and flung it at Lucy. "ENOUGH!! I've only been here two weeks and I've heard more than enough of your, *would you rathers!*"

Kat shook Freya's leg. "She's only teasing."

"I know." Freya smiled, pausing. "But it's hard knowing that my own mother is disappointed in who I am." Freya waved her hands dismissively. "But hey ho, her problem, not mine."

Kat saw the hurt and took Freya's hand. "It's okay, she-"

"Honestly it's fine; no one wants a melodramatic teenager as a flatmate. Come on." She turned to Lucy who was now off the bed and standing at her shelf getting the two miniature skeletons to hold hands and kiss. "Is the film ready?"

Lucy quickly tried to re-attach the arm bone that had fallen out of the socket. "Umm yes." The joint was fiddly so she placed the bone between the skeleton's legs instead. Looking up she offered a quick apology and then answered Freya's question. "We chose this film especially for you girls. It is about Maggie Thatcher. It's called the *Bronze Woman* or something like that."

"Really?" laughed Kat, grabbing Freya's hand and pulling her off the bed; both following the glow of Lucy's neon tracksuit into the dimly lit lounge.

"Ah sweet, look at you two love birds." Ben spoke from all fours in front of the complex DVD player. He was only just getting used to seeing Kat in such an open environment. As a colleague she was the epitome of professional, always striving to be the best for the school and its students, never turning a blind eye or taking the easy option. He had learnt many a lesson from her. The realisation that she had inadvertently kissed one of her soon to be Sixth Form pupils last year on a night out had caused great anguish, quickly followed by huge torture as she accepted her feelings were real and growing. Ben had not been part of the loop and Kat had tried her best to restrain her heart and do the job that she had been assigned at Coldfield - teach history to the best of her ability - a student teacher affair clearly not in the job description. They got there in the end though, he thought, looking back up and wondering when the sight of them together would cease to cause such a rush of blood to Mr Long. "Oh bugger!"

he sighed, waving the empty DVD case in the air. They've forgotten to put the disc in."

"Don't worry, we can watch something else," smiled Lucy, diving onto the leather sofa, secretly relieved.

"No, I'll dash back to the shop and get it."

Lucy hauled herself back off the comfy cushions. "Come on then, handsome. I'll keep you company."

"Sorry girls," he said, walking towards the hall and reaching for his brown bomber jacket that was hanging on the overcrowded coat rack. "Be back in ten."

Kat and Freya snuggled up on the free sofa.

Lucy pulled on her bright yellow puffa jacket and was about to slam the heavy apartment door when she turned back with a wink and added: "Have fun, scissor sisters."

Freya watched the door slam shut and rested her head on Kat's shoulder. "Where does she get it from?"

"I don't know, but they should bottle it." She paused and twisted a long piece of chestnut hair that was softly touching her bare arm. "Lucy has the ability to swallow, summarise and solve any issue in a matter of minutes. And to be fair to her, most of the time she's right."

"And what would she tell me to do?"

Kat straightened up and looked into Freya's green eyes, knowing intuitively what she was referring to. "Honestly?"

"Yes."

"She would have some crazy saying about living for the moment, doing what you want to do, sodding your mother. Then she would tell a joke about sodding your mother, and ask you a really rude *would you rather* question about sodding your mother," she paused and kissed Freya's forehead, "and by that time you'd be laughing so much that you'd realise she was right, and you'd be wondering what you'd been worrying about in the first place." She raised her eyebrows in apology. "But I'm not Lucy, and you're like me ... but you hide it much better than I do. We worry when things are not completely right."

Freya leaned her head back against the firm black sofa and sighed. "But should I care what mum thinks?"

"You wouldn't be you if you didn't."

"I guess I just want to feel that she truly loves me for who I am."

"She will ... one day. It'll just take time. I think at the moment this is more about her. About what her friends will think. About what the neighbours will think."

"What, that she was responsible for making me gay?"

"Maybe." Kat paused. "There's a lot of research that suggests a high proportion of lesbian women had a bad relationship with their mother whilst growing up. Hence why they seek the love of another woman in later life."

"Do you believe that?"

Kat smiled and shook her head. "No."

"Good, because I'm not looking to you for any sort of motherly love!" She took Kat's hand and gently kissed the long elegant fingers. "I just want her to get over it and get on with it."

"And she will, but can you understand how she might question it? She might worry it was something she did which made you turn out like this."

"So basically I just need to say - *Mother, I love tits! Nothing you did, I just love tits!*"

Kat laughed. "Lucy's already started to rub off on you." She smiled. "But yes, maybe you should. Or just show her. Show her you're happy. Show her how accepting people are. Show her that this is normal." She looked at Freya with passion, "Because it is. Nothing has ever felt as natural as this does now."

Kat could be mesmerising and any response Freya had planned was lost in Kat's penetrating blue eyes and their gentle meeting of lips.

****

Ben and Lucy strode arm in arm towards the bright DVD shop. It was a damp evening and the shining lights of the store glowed out in contrast to the darkness of the night, calling them in for refuge and warmth. Ben reached round to Lucy's shoulder and pulled her close. "Come on, babe, let's hurry."

She snuggled in tightly, marvelling at the way his strong-armed gesture made her feel so small and fragile. Womanly was the word she liked to use. She realised she was a powerful girl which made Ben's physique all the more appealing. Usually in a relationship she was the one with the muscles, the height, the strong personality, and very quickly the text message that read: *'Sorry Luce, great fun but just too much for me!'* This time it was different. This time he got her jokes, laughed at them, and then came back with something even more extreme. This time he praised her muscles without the slightest hint of jealousy, and encouraged her to train to the next level. This time he said *I love you* like he meant it. "Our one year anniversary soon," she giggled into his ear.

Ben squeezed her even tighter. "I know, babe, and what a fanfuckytastic year it's been." Her wide brown eyes dropped away, so he added, "... and Lucy Lovett, I want many more fanfuckytastic years to come." They eyes were back, eager and wide. "In fact I want every year from now on to be fanbloodyfuckytastic!" He stopped the walk at the edge of the pavement and moved Lucy in front, studying her strong features and sharp Betty Boo haircut. She was perfect for him, and he loved her completely. "I'm not going anywhere."

"Apart from the DVD shop," she added, smiling to herself and dragging him across the road with one hand.

"Yes, apart from the DVD shop," he laughed as she hauled him up the curb and in through the sliding electric doors. He'd let her win this battle of strength for now; confident in his ability to overpower her later on in the bedroom. Their muscular bodies made for explosive sex, and their matched stamina made for frequent explosive sex. He never tired of the way she returned from an afternoon of teaching at the local gym only to want a further work out of her own. She was incredible, and she was his. He grinned and yanked her back, pulling her in for a huge public snog just inside the shop.

"Mummy, Mummy. Kissing!" The little boy was pointing at the kissing couple and sticking out his tongue. He blew a loud raspberry. "Yuck!"

"Excuse me," said the boy's mother, trying to balance four DVDs, one handbag, two bags of popcorn and a wriggling, raspberry blowing three year old boy in her arms. Ben and Lucy didn't move, so the woman tried to quietly edge past, but lost control of the pile of Disney movies when another wet raspberry sprayed her cheek.

"Mummy, Mummy, Peter Pan on floor!" wailed the little boy in instant waterless tears.

The woman sighed in despair and crouched down to unload her arms and start again. "Stand absolutely still. There's a road out there." She sighed. Life had been getting easier as her son got older, but now every small outing and every seemingly simple task always took forever, and the smallest mishap could often bring her close to tears. She took a deep breath and composed herself, reaching for the scattered films. "Oh no!" She crawled quickly to the pick and mix stand and took a large wet jelly baby from his chomping mouth. "These are not for us."

The little boy reached inside his cheek and pulled out another one, carefully placing it back in the see-through box. "Sorry, Mummy."

The woman looked up. Nobody had noticed so she shuffled on her knees back to the scattered pile of belongings. *I really am a bad person*, she thought, seeing a heavily pierced teenage girl scoop a large mound of jelly babies into an already overflowing cup, aware that her son's wet one was in the mix. She reached for the two bags of popcorn and her handbag and slowly rose to her feet. Dizziness had become quite hard to avoid.

"Are these yours?" asked Ben, holding the neat pile of Disney DVDs.

She would have forgotten them. "Yes!" She took the films, shoved them under her arm, took her son's hand, made a mental check, then realised: *car keys!* She spotted them on the counter and turned back around to collect them.

"Lisa?"

She paused and returned to the man, realising she was indeed a bad person for her forgotten word of thanks. She took a tight hold of her son's hand and focused. "Thanks for that. Sorry, simple trips are just so difficult with a little one."

"Lisa?"

She hadn't even realised he had used her name.

"How are you? It's been ages." Ben felt an unexpected pang of emotion.

The woman squeezed her son's hand even tighter, lost for words.

Ben bent down and wiggled his head in front of the little boy. "And who is this big champ?"

The little boy giggled as the huge man with sticky-up blonde hair pulled funny faces and buzzed his nose with an enormous finger.

"My son. Thanks again, but we really must go." In one fell swoop she reached for the missing keys and headed back to the electric doors.

"Wow, well nice to see you." The exchange was awkward, but the anger and questions just weren't there. Nothing spilled out. *I must have grown up and moved on*, concluded Ben as he watched her leave. *She clearly has too* he smiled, seeing the cute little boy wrestling with her hand and peering back at them.

The glass doors were about to thud shut. "My name's Benny," came the final shout.

****

"You two took your time," joked Freya, now showered and snuggled back with Kat on the black leather sofa.

"Oooo, you two didn't have your pyjamas on when we left, and your hair wasn't wet either Kat!" She bashed Ben's chest. "We'd have caught them if we'd have hurried!"

He didn't smile.

Lucy slung her huge puffa on the coat rack. "Oh come on! I'm cool with it. It makes no odds to me."

"What?" Kat peered over her shoulder as she tied her wet hair into a high knot.

Lucy wiggled towards the lounge and chanted: *"We met Ben's old girlfriend."*

"And did you wipe the floor with her?" joked Freya, licking the tip of her finger and making a ticking gesture in the air.

"Of course!" She paused. "Well no. She was blonde, gorgeous, huge boobs - you know - one of those women who paint on their eyebrows. But..." Lucy put her hands together in front of her chest and started to jump like a kangaroo. *"...she had a ring and offspring!"* The chanting began again: *"...a ring and offspring!"*

Freya did an exaggerated wipe of her brow. "So no competition for you then." It had become common practice for the girls to gossip like Ben wasn't even there.

He huffed noisily. "It was years ago." Hanging his brown bomber jacket next to Lucy's neon sports coat he added: "I hadn't noticed the ring though."

"It was HUGE!"

He smiled and relaxed, taking the reinstated DVD from its box and kneeling back at the machine. "Cute kid. What was he, about one?"

"Give over!" Lucy bounced into her area on the sofa and lifted her feet to the black pouffe. "Oh bless you, babe! Why are men so rubbish with kids' ages? He was at least three."

Ben fumbled with the case. "You know what, I'm not really in the mood for this. You girls enjoy. I'm going to do the boring sensible thing and get an early night." He stood up and headed towards Lucy's room. "First day with my new Year Nine tutor group tomorrow and I need to have my wits about me." He spoke with more sensation than he actually felt.

"Oh no, come on! I'm not interested in watching about the Queen, but anything is bearable when you're cuddled up next to me." She widened her brown puppy dog eyes; that always seemed to work.

"No seriously, night guys. New school year, nice fresh face." He smiled unconvincingly as he waved goodnight and entered the bedroom.

Lucy waited for the door to click closed then immediately dived onto Kat and Freya's adjoining bit of sofa. "She called her kid Benny," she mouthed, with giggly facial expressions.

"What?" whispered Freya.

Lucy piped up. "The ex girlfriend called her kid Benny! How embarrassing for her! I think they must have been childhood sweethearts or something. I pretended not to hear. I don't want him thinking that I'm bothered."

"Are you?"

"No, of course not." She got back up and silently started the ridiculous kangaroo dance again. *"She's got a ring and offspring,"* she mouthed.

Kat reached for the remote. "Come on, this is meant to be fab."

Lucy pouted and plopped back onto the sofa, her voice back to normal volume. "If we must! But don't you two start telling me all about the fifteen hundreds."

Freya and Kat shared a secret smile. "Margaret Thatcher. The Iron Lady?" offered Kat.

"Oh no! It's not one of those films set in medieval England is it, with dusty streets and horses and blacksmiths and stuff?"

"Oh Lucy," sighed Kat, all hope lost.

CHAPTER SIX

Kat and Freya were sitting on the tall red stools at the breakfast bar, both enjoying their unique choice of cereal. Last night's film had been wonderful and a lovely way to end to a very special six-week summer holiday. It was now back to reality, and the sensible breakfast sitting in front of them was the first sign of things getting back to normal. They had been spending their time enjoying lazy breakfasts in bed, or leisurely brunches at the Coldfield Park café. But this morning was a school morning and Kat always opted for the same choice on a school day - Muesli with orange juice, instead of milk. Apparently that was the way it was traditionally eaten when introduced in 1900 by the Swiss physician Maximilian-Bircher-Benner, for patients in his hospital - or so Freya had just learnt.

Freya looked down at her own bowl of Golden Grahams, glistening with extra added sugar. "Well, did you know that Golden Grahams is a brand of breakfast cereal owned by General Mills and that it consists of small toasted square shaped cereal pieces made of whole wheat and corn, and the taste is a mix of honey and brown sugar?"

"Give it here," laughed Kat, reaching across the raised counter for the yellow box. "You know your mother would tell me off for allowing you to eat these." She pulled a couple from the box to try.

"Whoa there!" Freya's green eyes narrowed. "Let's get one thing straight early on in our relationship. Nobody, but nobody, *allows* me to do anything."

Kat could sense the naughtiness in Freya's tone, but was also mindful of her fiery independence and determined personality. She may once have been her student, but now she was more than her equal. "Sorry, wrong choice of words." She popped a couple of the squares in and smiled. "Oh my goodness, mmm, they're lovely."

"See, you can learn things from me too."

Kat swallowed the sweet tasting bites and spoke with sincerity. "You, Freya Elton, have already taught me more than you'll ever fully realise."

"Oh, lover, come here." She swivelled on her red seat and held Kat's thighs between her hands. Kissing her gently she teased. "Eugh, I just tasted that horrible Muesli stuff."

"You know what? I might just mix a couple of these in." Kat grabbed a handful of sugary squares and added them into her bowl of wet mush. "Lover?" she said, smiling. "I like that one."

"Better than sweetie?" questioned Freya.

"By miles!"

"And what am I? Your babe? Your honey?"

Kat smiled. "No, I think my favourite at the moment is Sexpot."

"I like it," grinned Freya. "But maybe a bit awkward when we greet each other in other people's company."

"Well *lover's* hardly any better!"

"*Teach* it is then."

"Just call me Kat. I'm your Kat."

"Yes, you are aren't you." She smiled. "You're my Kat."

Kat winked. "Well, you have got the best pussy in town."

"Don't start all that again." Freya slapped Kat's thigh and giggled. "And I still can't believe I never saw this side of you last year ... yet I still managed to fall head over heels in love with the professional, straight laced side of you." She took Kat's hand. "You had me at hello..." Freya jumped off the stool and grinned. "...hello, my name is Miss Spicer and I'll be your new teacher for this final year." She flicked her hair.

"I did not flick my hair!"

"Yes you did. And you sashayed around the classroom not even noticing that I was there, hiding in the corner, absolutely bricking the fact that I'd snogged the face off you on that Friday night." They both loved to reminisce about their first meeting and subsequent excruciating battle of wills.

"*Look at us now*," they almost sighed in unison.

"Any nerves?" asked Kat, swallowing her final mouthful and standing up. She stepped towards the door and reached for her beige rain mac.

"Honestly?"

Kat pulled the collar up around her neck. September had arrived and the weather was dreary. "Yes of course honestly."

"Have you got time?" Freya looked at the oversized red clock hanging on the tiled kitchen wall. "Ben left ages ago."

"I know, not like him at all. I think maybe seeing his ex must have knocked him a bit." She paused. "I'll check how he is at school; and yes..." She sat back down. "...I have always got time for you."

Freya pushed some soggy Golden Grahams around her bowl. "When do you think I should tell people?"

"That you're gay?" Kat looked at Freya's pretty face and bright green eyes that were touched with slight anxiety.

"Yes. We have an introductory lecture today and then it's the Freshers' Fair and then I think I get to find out my seminar group and meet my tutor. I just don't know when I should tell people."

Kat perched back on the red breakfast stool. "Okay, you know what? This one always used to get me too. I would wrestle with - do I say Hi, I'm Kat and I'm gay - or do I wait until I'm found out - or do I ignore it completely?"

"And what did you conclude?"

"I personally think the best thing is to drop it into a conversation early on. For example, if you meet someone new and you are chatting about ... say music?"

Freya nodded. Kat might be her old teacher but she would always love the way she taught.

"Okay music ... well you just drop in a comment like, *Yes, Adele is great isn't she. I went with my girlfriend to see her live in concert last month.*" Kat stood back up and reached for her black leather workbag. "Or, if you're talking about sport you can say, *I enjoy tennis and my girlfriend and I play for the Coldfield club.*" She smiled and hovered at the counter.

"Yeah, that makes sense, now go!" She knew Kat would stay for as long as needed, even with her timekeeping clock screaming to make a move. "You were never late to our lessons."

"Apart from duty days. Oh no! Duty days, I hope Kathy from Cover's been kind to me this year." She leaned in for a meaningful kiss; it was their first official morning parting, both about to embark on the next stage of their careers. "You have nothing to be ashamed of. Those uni girls will love you."

"I'm not ashamed, but you know what it's like. It's just a difficult one."

"Trust me, I know," smiled Kat, finally reaching for the door. She paused. "I'll miss you at school."

Freya grinned mischievously. "No you won't. There'll be some new hot chick in your A-Level history class to keep it all interesting."

"Yes, you're right." She opened the heavy apartment door. "Have I told you Chianne Granger's taking the course?"

****

Kat smiled to herself as she walked quickly down the long blue corridor of B Block. It had been a very interesting Monday morning briefing. Kirsty Spaulding had commanded the troops from the front, outlining her ambitious aims for the school year ahead and highlighting the fantastic achievements of the school year just past. Kat's name was mentioned several times as an example of excellent practice, causing a slightly embarrassed blush and reticent hand wave. Also mentioned were the names of the English department girls - Diane Pity and Fiona Mews. They had sunk down in their brown woven fabric chairs when highlighted as leaders of the worst performing department. It was in fact, Leery Old Lester, who was the actual Head of English, but he hadn't been allowed in front of an examination class in almost ten years. The three had subsequently been put on weekly observations, causing Kat's current private smile.

As much as she had tried to forgive their behaviour from last year, it was still quite difficult to forget, and even though she would never wish comeuppance for her adversaries, she was smiling at the fact karma seemed to be on her side. She made a mental note to ring Jess, who was the queen of karma, tarots and fate, after school and tell her.

"How can you look so happy on the first day of term?" Ben was leaning in his classroom doorway, large mug of coffee in hand, looking impressively dishevelled for 8.45 a.m.

Kat swerved to the right and checked her watch; she had time. "I'm just smiling about Kirsty." She looked up and down the corridor, still empty before the bell. "Is it a prerequisite for a Head Teacher to become more and more eccentric as the years go on?"

Ben scratched his blonde stubble. "I wouldn't complain if I was you."

"Embarrassing, wasn't it."

He removed his foot from the wall and stood up straight. "Are you kidding? What you achieved last year with your classes was incredible and it's about time some other teachers were told to up their games."

Kat sighed. "More reason for them to hate me." Pausing, she eyed the dark circles under his eyes. "I meant to ask ... is everything okay? It's not like you to miss out on a film, or get an early night on a school night, or walk to school on your own." Ben loved a good gossip and a whole variety of topics were usually covered during the short morning route.

"Actually there is something." He looked up, about to begin. "Hang on, speak of the devil-ess." He blew the steam from his coffee and rolled his eyes.

Kat heard the quick trotting first and inhaled the overpowering perfume second. "Oh great, here goes," she whispered, as the clipping heels pulled to an abrupt stop. "Diane, hi." She always tried to be polite, fully aware that the response would be derogatory.

"Good morning Kat. I like your blouse."

Ben sprayed the blue doorway with specks of brown coffee. He coughed and tried to compose himself.

Not the dirty look and snidey remark she'd been expecting. Kat glanced down at her white ruffled blouse. "Thanks," she said, unable to avoid a comparison with Diane's low cut red body top.

Diane noticed the stare and pushed her fake chest out even further, tapping a stylized false nail between her ample cleavage; *that ought to do it,* she thought, batting her false eyelashes and trying to look coy. "I need you."

Kat felt uncomfortable, the breasts were coming closer and she was already standing against the wall.

Diane could see it in her eyes, Kat wanted her. This should be easy. "I need you ... to give little old me ... a hand."

Ben returned from his desk with some extra large tissues, quickly cleaning the coffee from the door. There was no need for such a vigorous wipe, but the sight of Diane's tits so close to Kat's beautiful face was ashamedly arousing.

"With what?" Kat always gave people the benefit of the doubt, allowing second and third chances, but she was not a fool and the way Diane and Fiona had treated her last year was still too hard to forget.

Diane noted the tone and stepped back. How dare *Super Spicer* try and play hard to get? She was a lesbian wasn't she? What lesbian ever got the chance to see a hot body like hers? She paused, realising she had no other option, so tried again. "I need your expertise, Miss Spicer." Purring, she reached for Kat's arm.

"Um, okay, with what?"

Ben was back in the doorway, foot on the frame, enjoying the spectacle.

Diane gently rubbed the cool fabric of Kat's silk blouse. "Me and you ... period two? We could do a bit of brainstorming if you like?" She shook her bleach blonde hair and gave a seductive wink. That should do it.

Kat removed the fingers from her blouse and stepped to the side. "Am I allowed to ask what you're up to?"

Diane snapped out of it. "Oh, for fuck's sake, I've got an observation this afternoon and I need someone to show me the new lesson plan format."

Ben laughed. "What, the new format they brought in two years ago?"

"Yes, that format, you fucked up fucker." She spat the words, still not over the fact that his new girlfriend looked like a rugby playing Jessie J.

Kat knew how she would handle it. "Period two it is then," she smiled, tucking her register back under her arm. She told Ben they would catch up later, and sashayed elegantly down the corridor.

"I'm going to have to sleep with her aren't I?" gasped Diane opened mouthed. "I can't, I just can't." She wiggled her long pink nails. "Can you imagine? Eugh!"

"What planet are you on?" Ben gulped the last mouthful of coffee and wiped his stubble. "Kat wouldn't touch you with a barge pole."

"No, it would be the prosthetic pole strapped to her crotch doing all of the touching."

"In your dreams, Pity."

"Nightmares, actually. Now piss off, Mr Puller." She stalked to leave, giving her bottom an extra good wiggle as she went.

****

Kat stood still at her classroom door, guiding her children out into the fast moving corridor. She was lucky enough to have kept her tutor group and her beloved Year Sevens of last year were now feeling much more confident having graduated into the prestigious world of Year Eight. No longer were they the tiny ones of the school, wandering around forever lost, swamped in their new blazers, trying to navigate the always unreadable school maps. Now they had knowledge, authority and fast developing personalities; testing the rules on uniform and jewellery, already aware of the teachers who meant business and those who did not.

Kat had used her morning tutor talk to instil a sense of responsibility for the year ahead, guiding them on appropriate, expected behaviour. Now looking down the bustling corridor at Tracy James, helping a tiny Year Seven boy back up to his feet, she felt a pang of pride. The herd of Year Tens charging the wrong way down the one way system must have knocked him. Tracy had stopped to help. Kat concluded the consensus was wrong. Year Eights were not the *difficult* year group - at least her Year Eights weren't. Leery Old Lester and the English women had been moaning about them in the staffroom this morning, complaining about the bitchy girls and laughing about the monotone boys. Kat had silently sighed. Never would she become one of those cynical teachers, trudging through the school day with a bitter chip on her shoulder. No, she had confidence she would remain upbeat, forward thinking and optimistic, no matter what her career threw at her. She smiled to herself - even if that thing was Chianne Granger.

"Ai ai, Miss!" came the loud bellow.

Kat smiled and tried to ignore the inappropriate red basque and denim jegging combination, neither of which were doing Chianne's huge figure any favours. "Good morning, please take a seat."

Chianne waltzed into the room and flung her micro handbag onto the front table. She ordered to her lackey, who coincidentally had the extreme opposite build to her; lanky and thin: "Mann, get the seats!"

Chantelle Mann trotted in behind her idol and proceeded to pull the two front chairs out from under the desk.

"Further than that!" barked Chianne, unable to squeeze into the allocated space.

Chantelle quickly raced around to the desk behind and pulled it back to make more room. She wanted everything to be perfect; Chianne didn't choose just anybody to be her second in command. "Spray?" she suggested.

"Obviously!" snorted Chianne, sticking out her chin and tilting her head back slightly.

Kat watched in disbelief as Chantelle Mann reached into the sequined handbag for the travel sized can of super strength hairspray, immediately spraying Chianne's gravity defying black quiff. Kat took a controlled intake of breath and walked towards the front desk. The toxic smell caught in the back of her throat causing an impromptu cough.

"Alright, Miss! No need to exaggerate!" The top half of Chianne's oversized body was resting on the desk and the red basque had started to gape. Chianne caught the glance. "I wore this for you, Miss Spicer." She smiled and tried to look seductive. "I love the fact that us Sixth Formers can wear whatever we want. You can borrow some of my stuff if you want, Miss."

"Mine too," added Chantelle.

"Chants, I ain't being mean, but all of your gear is Tesco Two Stripe stuff. Miss Spicer ain't gunna wear stuff from Tesco. You like my gear don't cha, Miss ... I got this top from that posh stall on Brownhills market."

Kat crouched down in front of them both. The room had started to fill so she spoke quietly - the last thing she wanted was a confrontation during the year's first lesson. She started with Chianne. "Welcome to A-Level history, and thank you for your prompt arrival..."

Chianne straightened up in her seat and added a slight nod of self congratulations.

"...But can you please not enter the room so loudly, and can you please refrain from using hairspray in here."

Chianne leaned forwards on the desk, causing her puppy fat to spill out of the suggestive top. She whispered her response, deliberately rolling her final R, "Anything for you, *Miss Spicerrr.*"

Kat paused. "Right, okay, I'm glad we've cleared that up." She turned her attentions to Chantelle. "I'm really sorry but this is A-Level history."

"I know, Miss." Chantelle smiled enthusiastically, pulling a piece of paper from her pocket. "I'm on a conditional offer."

The school had a strict policy on Sixth Form entry which included at least five A*s to C in GCSE grades and at least a C in their chosen A-Level subjects. Kat recalled that Chantelle Mann had achieved neither. She studied the piece of paper that had been signed off by Janet Louza. A Head of Department could waiver the entry rules for the odd student who showed extreme enthusiasm and desire to continue their education at Coldfield. Basically they would have begged to stay on at school. The said student would then be put on a conditional offer. A trial that could be terminated by the school at the first sign of trouble. She smiled kindly at Chantelle. "Are you sure this is the subject you want to take?"

Chantelle looked nervously across at Chianne. "I had hoped to do the childcare course, but I think this might give me a ... a more bettered furthered education operations."

"Better further education options!" scowled Chianne.

Chantelle nodded approvingly. "Yeah, so I chose this, English and Media Studies just like she did." She thumbed across to her best mate.

"And this is *your* choice?" asked Kat, delicately trying to guide Chianne's loyal supporter in the right direction.

"Yes, Miss."

Kat nodded and tapped the table, standing back up. "Okay then, but please, if you begin to struggle, don't suffer in silence. Let me know and we can have an open and honest conversation about whether or not this is the right course for you."

"Oh yes, Miss, it definitely is." She spoke eagerly. "I love learning about the pyramids and how they were built and that big fire thing that happened that one time in London, and the plague and everything."

Kat crouched back down and tucked her blonde hair behind her ears. "Chantelle, this is modern day history. We're learning about Pitt, Lord Liverpool and Gladstone."

Chantelle stole a sideways glance, but Chianne had already lifted her podgy hand in reassurance. "Don't worry, Chants. Pitt was the youngest prime minister, Lord Liverpool was another PM during a recession in 1817..."

"We're in one of them now!" added Chantelle with proud knowledge.

"Yeah, well done mate ... and Gladstone was the PM four times."

Kat raised her eyebrows in surprise.

"So you see, Chants, this course *is* for us."

What a double act thought Kat, suddenly aware of the room full of Sixth Form students. There were ten in last year's class, but many more had opted for it this year when they heard Miss Spicer, their favourite all time teacher, would be teaching the course. Kat stepped back and took control of the room, beginning with her usual introduction. "Hello and good morning everybody. For those of you who haven't met me yet, I'm Miss Spicer and I'll be your history teacher for the next two years." She flicked her hair unintentionally.

Chianne let out an approvingly low wolf whistle.

"Thank you for that, Chianne, you've brought me onto my next point. This is *A-Level* history. Where I will treat you like the young adults you are..." she turned to Chianne and nodded, "...as long as you behave like the young adults you should be."

Chianne playfully tapped herself on the hand in punishment.

Kat leaned back against her wooden desk and eyed the large group. "So ... can we go around the room and say a brief sentence about yourself and why you chose history?" She smiled and her genuine warmth and reassurance immediately put the nervous amongst the group at ease. "Okay, how about I start." She paused, stood back up, flattened her white silk blouse and began. "My name is Miss Katherine Spicer, this is my second year teaching at Coldfield and I chose to become a history teacher so I could help to ensure that the generations of the future learn from the lessons of the past."

A couple of the group nodded in admiration. Chantelle started to panic, what was that rhyme about Henry the Eighth and his nine wives?

"So let's start at the front..."

Chianne had already hauled herself up. She spun around to face the rest of her peers and began to sing in Nicki Minaj style. *"My name's Chianne, I bet you all know who I am..."* The urban rap song was matched with a couple of attempted hip and shoulder pops. *"...so listen to me, I'll tell you why I chose history."*

"Whoa, whoa, whoa." Kat had quickly positioned herself next to the dance performance. "Chianne, I'm not quite sure where you think you are, but this is an A-Level class." She exhaled, annoyed by the show of immaturity. "Now please sit down. I don't find that behaviour at all appropriate. Chantelle, your turn, stand up. Tell the class why you chose history."

Chantelle stood slowly and turned to face the group. "Well I love the poem about that King Henry who had all of those wives. *Divorced, beheaded, survived ... divorced, died, buried alive.*"

Kat sank back onto her desk. This was not at all what she had been expecting.

CHAPTER SEVEN

Freya took her time getting ready. It had been strange seeing Kat leave for school. She had pictured her entering her classroom and smiling at her classes, instantly putting them at ease. She knew from experience that the students would quickly warm to her kind and caring manner, hailing Kat as their new favourite teacher for the year. Her own time at Coldfield had been wonderful and her final year certainly one to remember. Now it was the next phase of her education and she wanted to get it right. She knew it was just an introductory lecture, but she wanted to look the part so she delved into Kat's work wardrobe and selected a pair of black high-waist trousers and a tight black shirt.

She rifled through Kat's well organised jewellery drawer and picked out a matching pale blue necklace and bracelet set. She tied her long brown hair into a high pony and stood on her tip toes. The trousers were slightly too long, so she nipped back into her own bedroom across the laminate floor and pulled out her largest pair of black heels. She pulled them on and walked slowly back into Kat's room towards the full length mirror, deliberately crossing her legs over in a sexy walking action.

She lifted her eyes to herself and started to speak. *'Hi, I'm Miss Elton, your sexy new teacher...*" She started to laugh. *"...and I look like a complete prat!'* She kicked off the shoes and flopped onto the end of Kat's double bed. *Who was she trying to kid?* She would never be as hot, yet professional, as Kat was. As sexy, yet demure. As stunning, yet slightly shy. She pulled herself back up and looked in the mirror, slowly unbuttoning the black shirt. She put on a husky voice. *"Hi I'm Kat Spicer, it's Freya isn't it? I think we met on Friday night. I'm your new history teacher.*" Freya unbuttoned the final button and threw the shirt to the carpet. She kept her own eye contact in the mirror and pushed up her boobs in her bra. "*Will you let me teach you some other stuff as well?*"

Lucy's tutting was slow and prolonged. "So, this is what you're into then!"

Freya grabbed the shirt off the floor and dived back onto the bed. "I thought you were out!"

Lucy burst into fits of laugher. "I was! But boy, am I glad I came back!" She signalled to the mirror. "Kat's eye contact is better than that though."

Freya quickly pulled the shirt back on. "Thanks, I'll remember that next time I'm pretending to be my ex-teacher and talking to myself in the mirror."

Lucy sidled up to Freya with her chin pushed out and her head slightly titled upwards. "She has a poise, kind of like this."

Freya grabbed a fluffy cushion and hurled it at Lucy. "Can we just forget about this now?"

Lucy laughed. "No way!!! I'm going to use this for years to come! What are you doing anyway? Apart from getting yourself off in front of the mirror."

"I'm getting ready for uni, believe it or not. I have my first lecture in a couple of hours and I'm not sure what to wear."

Lucy snorted. "Well, for god's sake don't wear any of Kat's boring shit!"

Freya grinned and returned to the open wardrobe. "I think she looks hot in her work stuff!"

"You bloody would, you dirty dog. No need to ask what you dream of at night!"

Freya reached back to the bed and hurled another pillow, narrowly missing Kat's dressing table and cluster of fancy perfume bottles. "So what do you dream of then? Let me guess. Mr Puller and his tight trousers?"

Lucy sat down on the end of the bed and looked at Freya seriously. "You honestly want to know what I dream of?"

Freya was taken aback with the change in her tone so sat back down on the bed, giving Lucy her full attention. "Yes. Why? What is it?"

Lucy kept her face serious. "I dream of a world where chickens can cross the road without having their motives questioned."

Freya frowned, then burst out laughing. "What are you on?!"

Lucy continued straight faced. "You know how it is, everybody always asking why the chicken crossed the road."

"Yes, yes, I got it first time, you weirdo!" she giggled.

Lucy jumped on top of her. "Says you, Miss *look at me, I'm so sexy in the mirror!*"

****

Lucy's distraction had actually been a great way to calm her nerves and Freya's day was turning out to be very exciting indeed. She had filed into the university lecture theatre with a buzz of nervous anticipation, eager to discover exactly what her three year course would entail. She had not, however, been expecting to find out that the first school placement would be as soon as January, and nor had the girl sitting next to her if the crazy expression on her face was anything to go by. Freya acknowledged the gasp sent in her direction and mouthed the word *"January?"* back.

"Shit!" came the silent, wide eyed reply.

Freya smiled and returned her attention to Elaine Springer, the principal lecturer, who was talking in a very animated and energetic fashion at the front of Theatre 32, as it was named. It was a modern, spacious, and very high room, with rows of seats cascading down to the stage at the front. Freya had done the predicted thing, as had the majority of her new course mates, and opted for a seat near the back. The ten front rows remained empty with the plush red chairs still in the upright position.

"I bet you lot can't even hear me!" joked Elaine, trying to put the nervous batch of newcomers at ease. She rose onto her tiptoes and made a loudspeaker with her hands. "Come on, all of you hurry down here to the front. Onto the stage. Come on!"

Freya and her new friend shared another frowned expression.

"I mean it! Come on, shuffle out of your seats and get down here. I won't bite. I promise!" Elaine spoke with a real bounce in her voice which matched the tiptoed stance and beckoning hand gestures.

Freya edged out of the row and made her way, with the other mix of characters, down the freshly carpeted steps to the front of the theatre. There seemed to be a very complicated network of computers, television systems, and loud speakers at the front, enabling the lecturers who chose to use it, a variety of modern technology to aid their quest of imparting their knowledge on the new undergraduates. Freya studied the people who were starting to form a circle, and realised just how diverse the group actually was. She had assumed they would all be recent A-Level graduates like her, but the varied age range proved her wrong.

Elaine lifted her arms out to the side and wiggled her fingers. "Righty-ho, hold hands please everybody."

Freya looked to her left at the fresh faced girl from her row. The girl instantly lifted her eyebrows and smiled in response. Freya was just about to reach for her hand when the petite lecturer jumped into the centre of the circle.

"Just joking! Just joking! You lot look petrified. Relax! This isn't school, this isn't work, this isn't that awful job you've given up to follow your calling. This is university..." she did a little spin, "...and you are going to have the time of your lives!" quickly adding, "and also learn how to be the best possible history teacher known to mankind!"

Freya smiled. It had been Elaine Springer who had shown her around the university on open day last year and she had been instantly drawn to her nonconformist approach. Elaine had openly praised the new modern university facilities and loudly criticised the tedious old lecturers they housed; her, obviously not included. She watched as Elaine grabbed the blue clipboard from the podium, sending her notes flying to the floor. A middle aged woman with a tight brown bun and long ankle length skirt bowed to pick them up.

"*Teacher's pet*," mouthed Freya's new acquaintance.

"Please, just leave them," insisted Elaine, "...they were just for show anyway."

Freya caught a glimpse of the detailed notes being collected by the woman and knew her new tutor would probably be one of the cleverest, most inspiring women, she would ever meet.

Elaine lifted her funky triangle shaped glasses and studied the list on the clipboard. "I remember that I met a number of you on different open days, but I would just like to refresh my memory and give you all a chance to get to know one another. So, could I please have Gaynor Newman first." She looked up. "Can Gaynor Newman step forwards please?"

The middle aged woman placed the last of the notes back on the podium and flattened her floral skirt. Stepping into the circle she spoke with authority. "That will be me."

"Gaynor, I need age ... history ... hopes."

The woman performed a regretful curtsey. "I do not feel at liberty to disclose my age."

Elaine entered the circle and nudged her gently. "Oh come on, Gay. We're all friends here."

The woman stiffened up. "No, a woman's age is her best kept secret," she nodded at the balding man wearing the tweed jacket and red cords, smiling shyly at his approving return nod. "*History* ... well I have been a librarian for the past twenty five years, and my *hope* is to impart the knowledge I have gained from twenty five years in the library to the youth of today."

Freya couldn't help but look at her new acquaintance.

"*Good luck with that,*" was the mouthed response.

A stifled laugh slipped from her mouth and she glanced up, praying that Gaynor hadn't heard; she hadn't, she was too busy listing her favourite history periodicals to have noticed.

"Fantastic, Gaynor, just what I was after." Elaine lifted her black triangle glasses and added, "I can call you Gay, can't I? ... Can I call you Gay?"

"No." The answer was abrupt.

Elaine took a step back into the circle. "Sorry ... Right .... Okay. Freya Elton next please."

Freya stepped forwards. "You can call me gay, if you like." It was too good an opportunity to miss. Kat would be proud.

"I like it," grinned Elaine. "Visibility is paramount in schools today." She quickly turned back to Freya. "You did just declare your sexuality didn't you?"

Freya nodded with a smile.

"Good, good!" Elaine lifted up her triangle glasses, as if letting the group in on a little secret. "Sometimes I get the wrong end of the stick and I just wanted to check," she clapped her hands, "but great, great! If everyone was open and honest about their sexuality then issues with small minded bigoted people would disappear. Honestly, some people forget that we're in the year 2012 and it's people like these who need to be educated ... or alternatively ignored. So yes, hoorah for you, Freya!"

Freya's heart was racing, but it felt good. She noted the pause and began. "Well, I'm Freya. I'm eighteen. I've just finished my A-Levels and I hope I'm good at teaching because I love history and I want a job that I really enjoy."

"Fantastic!" Elaine gave an impressed thumbs up. "Can I have Gregory Taylor next please."

As Freya stepped backwards into the circle she sensed the eyes from her new acquaintance, penetrating her from the left.

****

Kat waved the last of the Sixth Formers out of her room, aware that the lesson had been a lot harder than anticipated. The constant interruptions and outbursts from Chianne, and ill-timed redundant questions from Chantelle, had slowed the pace of the lesson. She slid back onto her padded chair. *Had she been spoilt with last year's small group of ten? Were the results from last year a fluke? What on earth was she going to do with Laurel and Hardy at the front?* She heard her phone vibrate in the desk drawer and felt instantly warmed as she saw the picture of Freya and a small flashing envelope. She clicked the message open.

"Already out at uni. It's all cool ;)"

She smiled to herself. Freya was so headstrong and determined that she had never doubted it would be any other way. Closing her eyes she pictured the mischievous grin and sparkling green eyes that had greeted her as she had turned over in bed this morning; still unsure if it was a natural stirring or the result of Freya's soft fingers caressing her back. She inhaled slowly, aware of the wave of contentment that washed across her whole being. She was happy, blissfully happy. *Life is great* she thought, opening her eyes, immediately shocked at the sight in the doorway. Diane Pity's head was peeping around the battered blue door and her tits were angled to ensure they stuck out as well.

"Having a moment were we?" Diane flicked a leg forward and purred. "Can I join in?"

Kat looked at the patchy orange leg, huge boobs and heavily made up face that was sticking out into her classroom. "Please just come in, Diane." She stood up and brought one of the plastic chairs to her desk.

"Ooo, you are in a hurry." Diane tottered into the classroom that was noticeably more educational than her own, with wonderfully colourful displays on each wall, and thought provoking posters that encouraged the reader to strive for perfection and always give ones best. The only posters that adorned her classroom walls were those of her idol Peter Andre. She realised that she might have to make an effort this year, what with the approaching observations, and tape some of her students' crappy work to her walls.

Diane eyed the neat exercise books on each clearly labelled shelf and wondered what it would be like to be a proper, well-organised teacher, who actually cared that books didn't get lost and actually marked things on a regular basis. No, not for her, she concluded as she approached the desk, flapping a piece of paper in her right hand and using her other hand to straighten her tight red top which she'd deliberately lowered for the spectacle at the door. "Right, let's get this out of the way first." She picked up the plastic chair and placed it within touching distance of Kat's knees. "Here's my lesson plan." Plonking the printed sheet onto the well organised wooden desk she took a seat and continued. "Apparently this is not a properly formatted lesson plan, and for some reason Cuckoo Kirsty and that drongo James Dapper have decided that we should be the focus of the first departmental review."

Kat picked up the sheet and read the bold headline: FREE PRINTABLE LESSON PLANS 4U – ENGLISH.

"I mean what's their problem?" Her beady eyes narrowed even further. "There are far bigger problems in this school than the way I format my lesson plans."

Kat studied the brief piece of paper and turned her attention to Diane, noticing the normally hidden crevices and wrinkles under her thick layers of foundation. She was even close enough to spot the brown staining on her teeth. Diane was not much of a smiler and Kat suddenly wondered if she smoked.

Diane clocked the way Kat was drawn to her mouth and began to turn her lips at the corners, testing out her seductive smile. "So here I am, in your more than capable hands. Apparently, you're the one to come to when it involves the latest educational initiatives. I prefer to be all *old school*. It's never done me any harm in the past, and the powers that be seem to change all of the crappy specifications and initiatives on such a regular basis that I think it best to stick with what I know." Diane had no idea about any new initiatives but she thought her spiel sounded good. She gave another alluring smile.

Kat thought Diane looked slightly in pain and desperately tried to ignore the knees that were now resting against her own. She reached into the second drawer of her desk and pulled out a blank lesson plan. "This is the format that you should be using." Diane had five more years experience than Kat, but both knew who was the more knowledgeable. "All you have to do is follow your department's scheme of work and fill in these boxes." She pointed with the end of her pen. "You have to fill in the Date - Class - Lesson - Overview and Purpose - Education Standards Addressed - Objectives - Information - Verification - Activity - Summary ... and then over here..." Kat lifted her pen to point to the final three boxes. "...you fill in, Materials Needed - Other Resources and Additional Notes."

Diane lifted her lip and scowled. "All that for one pissing lesson on poems?"

Kat reached into the third drawer down and pulled out a lesson evaluation. "And then they will expect you to fill in one of these." She lifted her pen again and began highlighting the boxes. "Were the objectives achieved? What role did ICT play in supporting the success of your lesson? Which other key factors supported the success of your lesson? What difficulties did you find in delivering your lesson?"

"I found difficulty filling in all of these pissing forms!"

Kat carried on and tapped another box. "How did you deal with these difficulties?"

"By not bloody doing it!"

Kat was enjoying the shock so she continued. "What feedback did you get from your students? And finally..." She tapped the last box. "...what changes would you make to this lesson, if any, in the future?" She calmly looked up at Diane, who was now completely flustered. "So that's it really. Just transfer your lesson onto this plan and then evaluate accordingly." She smiled. "Now, is there anything else I can help you with?"

"Oh for fuck's sake! I'll flash you my tits if you fill in these frigging forms!" Playing the slow seductive card would take too long; she needed to get this relationship up and running.

"Excuse me?" Kat was relishing the feeling of power that Diane had stripped from her last year. It felt good, but she wasn't going to gloat.

"Everyone knows you're *Shit Hot Spicer* who gets everything right." She flicked her bleach blonde hair and stuck out her chest. "You do something for me and I'll do something for you."

Kat tapped her pen between her teeth, she'd had her fun; enough had been said. "Of course I'll help you, Diane. But I don't need anything in return."

Diane stared at the genuine blue eyes. "You'll fill in this goddamn awful form for me? What's in it for you?"

"You asked for my help, so I'll help you."

Diane scrunched her nose, perplexed. "Why?"

"Because you asked me to help. Now look," she reached for her pen and started to write in the first box, "English - Year Seven - Period Five." She tapped the second box. "Objectives?"

Diane leaned into the desk. "To write a poem."

"Okay great, good start." Kat smiled.

The door handle hit the grey filing cabinet and both jumped at the noisy bang. Fiona Mews stood hand on hip in the doorway, with her long black plait swishing from side to side. She flared her abnormally large nostrils. "Lester said you were up here. What are you doing?" She looked down her nose at Kat.

Diane blurted her response. "I'm being observed lesson five and I wanted to check my lesson plan." The admission was rather sheepish.

"With her?" It was one of the things binding together their fake friendship - a mutual dislike of Kat sodding Spicer.

Diane shrugged her shoulders. "Yes, why?"

Fiona was fuming, how dare her best fake friend switch allegiances? She tightened her chintz scarf, hiding her large walnut shaped neck mole, and spun to leave. Stopping in her tracks and taking two steps back she added in Kat's direction: "Just so you know, Diane calls you Spicer the Slit Sucker."

"I do not!" The outrage was poorly performed.

Fiona nodded and flicked her neck scarf. "Sorry, no, what was it this morning?" She flared her nostrils. "That's right, this morning Diane called you Kat the Crack Cleaner." She hissed with her tongue and marched out of the room.

Kat picked up the pen. "Okay, so next you fill in *Activity*."

****

Ben and Kat made the short walk home together, both asking the same question; where on earth had the summer holidays gone? It had been a long day, but it was always the same; returning to school and feeling like you had never been away. The chatter was upbeat and pleasant as they strode from the school along the wide cycle path towards Coldfield Park and the modern apartments that backed onto it. The gossip was there but Kat could sense Ben's distance. He was a great guy and perfect partner for her best friend Lucy. Yes there had been a minor hiccup early on in their relationship, but now it seemed it would stand the test of time and Kat was pleased. Lucy deserved someone like him. He was a man's man by anyone's standards. Tall and muscular, with the ability to grow an inch of blonde stubble moments after his morning shave. The students loved him and he cared about his job, always trying to make lessons memorable and fun. Yes, he was a keeper thought Kat, noticing his eyes glaze over once again.

"Was it that bad?" She gently linked her arm through his brown bomber jacket.

"What?"

"Your first day back?"

"No, no ... pretty good actually. Great new tutor group. Great examination classes." He nodded his head. "Yep, all good."

Kat wasn't sure who he was trying to convince so she squeezed his strong arm. "You just seem a bit preoccupied and I think you were going to tell me something this morning in the corridor before Diane made her embarrassing appearance."

He put his hand to his stubbled chin and stopped.

Kat unlinked their arms and looked across at his troubled face that was pale with nerves.

He finally spoke. "Shit Kat ... I think I've got a son."

CHAPTER EIGHT

Kat and Freya were lying in the warm double bed, laughing about the events of the evening, having each arrived home with flowers and chocolates to celebrate the other's first day back. Kat's flowers had been the most spectacular but Freya had claimed the points for the best chocolates.

"You really shouldn't have," said Kat once more, reaching out from under the duvet for a Bucks Fizz truffle. "It's not like I've done anything good today."

Freya rolled onto her side. "I just wanted to say I love you." She watched as Kat delicately nibbled the sugary chocolate shell from the truffle. "That's all."

Kat paused and smiled. "Well I love you too, and you deserve your flowers and chocolates. Coming out on day one of uni is something to really be proud of."

Freya looked across to her bedside cabinet at the arrangement of deep crimson roses and purple calla lilies. It had been a truly beautiful surprise, hand tied with luxurious gift wrapping and placed on her bed for her arrival. They put the bunch of yellow carnations that she had bought from the garage to shame. "So were there any new hotties in your class this year then?"

"None that I accidentally kissed, no. And this year's bunch will certainly not be able to live up to you guys, I can tell you that now. I don't know if I'm getting old, but they all seem so young."

"No one with my level of mature alluring personality then?"

"No. And I'm not planning on making a habit out of seducing my students."

"Is that what you did? Seduce me?"

Kat laughed. "I think we both know that I didn't stand a chance. Remember that time we played tennis and you stood in front of me and asked me to take a shower?"

Freya pulled the pillow onto her red embarrassed cheeks. "Oh don't remind me. I still cringe at that now."

"You shouldn't, I was so tempted."

"Were you really?"

"You know I was, but you know what?" She paused and looked at Freya's pretty face, still slightly flushed from their gentle love making. "We wouldn't be here now if I'd have said yes. But it would no doubt have been a highly pleasurable, if not somewhat elicit, shower."

"Do you really believe we wouldn't be together now?"

"No. We would have been caught out somewhere down the line and we would never have been able to hold our heads up high like we can now."

Freya sighed. "Yeah, I guess not. But I was gutted that you rejected me."

"I hardly rejected you."

"Well it felt like it at the time."

"Is that why you went running into Bea's arms?"

"We said we weren't going to talk about that."

"I know, I'm only teasing. And anyway, I'm glad that I wasn't your first. I'm glad you had a chance to grow in confidence with someone else."

"Okay, okay, let's not go there please!"

"Am I allowed to talk about the time you tried to hold my hand in the jacuzzi at Cross Hall?"

"Only if I can talk about the time you dry humped me when we partnered at Judo."

Kat laughed. "Right, let's call it a truce. Tell me more about uni."

Freya thought back to the people on her course and the way her new acquaintance, a Miss Renee Eves - as she had learnt when it was her turn in the circle - had been slightly over familiar. "Can I ask you something?"

Kat edged up the bed and got herself comfortable at the padded headboard. They seemed to be spending most of their time in Freya's room, enjoying the reprieve from Ben and Lucy's noisy antics. "Anything."

"How does your Gaydar work?" It was an ongoing joke that Kat had the most sensitively tuned Gaydar, able to spot a lesbian, bi-sexual, bi-curious, or deeply intrigued woman from any given distance.

Kat edged back down the bed and rested her head on her elbow, looking deep into Freya's green eyes. "Why?" she asked with mock suspicion.

"You just need to teach me. Especially now that I'm out in the big wide world."

"Does someone at uni fancy you?"

Freya flicked a piece of Kat's blonde hair. "Don't be daft! It's just something I need to learn."

Kat smiled. She was pretty good at spotting when people were losing the truth. "I'm not sure I buy that, but anyway you don't learn it, you just have it." She smiled. "And I'm sure you have it, otherwise you wouldn't be asking me this question." She leaned into Freya and lifted her eyebrows in curiosity. "Come on, who is she? Who made you ask me the question about Gaydar?"

Freya was the one who now pulled herself up to the top of the bed, out of sight of those knowing blue eyes. "There's no-one!"

Kat rolled onto her back and looked up at the white ceiling and textured swirls. "Okay, if you really want to know, then it's all in the eyes. Follow her eyes. What does she look at? Where are her eyes drawn? For example, you're walking down the street with her. Does she glance at the man's bottom in front or the woman's?" Kat raised her eyebrows once again. "Or you go for a coffee with her and there's a woman sitting at a table alone. Is your *friend* admiring the woman's designer handbag that's resting on the floor, or is she admiring the way the woman's long bare legs are crossed at the knee?" Kat thought for a moment. "Does she eagerly await news of your latest lesbian escapades, with her eyes wide at the juicy details?" Kat coughed. "Does she flirt with you?"

Freya sensed it was a question. "There's no-one!" she giggled.

Kat joined her at the headboard and took her hand. "Or you have the other extreme where the woman is constantly talking to you about the men she fancies and how she is not at all bi-curious and how she could never imagine being with a woman-"

Freya cut in. "Which obviously means she has imagined being with a woman!"

They laughed together and Kat squeezed her hand gently. "There's something completely wrong if you go through the next three years of university without anyone fancying you, Freya. I've been there. I've seen what it is like." She smiled in remembrance. "Crikey, it was compulsory for us girls to snog each other during our sports beer circles."

"Really?"

Kat laughed. "Yes, and some of the games of truth or dare got totally out of hand." She patted the soft fingers wrapped around her own. "I would understand if you wanted to go out and experiment, there are so many amazing women and you are only eighteen-"

"Almost nineteen."

"Well you're young and fairly new to this and I don't want you to look back and resent me for holding you back." She meant every word.

"How can you say that?" The shock was genuine. "You are all I want. You are all I need. Why would I waste my time exploring my sexuality with other women when I've already got the ultimate woman lying right here, holding my hand?"

Kat smiled and wondered if she would ever truly believe it. She held the gaze and spoke quietly. "I want you to tell me. I'm not going to freak out or go crazy or anything."

"Tell you what?" She would never fully understand Kat's insecurities, no matter how hard she tried. She was beautiful; stunningly beautiful. Kind, caring, smart, sophisticated, funny, generous. She was perfect in every way.

"Tell me when people like you. When they come on to you. Please just tell me and we can talk about it. It won't make me doubt you ... it will make me trust you further." She tucked a wave of long chestnut brown hair back behind Freya's warm ear. "Because it will happen ... trust me."

Freya didn't know whether to be offended or flattered.

Kat sensed the tension so returned to her teaching mode. "Okay, so anyway, the other part of Gaydar is being able to tell when the woman in question likes you ... and again it's all in the eyes. It's like a silent code between lesbians. You hold the stare for just that fraction too long. Both of you do it and it's deliberate. You look ... you smile ... you maintain the look, until you both smile again." She paused. "You smile that knowing smile. That lesbian smile."

Freya thought back to the way her new acquaintance had held her eyes.

"That's Gaydar."

"Are you ever wrong?"

"I don't think so, no," smiled Kat.

Freya laughed and rolled over, easily straddling Kat's flat stomach. "You're one shit hot teacher, you know that?"

Kat spanked her backside. "You know I don't like swearing."

"Oh yeah right, Miss *Fuck My Wet Pussy Right Now!*"

"Shhhh! Lucy will hear!" she laughed.

"No way, they would beat us hands down in a shag-off!"

Kat shook her head. "Right, enough! Recite an eloquent A-Level English poem for me please. My ears are not used to this vulgarity."

Freya whispered something into Kat's ear causing a loud burst of laughter.

Kat composed herself and looked into her naughty green eyes. "I love you so much, Freya Elton."

"And I love you too, Miss Spicer."

****

Ben closed the heavy apartment door, wondering if that had been the first of many lies. He felt dreadful but he needed to know. Padding slowly down the stairs to the communal lobby he rehearsed his speech. It was a long shot, but it was all he had. Crossing the empty parking bays he glanced back up to the glowing window of

Lucy's room. A shadow moved past the curtains and he felt a pang of anxiety. He stopped and seriously contemplated dashing back up to tell her everything. The only thing that made him turn back around and continue his walk was the echo of Kat's words in his ears. *Wait until you know*, she had said; and she was right. Why go upsetting Lucy and dragging up the past for a faint whimper of a slight suspicion. He walked quickly along the damp pavement, guided by the soft glow of street lamps. Two minutes and he'd be there. He dug his hands deeper into the lining of his favourite bomber jacket, comforted by its familiar feel, suddenly stopping and scrunching his fingers into a tight ball. It was more than a suspicion. Benny had to be his.

The automatic doors opened and he narrowed his eyes at the bright lights. Great, he thought, the new girl's on. Turning left, he stopped at the jumbled family section of DVDs and reached for a Disney classic. He tapped the empty case as he made his way to the counter. It was late and the shop would only be open for another fifteen minutes, maybe he could catch her off guard.

Ben spoke confidently. "Dumbo! My son's favourite. He's got a bad cold and he's not been sleeping well. I promised him a film tomorrow if he took his medicine tonight."

"And did he?" smiled the girl behind the counter.

"Yep! So good old daddy has to keep his end of the bargain." Ben pretended to be interested in the display of popcorn, not really noticing there was an offer of three for two. He picked up two bags.

"Ah sweet. I hope he gets better." She indicated towards the popcorn. "Three for two."

He grabbed another bag and reached into his pocket for his wallet. Pushing each card up and frowning in confusion. He patted the back of his jeans and reached once more into his jacket. "Lisa gave me the card." He shook his head. "Where did I put it?"

She tilted her head in annoyance at the staff office behind her. "Sorry, but they say you have to have your card. It's company policy."

He sighed and tapped Dumbo on the desk. "Benny will be so upset."

The girl's face lit up. "Oh I know Benny! Cute little guy, likes to sample the pick and mix. Your wife came in this morning with him, brought back about five films!"

Ben smiled convincingly. "That's the guy."

The girl winked and checked over her shoulder. "Oh it should be okay, what name's the card in?"

"Lisa Faith." He held his breath, absolutely no clue of her married name.

"16 Winterton Lane?"

"That's the one," he nodded, handing over a ten pound note.

She frowned, checking her buzzing computer screen once more. "He brought that Dumbo back this morning."

Ben kept his hand outstretched for the change. "I know! I should buy it really."

"Here, give him one of these from me." She reached across the counter to the stand of lollies, pulling one out and checking behind her as she passed it to Ben. "That popcorn's way overpriced."

"Thanks, he'll like that," he said, smiling. "Best be off." He waved nervously as he made his way to the electric doors, dashing around the corner of the building and reaching for his phone. Opening up the notes application he tapped in the address. *16 Winterton Lane.* There was no way he would forget, but he just wanted to make sure.

****

Kat and Freya heard the loud click of the apartment door and the sound of Ben kicking his shoes towards the rack. It amazed them all how he was the only member of the group unable to bend down, pick them up and place them neatly next to the other slightly more delicate pairs. But to be honest that and the fact he always put the recycling in the normal bin were their only gripes; not bad for a man, they reasoned.

"Probably went to get some more Trojans."

"Eugh," shuddered Kat, gently stroking Freya's bare back.

"Do you have any idea how many of the girls at school fancied him?"

Kat smiled. "I can imagine."

"Never did it for me though," she grinned.

"And what does do it for you?" whispered Kat, checking the clock and reaching down to dim the lights. She returned her hands to Freya's body.

"You," moaned Freya, enjoying the searching fingers.

"What in particular?"

Freya buried her head into Kat's neck and smelt her deep intoxicating perfume; a scent so consuming, never to be forgotten. "You know what does it for me." She lifted herself onto her elbow and gently kissed Kat's lips. "Teach me. Teach me how to do it."

Kat noticed a slight red tinge to Freya's high cheekbones, so she whispered even quieter. "What do you want me to teach you?"

"You know what."

Kat smiled and whispered. "The multiple orgasm thing?"

Freya nodded. "Nobody has even been able to do that to me before."

Kat wondered when they would have the chat about her past relationships and conquests, but realised that that time wasn't now. "Shall I talk you through it?"

"Mm hm," said Freya already enjoying the sensations of Kat's fingers parting her hair and massaging her scalp.

Kat propped herself up on her left elbow and stared at the beauty of Freya lying on her back, half covered by the white duvet, with her eyes closed. She slowly started to touch her cheeks with tiny quiet kisses, using her right hand to lightly caress her neck. "Everything has to be slow, soft and delicate." She continued the movement. "There's no teasing. It's just really slow. I will kiss your lips, your cheeks, your neck and your shoulders, always making sure my fingers are gently grazing your skin, sending quivers of anticipation across your body."

Freya breathed in. Kat was right. They were quivers of anticipation. It was an anticipation of the fingers getting lower and the kisses getting closer. She let out a soft moan.

"You see, I'm not going anywhere and then taking that pleasure away, I'm just building that pleasure in all of these different areas." She moved her mouth to Freya's neck, biting ever so lightly with her teeth, using her fingers to trail up and down Freya's right arm. "The most important thing is to be slow and gentle. I'm barely touching you but I know that you can feel every single contact like it's deep and pressured."

Freya kept her eyes closed. Every receptor in her body was in overdrive. Kat was right. She was getting lost in the build up, falling into a place of intense arousal. "Keep talking," she whispered. "I like it when you talk."

Kat continued to describe her movements. "I'll kiss your shoulders and your arms, moving down to your hands and your fingers." She made sure that every tender kiss was accompanied by a searching touch, tenderly arousing every inch of Freya's aching body. "Just enjoy it," she said, deliberately taking her time, herself gaining pleasure from the detailed attention. Freya's body was perfect and she could worship it for hours.

Freya finally felt Kat's fingers on her thighs and her mouth on her breasts. The sensation was overpowering even though the touch was so slight. She gasped in pleasure, unbelievably close to orgasm.

Kat slowly parted Freya's legs, trailing her fingers carefully around her neat triangle. Gently she moved her fingers down and carefully opened her lips.

Freya cried out in pleasure, even though she had yet to be touched.

Kat placed her middle finger in the moist warm parting and began a delicate upwards movement.

Freya tried to hold her breath, but the simplest touch was ecstasy.

Kat moved her finger back down and knew she was close.

As the tender finger made a final journey back up, Freya screamed out in pleasure, bursting with satisfaction.

Kat resisted the temptation to press down hard or plunge inside her. She could feel the tightenings and knew by the way Freya was squeezing her arm that the orgasm was intense. She paused for a while, allowing the pulses to subside, then quietly spoke again. "You have to wait until the pulses have stopped and then you increase the pressure."

Freya eventually opened her eyes which were glazed with pleasure. "Show me," she whispered.

Kat spoke softly. "You can either use your fingers again, slightly harder and more rhythmic, or..." she kept eye contact as she moved gracefully into the gap between Freya's legs, "...or you can use your mouth." She rested on her own stomach and looked up at the exposed pert breasts. "But still you must be gentle and slow." She turned her attention to the wet lips and tenderly kissed both sides.

Freya threw her head back on the pillow. This was incredible. It was a complete surprise the first time Kat had done it. She had no idea it was possible, especially not to this extent. She groaned in enjoyment. The kisses were timid, yet exploratory, and the flicks of the tongue were occasional, but perfectly timed.

Kat brought her mouth up higher and encased Freya between her lips. Gently she started a slow rhythm with her tongue. The pressure was minimal and she listened to Freya's moans for guidance. It wouldn't take long. The temptation to reach around for her bottom, draw her close and swallow her completely was huge, but she resisted. This was about Freya, not her. She heard the gasp of anticipation and knew it was coming, so she quickened the pace without increasing the pressure. She wasn't finished yet.

Freya cried out for the second time that evening. This time it was deeper and more prolonged; seemingly impossible, given the strength of her first orgasm. She gripped the sheets to the side of her. Kat was incredible, she had no idea it could be like this. Suddenly she felt Kat sliding in underneath her, pulling her back onto her stomach. Their heads were touching and they looked up at the ceiling, Freya on top, Kat underneath. "What are you doing?" she whispered, still gasping for breath, "am I not too heavy?"

Kat enjoyed the feeling of Freya's whole body lying on top of hers. "No, I need you like this."

"What for?" She felt exposed lying face up on top of Kat.

"This," Kat reached down with her hand as she would if she were about to pleasure herself, but instead of her own warm opening it was Freya's. She took her left hand and reached for Freya's nipple. She squeezed it roughly and thrust her fingers in between Freya's legs. The pace was quick and the pressure was intense.

Freya screamed out in pleasure. "Oh, fuck, Kat! Yeah! Fuck, fuck, fuck!"

Kat was hard and fast, pulling Freya's nipple and rubbing her roughly. She could feel it with her, the huge ripping orgasm that made them both lean up in contraction. She pushed her fingers deep inside and shuddered at the way Freya gripped them with mammoth pulse after pulse. She waited for what seemed like an eternity for the tightenings to stop, slowly sliding her fingers back out and wrapping both arms around Freya's shaking body.

Freya gasped. "What the fuck was that?"

"*That* was the multiple orgasm thing."

"Well fuck me!"

"I think I just did," smiled Kat.

CHAPTER NINE

Ben was determined to sit in the cluttered staffroom and waste his free period. He needed some thinking time, but wasn't really in the mood for thinking. Instead, he chose to study Hannah Phag's intricate movements around the staffroom. She was only in her early twenties, but looked much older, with awfully drab clothing and a blotchy make-up free face to match. First, she hovered around her pristine IT area, tapping her wispy chin and shaking her head. Then, she moved to the kitchenette and wandered around the island which was covered in dirty mugs. Pausing every so often to bite her chapped bottom lip and look up at the polystyrene ceiling tiles.

On any other day he would have bounced over, flung an arm around her plump shoulder and asked how he could help. She would have turned the colour of beetroot and mumbled some incoherent answer, always made worse by his immediate outrageous flirting. He liked Hannah Phag and admired her determination to stick out last year's probationary year. A difficult feat given the fact most students and staff referred to her as *Faggy*. He watched as she circled the various clusters of brown fabric chairs, rubbing her eczema covered palms together in thought. Ben suddenly pictured a monk and smiled to himself for the first time that morning. Hannah had taken the advice from the Head of IT to try and *up her image* in order to avoid undue ridicule from the kids. The upping on her part had consisted of a bowl-esque type haircut and new ankle length green felt skirt. She was now lifting up the discarded bicycle wheel in the geography area and looking at the ground.

Ben finally broke. "Come on, Hannah," he said, clambering out of his seat and wrapping a firm arm around her shoulder. "What are you looking for?"

Hannah felt the itching immediately intensify. The ever so handsome Mr Puller always had that effect on her. She tried to play it cool. "The remote got bored and went walkies." She heard the way it came out and tried to quickly rectify her mistake. "The remote for the board ... my board, my interactive white board, it's gone-"

"You're bored?" Ben thrust an imaginary dagger into his heart. "Hannah, how could you? I'm offended. Am I that bad?"

She shook her head frantically. "No, I'm not bored of you. My interactive white board remote has gone-"

He held her waist and spun her around. "You can interact with me any time you want, Miss Hannah Phag."

"No, I, well-" She giggled childishly, her occasional moments with Ben were key events in her rather slow paced life. In fact, it was only in times like this, and of course the time spent on her flame-etched moped, that ever caused her a real thrill.

Ben took her by the hand, ignoring the abrasive feeling, and guided her to the red lost property tray by the door. "Okay," he said rummaging through the items. "We have a Year Seven boy's English book. A large set of PE keys. Mr Lester's planner and ..." he tapped the item in his hand, "an interactive white board remote."

"The caretaker must have found it then!" she giggled, too hysterically.

As he passed it over he patted the top of her hand which was now starting to perspire. "Now, is there anything else I can do for you, my love?"

Kat pushed her way through the glass-topped staffroom door carrying a large box of unmarked exercise books. "You could make me a cup of tea," she whispered in passing.

Ben nodded. "Hannah, can I get you one too?"

A half baked idea shot through Hannah's mind. She'd try an innuendo. "A cup of tea?" She tried to look seductive, but knew immediately that she had failed. She scurried towards the door. That was the last time she would be trying a provocative one liner. "Umm, no no, the remote is missing the board ... bye."

"Oh bless," said Kat, watching Hannah rattle out of the staffroom, clutching her remote like her life depended on it. "I think she might like you." Smiling, she lowered the box to the tiled carpet floor and made her way over to the pigeon holes.

"Who doesn't" he replied, performing an imaginary dust of his shoulders.

"Me?" offered Kat apologetically.

Ben began to fill the lime scaled kettle and sighed. "And for that, I will be forever scarred." He dropped the ancient kettle onto its dusty stand and flicked the switch. "This time last year I thought all of my dreams had come true. You were a new, hot, sexy, smart, young teacher and I fancied the pants off you."

"No you did not."

He plonked two tea bags into the old mugs and looked up. "Yes I did."

"Does this stuff really work for you? ... With the women I mean?" Kat pulled out the pile from her pigeon hole and flicked through the bundle of letters, announcements and flyers. She paused, remembering the date. "And anyway, this time last year I'd already come out."

"Well, whatever *you do* with the women certainly seems to work," he winked and smiled cheekily.

Kat doubled checked the staffroom. She knew it was empty but she felt the need to be sure. Scowling at Ben she spoke quickly. "Yes, okay, thank you! Change of subject please."

"No seriously, I think I need a few tips if the noises coming from Freya are anything to go by."

Kat felt devastated by embarrassment. She knew Ben was only teasing, but even so. "Seriously, stop right now."

Ben had fast learnt that Kat was a complex character, never fully sure of herself; always tinged with self doubt. The only area where her confidence really shone through was in her teaching. "Oh babe, you know I'm only messing!" He grinned. "And anyway, I could make my woman shout louder than your woman."

Kat smiled, meaning every word. "We both know that's not true."

Ben chuckled loudly and used the cleanest spoon he could find to squeeze out the dripping tea bags. "I thought you did that thing with *Diane* on a Monday?"

Kat looked up from her memo and ignored the sarcasm in his tone. "She has a break from observations this week. Apparently her last few lessons have been good."

"Yeah, only thanks to *you*," he said, making his way over with the two steaming mugs. "*Mug*." He handed it over.

Kat shoved the unimportant pieces of paper back into her pigeon hole but kept hold of the memo. "Well maybe I am, but I would rather walk that extra mile and end up falling off a cliff, than never find out what's at the end of the road."

"Is that one of Lucy's sayings?"

Kat smiled, pleased that he wasn't going to give her another serious lecture about the dangers of Diane Pity. "Mine actually."

"What are you so engrossed in anyway?" He peered over her shoulder, making sure his mug of tea didn't touch her back, and read the memo. "Oh wow, Kat - that's great!" He read it once more. Janet Louza was officially informing her that she would be playing a key mentoring role in January's teacher training programme. "At least you get some of your lessons taught for you."

Kat folded the note and returned it to her pigeonhole. "That's just it. I'm not sure I want an unqualified, inexperienced person teaching my classes."

Ben walked towards his area and patted the brown sunken seat next to his own. "Ooo, listen to you! We all had to start somewhere."

Kat sat down and took a slow slip of tea. "That sounded awful didn't it! I just mean I love my classes and we have our own little routines and..." she paused, "...you're right, how selfish of me."

Ben shook her knee. "It's started - your transition from fresh faced enthusiastic young teacher, to embittered old trout!"

"Well you've perked up a bit," she said, returning his jibe with a slap on the thigh. She blew some of the steam from her mug and studied him carefully. "How are you?"

Ben took a large gulp of hot tea and tried to ignore the burning feeling scalding his throat. "All good, all good."

Kat puzzled for a moment. It had been over a month since he had confided in her about his suspicions, and as yet there had been no other news - or none that he had told her about in any case. She didn't like to pry and always felt people would talk when the time was right, but now she sensed something was wrong. "Do you know where Lisa lives? Can you get in contact with her?"

His ability to lie had improved over the past few weeks and the copious amount of practice he was getting made the current head shake fairly easy.

There was a loud and repetitive bang on the glass-topped staffroom door, so Ben jumped up, relieved at the interruption. He hooked his hand over the top of the frame and rested his head on his arm. "Chianne, to what do I owe the pleasure?"

"I've got something for Spicer. Is she in there?"

Kat heard the gruff voice and saw the huge shadow in the doorway.

"Miss Spicer, *it's for you-hoo!*" sang Ben, grinning from ear to ear and walking back over with his cheeks puffed out.

Kat slapped him on the chest as she made her way to the door. She smiled, trying to ignore the fresh coating of make-up that had been applied since the end of their last lesson. "It's only been fifteen minutes since our last class, Chianne."

"Yeah I know, but I didn't want to give you this in front of the others." She thrust a small envelope at Kat. "My seventeenth. It's an invite." She plonked her hand on her protruding hip. "There'll be loads of alcohol and shit."

"Please don't use language like that Chianne, but thank you for the invitation. I'm very flattered." Kat opened the envelope and looked at the childish party invite: *Cinema, bowling and booze up*, it said. She pursed her lips and frowned. "I'm so sorry. I'm away at my parents that weekend."

Chianne huffed, blew hot air up towards her solid black quiff, and was about to have a tantrum. Suddenly she decided to change tact. Instead she fluttered her stubby eyelashes. "Maybe we could just do something another time?" She tried to lean against the door-way and look sexy, but ended up missing the frame and struggling to keep her balance.

Kat reached for her hand. "Oops, there you go. Thanks for the offer, but no, we can't do anything for a number of reasons." She smiled. "But I'm pleased I'm back in your good books." Trying to make light of the situation was her only option.

Chianne flung the supporting hand back towards its owner and stomped off down the pale blue corridor. "Well you ain't no more!"

"I think somebody likes you," whistled Ben, enjoying the opportunity to return Kat's earlier comment.

Kat watched as Chianne strode heavily towards the double doors, banging her fist against a bullying display as she went. Kat shook her head and returned to her seat, genuinely confused. "I have no idea what to do with that girl."

"That was a girl?!"

She laughed. "Stop it, Ben! It's just that one minute she hates me and is trying to get me to make mistakes in the lesson, questioning everything I say and offering alternative arguments."

"That's a good thing, isn't it? I'm being serious now. We always want the students to have their own views and develop their own arguments."

"I know, and she's smart ... and I mean abnormally clever, but she has no clue on how to behave. She's clearly doing all of Chantelle's work for her and I know Chantelle will fail the end of term test next week ... and then I'll have to ask her to leave the course ... and then Chianne's going to be even harder to handle!"

Ben grinned. "Does she get on your bus?"

"Chianne?! Will you stop it!" Kat laughed. "I came in here for a quiet free period."

"So did I," said Ben, momentarily pulled back into the place he wanted to avoid.

"But no, she doesn't get on my bus. She's constantly showing Chantelle footage of her latest escapade with Davey Jakes."

"Good old Davey Jakes. It takes a real man to master something like Chianne."

Kat paused and thought carefully. "But I can't figure her out. I have no idea who she is."

"Do you really want to know?"

"Yes, actually I do. I'd just assumed that she was a bottom set bully who got the jibes in before others had the chance. Did you realise she was so clever?"

Ben shook his head. "No, I've never actually had the pleasure of teaching her, but she certainly hides it well."

Kat nodded her head in decision. "I think I need to peel back all of her layers and discover her inner beauty."

"Well you'll need an industrial-strength potato peeler to get through all of that lot!"

Kat stood up and smoothed her tight black skirt down to her knees and smiled. "Right that's it. I'm going to finish this free period in my room."

Ben didn't complain; the turmoil was pulling him back in, begging to be resolved. "Meet you in here at four?"

"Yep," she said pausing at the door. "Freya's got her new friend *Renee* coming round this evening."

Ben grinned. "So we finally get to meet her then?"

"We do indeed," said Kat with an official nod.

****

Kat actually felt quite nervous entering her own apartment, and judged it as a strange apprehension of the confirmation of her suspicions. Freya had settled into university life with the expected ease, quickly adjusting to the diverse timetable of lectures, seminars and practical classroom based lessons. Kat had heard all about the gloriously traditional Gaynor Newman, who clearly had a crush on the ever so shy Gregory *'who always wears elbow patches'* Taylor, and Elaine Springer with the triangle glasses, crazy dress sense and refreshingly inspirational approach to education. Yes, thought Kat, Freya's descriptions were clear ... well mostly. The only person on the course that she couldn't properly picture was Renee Eves.

Freya had returned from her first day absolutely full of beans, clearly confident in her chosen course; the fast approaching school placements her only slight concern. She had rattled away about the wide variety of characters, all with the aim of becoming qualified history teachers. Kat knew from her experience on the same course that at least forty percent wouldn't make it. The majority of that number leaving straight after the first school placement, suddenly realising that teaching wasn't for them after all. The others would be picked off due to poor assignment grades, unprofessional behaviour on school placements, or even the inability to pay their university course fees.

Renee Eves had been described as *'a right laugh,'* and *'looks a bit like Rihanna.'* Freya was constantly going on about some outrageous face she had pulled, or some hilarious comment she had made; but Kat's picture was still quite vague. Freya had insisted that Renee was straight, but for some reason Kat's own Gaydar was pinging loudly, and she'd not even met the poor girl yet. Her comment of: *'I think I need to meet this Renee,'* had caused their very first minor argument. Freya had literally taken a step back with offence and asked Kat if she was serious, to which Kat coughed lightly and said yes, she was serious; she did want to meet her. Freya had shaken her head and sighed loudly, before deciding to take the huff. Both felt a sense of regret at their own defensiveness but continued to spend the next hour sneaking glances at the other, not actually wanting to be the first one to break. A glance, met in the middle, finally broke the silence and both smiled with relief. Their standoff had been brief and their behaviour silly. The discussion, held from either ends of the kitchen table, was lengthy and tended to go over the same ground with Freya always coming back to the point that Renee was straight, and Kat always reminding her that declared sexuality made little difference. But in conclusion they felt a sense of achievement in their ability to talk sensibly ... if not slightly heatedly on Freya's part. They had made up quickly and their love for one another had been swiftly and wholeheartedly declared; but there was still that slight niggle in the back of Kat's mind, and it was that niggle that was causing her nerves this evening as she opened the heavy apartment door.

Freya heard the click and raced over from the pouffe, flinging her arms around Kat and acknowledging Ben with a quick head nod. "Hi guys! I got eighty five percent in my first assignment!"

Kat's offer of congratulations was interrupted by Freya's warm, soft lips on her own; their usual hallway greeting. Kat wondered why she had assumed it would be different tonight.

"I love you," whispered Freya beaming from ear to ear. She took Kat's hand and they walked the three short paces into the open plan lounge. "Renee meet Kat. Kat, Renee."

Kat shook the outstretched hand and placed a light kiss on the rosy brown cheeks, literally dazzled by the flash of perfect white teeth.

Renee smiled again. "Hi, pleased to meet you." She shifted her weight onto her other hip and nodded in approval. "Girl, have I heard a lot about you?"

"You too," said Kat with possibly more meaning than she would have liked. "Hang on, I've still got my coat on, give me a second." She fiddled with the buttons as she spoke. "Freya, that's an amazing result, really well done!" She turned back towards the door where Ben was deliberately messing around with the shoe rack. "Don't forget Ben," she said, turning just in time to catch Renee making an hourglass figure shape at her with her hands, and a smokin' hot wolf whistle signal with her mouth. Both seemingly to Freya's amusement.

Freya stopped grinning and stretched out her hands at both parties. "Ben, Renee. Renee, Ben."

Ben padded into the lounge. "Hi, nice to meet you. Hey! Has anyone told you that you look like Rihanna?"

Kat knew the remark was aimed at her and rolled her eyes at the cluster of coats hanging from the rack. Ben was such a pain.

Renee fingered one of her intricate cornrows. "Yeah, I get that a lot."

"I'm going to be her bodyguard tonight," giggled Freya, jumping onto the black leather sofa.

Ben nodded. "Oh yeah, Lucy mentioned that it's your big tennis beer circle. I thought our rugby circles were bad, but the girls are a million times worse!" He paused, maturity getting the better of him.

"Seriously though, just take it steady. I've seen some dreadful sights after the beer circle booze ups. It's not funny if you end up in hospital having your stomach pumped."

Renee took a seat next to Freya. "Don't worry, Gramps, you can trust me to look after her."

Kat noticed the tone and felt a pang of anxiety. Was it nerves? Was it jealousy? Or was it her deep seated insecurity once again rearing its ugly head? She walked around to the other side of the sofa and rested gently on the arm next to Freya.

"Shove up a bit." Freya nudged Renee and made enough room for Kat to squeeze in.

Renee took the hint and moved herself onto the pouffe.

"So, how was uni?" asked Kat, reassured by Freya's small gesture. She knew she was being ridiculous and she had every faith in Freya and her vow to be faithful. But she would always worry; worry that she wouldn't be enough.

"We're loving Elaine Springer, aren't we Frey?!" Renee leaned over and slapped Freya's thigh.

Kat was taken aback. First by the thigh slap, but more so with the tone in Renee's voice, speaking as if they were lifelong best friends ... *and Frey?!* Kat straightened in her seat. *Other girls weren't allowed to call her Freya, Frey!*

Renee carried on. "Elaine's so cool and she has this really funky dress sense and she wears the cutest pair of glasses."

Ben was hovering around in the kitchen. "Is that what you're into then? Women with cute glasses?"

Kat had to stifle her laughter. Ben was a true friend.

Renee gasped and fanned herself in mock embarrassment. "Look at you, sneakily checking out if I'm available." She smiled at Ben. "But no, I'm not into women." She slapped Freya's thigh once more. "Much to this one's disappointment."

Freya laughed loudly and confirmed her assessment. "See, I told you she was a right laugh!"

CHAPTER TEN

Freya and Renee raced down the sticky steps into their heaving Student's Union bar. They were half an hour late. Kat and Ben had kept them talking in the apartment, warning them of the dangers of downing drinks and doing dares. The chat actually managed to have the opposite effect and increase their already heightened level of excitement. The evening was going to be raucous and both were in the mood to celebrate. The term had started well. They were holding their own in seminars, up to date with coursework, and their first assignments had been returned with distinctions. Yes, they had declared on the way over, it was time to let loose and party.

Freya had been instantly drawn to Renee's wild sense of humour and their stifled giggles from the very first lecture had been quickly followed by uninhibited laughs at the bustling Freshers' Fair. Upon entering the lively hall, Renee had immediately pointed Freya in the direction of the LGBT table and laughingly instructed her to go and sign up. However, the lone woman who was sitting at the rainbow decorated table, with crazy hair and crossed eyes, looked like she was more into segregation than inclusion. Freya had politely declined Renee's request and made her way over to the bustling tennis stand instead, signing up and promising to be at trials the following Friday. Renee had taken the pen, declared she was the third Williams sister and stated her playing level as regional; which much to Freya's surprise, she actually was.

The tennis trials had been more like a round robin tournament, with each of the first year students playing against the other, until the six with the most points played a match against a member of the university's current first team. Freya had made it into the final six, securing a place on the squad, but had lost her last match which meant a position in the second team; which in itself was a real achievement. Renee, who impressed in the early rounds, was put against the university's number one seed. Renee won in straight sets and became the only Fresher to make it into the top team. Freya had assumed from their brief friendship that she would be whooping and dancing and ensuring no one ever heard the end of it, but she didn't. Renee was actually really modest about it, which Freya found very interesting indeed.

"Do you think they'll fine us?" giggled Freya, hopping down the last step and pushing open the double doors to reveal a bar full of students in various states of undress. The Student's Union had been a real highlight of the open day tour, with Elaine Springer allowing them to stop and sample a beverage of choice. Freya had sipped her half pint of cider - it was what all of the others had chosen and she didn't want to appear unprofessional by drinking a pint, or lacking in spirit by choosing a soft drink. So, she sipped her beverage and fell in love with the room's unique design. It was set out like an athletics stadium with a four sided bar in the middle, a circular race track running all the way around the outside of the bar and a large outer area full of big round booths and clusters of moveable tables. Each booth was now full of one sports team or another and the groups that had arrived late had to create their own circles with the lightweight metal tables. She spotted the tennis girls in one of the first booths and felt a rush of adrenaline. This would be a night to remember, her first ever university beer circle. They were the stuff of legend ... or so she had been told.

Renee felt the same buzz and shouted her response, the noise of drinking songs and forfeit commands was deafening. "Yes! We'll definitely get a fine ... or possibly a dare," she smiled.

They sheepishly approached the beer circle and were met with a roaring shout. "What time do you call this?" Big Bird, the tennis club's ever so boisterous social secretary was leaning forwards across the table and pointing her stocky finger. They had been to a number of social dos, fundraisers and post match drinks in the bar before, but nothing had been as full on as this. As a club, they were currently unbeaten, and Renee and Freya were both quickly becoming the weekly star players for their respective teams. Freya still found post match showers embarrassing though, and it was fine when the games were at home as the university had modern facilities with individual shower cubicles; but some of the away matches were at old decrepit universities with rows of wobbly, always dribbling, always cold, showers. It wasn't that she was embarrassed about her body, more that she didn't want the other girls to be embarrassed around her. Deep down she knew it was a non issue, especially since Big Bird made it her duty to sit and comment on everyone's tit size, arse size and style of trim. Freya thought back to the most recent away fixture, trying to pinpoint what exactly it was about the showers that had made her feel uncomfortable. Renee's staring eyes suddenly came to mind.

"I said, what time do you call this?!"

Big Bird's bark pulled her out of it.

The pair stood nervously in front of the other on-time tennis players, unsure of the seriousness of the question.

"Seven thirty?" offered Renee, glancing at her watch.

"Right! That's thirty minutes late." Big Bird turned to her circle. "Who thinks it should be a mouthful of beer for every minute late?"

The cheers were thunderous.

Big Bird stood up, which due to her height and width, commanded even more attention. "There are fifteen girls in the circle. Get on the table and have a glug of everyone's drink, sing the uni song and then go round the circle taking a second glug."

The cheers became even more thunderous.

Freya looked at the sticky wet mess on the large round table and instantly regretted opting for her white jeans.

Big Bird noted their reticence. "That, or go and snog *Weener*." She pointed at Martin '*Weener*' Webley who was standing naked in the centre of the boys' football beer circle, with the group in the middle of some raucous, vulgar song.

"I'll take Weener," said Renee, immediately making her way towards the chanting footballers.

Freya watched in horror and admiration as Renee clambered onto the sodden table and made her announcement. "Sorry lads, I just need to snog Weener."

The group of lads jeered and started the required song. Each beer circle had its own rules and all participants knew best to follow them to a tee, no matter how harsh they were. *"Who let the dogs out? Woof, woof, woof, woof,"* the required chant for whenever a girl entered their domain.

Freya watched with her mouth wide open as Renee ferociously snogged Martin Webley, a really shy, apparently great footballer, also on their history teaching course.

"What's it to be then, Sparkles?" Big Bird referred to the name splashed across the back of Freya's bright yellow tennis t-shirt, an absolute essential for any social event and an instant dismissal from a beer circle if not worn. She had got off fairly lightly when the t-shirts were presented at the end of the first match and felt sorry for the one's labelled 'Sticky Fingers' or 'Anal Annie.'

Freya lifted herself onto the table and sat cross-legged in the middle, instantly conscious of the cold, wet liquid seeping through to her knickers. She reached for the first drink offered. "I guess I'll take the drinks."

Big Bird roused the group in song. *"Get it down you student warrior, get it down you student chief, chief, chief, chief."* She loved her job as social secretary and lived for the lively buzz of evenings like these. Newcomers always saw her as hard faced and fearsome but once they got to know her they quickly realized she was a softy at heart.

Freya took swig after swig of the outstretched drinks, pausing only to catch her breath and shimmy herself on her bottom around to her next teammate. The drink of choice seemed to be a mixture of cider and lager with some blackcurrant cordial or something added. Whatever it was, it wasn't great. Freya had spun full circle and reached out for Big Bird's plastic cup. She took an impressively large mouthful and rose to her feet, singing with gusto. *"With a B and an I and an R and an M, and an I and an N and a G and an H, and an A and an M, and a shout with me, we are Birmingham Uni! La, la, la, la, la, la ... la, la, la, la, la, la, la ... la, la, la, la, la ,la, la, we are Birmingham Uni."* It had been made very clear that all Freshers needed to learn the university song if they wanted an easy ride on their first beer circle and Freya had sought help from Kat on perfecting the lyrics. It had obviously worked as the group of tennis players erupted into cheers of congratulations.

"Sparkles, you've saved yourself, no need to do another round of drinks." Big Bird signalled Renee who was clambering down from the footballers' table. "Right, Colgate, get yourself up here and sing us the uni song."

Renee jumped onto her second table of the evening and tried to remember the words. She stumbled, "I'm a B and an I, I'm an R, no we're-" She raised her hands in apology. "I don't know it!"

The drum roll of hands on the table got faster and louder and Renee actually seemed to be wobbling with the force of movement.

"CONTRIBUTIONS!" shouted Big Bird, emptying a discarded plastic pint glass onto the floor and offering it into the circle to be filled by the other members' drinks. What was produced was a slushy mess of dark red liquid. "Down in one, then balance the empty glass upside down on your head. Go!!"

Renee did exactly what was commanded, necked the drink in four swift gulps and balanced the empty cup on her head with only the smallest amount of liquid trickling down her face and towards her cleavage.

"Bloody hell! You drink as well as you play tennis! Now put those pearly whites away, Colgate, and grab a seat!" Big Bird was impressed.

Renee dropped down into the booth next to Freya and let out a giggle of nerves. She whispered. "Shit, maybe Kat and Ben were right!"

Freya ignored the comment and focused her full attention on Big Bird; she didn't want to give her any more ammunition.

Big Bird let out a huge belch. "Right! Now that we are all here, we can begin!"

"We haven't started yet?!" laughed Renee.

"DREGS!" bawled Big Bird reaching for the discarded plastic pint glass. She started to sweep the spilt liquid from the table into the cup, passing it around the circle for her comrades to do the same. "Rule number one, newbie ... no one ever speaks when the social secretary is speaking." Big Bird reached for the cup, now filled with a centimetre of dirty brown liquid. "The punishment for this offense is dregs! Now get it down." She thrust it towards Renee and started to sing. *"There was a lady in red..."*

The group sang the responses in perfect unison. *"There was a lady in red."*

"...and she liked to give good head."

Renee held the cup above her head and studied the bits floating around.

Big Bird carried on singing. *"There was a lady in glitter..."*

"There was a lady in glitter."

"...and she liked it up the shitter."

"One more and it needs to be gone!" bawled Big Bird. *"There was a lady in fluff..."*

"There was a lady in fluff."

Renee closed her eyes and downed the drink.

"...and she liked a bit of muff." Big Bird slammed her fist on the table. "Well done! Right girls, it's a three minute pit stop! Piss, puke and pints. Make sure you're back here with three full pints and no sloping off, newbies!" She gave Freya and Renee the daggers.

"Why would we do that when we're having so much fun?" shouted Renee, trying not to retch.

"You're going to be trouble, aren't you, Colgate!" smirked Big Bird, pulling herself out of the booth and staggering towards the ladies.

Renee reached for Freya's hand and yanked her out of the sticky seats. "Come on, purple ass, we only have three minutes!"

Freya patted the back of her previously white jeans now ringing wet with a concoction of booze. But instead of feeling panicked and self conscious, she studied the other 'ladies' now making their way to the bar or the loos. All were in some sort of disrepair, and the tennis girls did actually seem to be one of the more restrained groups in the noisy and chaotic Student's Union. All of the hockey girls looked to be on their last legs and the rugby girls didn't have a bra between them. She stopped and waited for the naked running men to hurtle past her on the track.

Renee spanked a pert bottom as it raced past.

"You seem so calm about all of this!" said Freya, hopping over the track and making her way to the toilets.

"My sister was at Leeds and I joined a couple of her netball beer circles," she paused, "...and Sparkles ... you ain't seen nothing yet!"

Undergraduates at all universities across the UK, who weren't a member of a sports team, knew instinctively to stay away from the Student's Union on a Wednesday night. It was messy and always chaotic.

Freya pushed open the double doors and joined the back of the queue for the toilets. "Don't call me Sparkles."

"But your eyes, they're so pretty and so sparkly." Renee giggled, fluttering her eyelashes.

"Oh and your teeth are so glowing and white." Freya laughed. "Colgate and Sparkles, not exactly cool names are they?"

"Well I'm not complaining! That Big Bird's a monster."

Freya lowered her voice as it was mostly the tennis girls in the queue. "Well my Gaydar thinks she may have a little crush on you."

"In her dreams!" laughed Renee. "Martin Weener Webley has more chance than her! Did you see his little pencil? It definitely got more pointy when we were kissing."

"Gross. No, I was too busy drinking fifteen drinks!" She stepped into the vacated cubicle and closed the door, suddenly propping herself against the wall. She was already starting to feel unsteady.

"Piss it out! Puke it up! But whatever you do, hurry up! Bar and booth in one minute!" The bawl was unmistakably Big Bird's, so Freya yanked her white jeans back up, crashed out of the cubicle, sprayed a dash of water on her hands and raced to the bar. She ordered three pints of cider and proudly lined them on the table, one of the first back in the booth.

Big Bird edged in next to her. "Well done for being so game." She lowered her voice. "Seriously though, it's all just a bit of fun. Give me the nod if you're feeling rough and I'll ease off."

"Really?"

"NO! Now get that pint down you!"

The shout was so loud that it made Freya jump. She reached for her first glass.

Big Bird laughed. "Yes really. You Freshers' are so gullible!"

Freya wasn't sure if she was supposed to drink or not so she lifted the glass and took a couple of small gulps.

"Seriously, take it steady. The women's priority minibus will be here at nine and I want all of us on it." Big Bird looked up and noticed that most of her flock had returned with cradles of pints in tow. "Right, ladies. I think a game of *never have I ever* is called for."

Renee was the last to plonk herself down in the booth.

"Colgate, you're first. Never have I ever."

"What?"

"It's a beer circle game, Colgate. You say *never have I ever*, and say something you've never done."

Renee screwed up her nose. "Why would I say something I've never done?"

"Because you're trying to drop other people in the shit. If they've done it, then they have to drink." Big Bird knew the games like the back of her hand.

Renee smiled. "Never have I ever been a Tennis Team Social Secretary."

"You've got it! ... You bitch!" Big Bird laughed and took three gulps of drink.

The game took off quickly with Freya actually getting off rather lightly since most of the statements involved sordid experiences with men. It was her turn and she had one that would get them all talking. "Never have I ever had sex with a man."

Big Bird sprayed the table with the contents of her mouth. "Sparkles, we're changing your t-shirt to Virginia."

Freya shrugged. "I didn't say I was a virgin. I just said I'd never slept with a man." Some of the girls from her team knew about Kat, but it was clearly not common knowledge yet, so she smiled and repeated her offering. "Never have I ever slept with a man, who's drinking?" All fifteen lifted their cups.

"Right then, you dark horse." Big Bird was grinning. "Never have I ever slept with a woman?"

The adjacent women's hockey circle heard the statement and all cheered, downing the remainder of their drinks; lesbianism seemed to be a prerequisite for a place on the university hockey team.

Freya lifted her cup, as did two other girls in her circle ... and Renee. She looked over and frowned.

Renee saw the questioning eyes. "Well you have to try everything once don't you!"

"Snog, snog, snog, snog." The chanting had begun.

"Sparkles, Colgate, you're up first."

Freya made a stop sign with her hand. "I'm taken, sorry."

"Pucker up, Sparkles. Everyone knows what happens in a beer circle, stays in a beer circle." Big Bird started the chanting again.

"Snog, snog, snog, snog."

"Well I'm game," said Renee clambering onto the table and resting her feet on the seat either side of Freya's legs. "Come on, Sparkles. Take one for the team."

Big Bird offered Freya a lifeline. "Snog your bezzie, or down your pint in one."

"Sorry, I'll have to take this." Freya reached for her drink and started to gulp, spotting Renee through the base of the plastic cup sliding backwards and edging down into her seat on the opposite side of the table. She balanced the empty pint glass on her head. "Done," she nodded, causing it to fall into the lap of her neighbour. She lifted her eyes to Renee who was now staring in the opposite direction.

The evening rapidly deteriorated into a mess of dancing, dares and downing, but for the most part Freya was having a whale of a time. The highlight was possibly the boat race against the women's rugby team. Both groups stood in a line on one of the race tracks next to the bar. On the starter's orders the first women in each line downed their drinks, slammed their plastic cups upside down onto their heads, and raced around the bar to tag the second in the line and so on. The winning team was the one with all members back to the starting position. Every other person seemed to be slipping at the second corner and the drinks being thrown their way from the men's swimming team failed to help. Freya managed a clear run and collapsed back on the track in fits of laughter. Tina, who followed on from her, forgot to down her drink before turning the cup upside down on her head and covered herself in a full pint of lager.

Renee skidded to an unintentional stop on her bottom next to Freya's feet. She looked up and laughed. "I'm so frickin smashed, mate!"

Freya's words had become slurred. "We've got to get on schum buss yet."

With perfect timing, a long horn blared from outside. Big Bird gathered her troops. "Women's priority mini bus is here. Get on it now. No sloping off," she shouted, deliberately aiming her voice at Renee.

"Where does she think I'm going?" she frowned.

"Sche wants to schit nexst to you, babe."

"I like it when you call me babe," winked Renee, pulling Freya to her feet and guiding her out of the double doors and up the treacherous steps to where the mini bus was waiting. It was a new university initiative that had the aim of increasing female safety on campus, and on a Wednesday night a list was clearly displayed showing the order in which each of the women's team would be picked up. This evening they were third on the list to women's rugby and women's football and everyone knew the stench of sick on the bus would already be overpowering. They would all be carted off to the city campus where the partying would continue. The boys were left to fend for themselves and great prestige could be gained amongst mates if any males managed to board the bus as a secret stowaway. Most of the time they were left standing on the curb, waiting for their extortionately expensive taxis, watching the numerous exposed breasts pressed up against the steamy windows of the battered minibus.

The tennis girls all piled in and started to recite the heartfelt, yet vulgar beer circle songs, causing the windows to fog up instantly with a potent mix of alcoholic condensation. Freya joined in to the best of her ability, conscious that everything whizzing past the wet windows looked a bit of a blur.

Big Bird threw the new pieces of paper into the back of the bus. She took her job as Social Secretary very seriously and wanted the girls to learn this new song. She lifted herself onto her knees, trying to look unaffected by the bumpy journey, and spoke. "Right, ladies. This is the tampax factory song. It's a new one that I want us all to learn. I'll start off and then I want to go round this way." She signalled to her right at the minibus crammed full of very drunk girls. "You and the person sitting next to you sing the next line."

Freya couldn't even read the hazy words, but knew Renee would be loud enough for the pair of them.

Big Bird began the tuneful holler as the minibus rounded another sharp corner. "*We're the girls who work in the Tampax factory. Shout your orders loud and clear, loud and clear. We've got thin ones, fat ones, sannys big and small. When the end of the month comes around.*" She pointed at Tina and Tracy sitting on the first row of seats.

They hollered their line with full gusto. "*You can tell by the smell that she isn't very well, when the end of the month comes around.*"

The bus erupted into fits of laughter and Big Bird sang the chorus once more. "*We're the girls who work in the tampax factory. Shout your orders loud and clear, loud and clear. We've got thin ones, fat ones, sannys big and small. When the end of the month comes around.*" She nodded and signalled the couple in the next row.

They were equally as loud. "*You can tell that she's blobbin cause she losing haemoglobin, when the end of the month comes around.*"

The responses following each tuneful chorus were becoming more outrageous. "*You can tell by the taste that it isn't salmon paste, when the end of the month comes around.*"

The minibus was literally shaking with laughter. "*You can tell by the string that she's got the bugger in, when the end of the month comes around.*"

The lines were hilarious and Freya was properly trying not to wet herself. "It's us!" she wailed, seeing Big Bird's waving finger.

Renee took the lead and shouted: "*You can tell from the frown that you'll have to pot the brown, when the end of the month comes around.*"

"Woo hoo and again girls!" Big Bird was kneeling on the front seat, conducting her crowd like a professional.

Freya thought the journey seemed to be super bumpy and super long, but that was probably because she was having to concentrate very hard on not being sick. The minibus pulled to an abrupt stop and she hit her head on the seat in front with a heavy thud. She had no idea who the driver was, or why on earth they would agree to a route like this one. She pulled back and looked up to see Big Bird ringing a pretend bell which appeared to indicate the end of the beer circle.

The holler had become really gruff. "Stay safe, have fun and be at tennis training by nine a.m. on Saturday morning." Big Bird glanced over at Renee. "I'll be next to the main bar if anyone needs me."

The gaggle of girls piled off the minibus and charged into the cheesy university club.

Freya and Renee were the last ones off. "What happens now?" slurred Freya, clumsily falling out of the sliding doors and not rushing to pull herself back up.

Renee took her hand and yanked her across the road, towards the burly bouncers and into the pumping club. "Now we have a chat in the toilets," she said.

Freya had a vague recollection of being in the building before, but she couldn't quite place it.

"Looks different to Freshers' Fair hey?" shouted Renee.

Freya couldn't focus and closed her eyes as Renee pulled her into the noisy toilets. She opened them briefly to enter a cubicle and reach for the lid. She dropped it down and sat on the seat.

Renee followed her into the tiny space and closed the door behind them.

"Don't worry, I'm not pisssschin. Jusscht sittin on the ssheat." She looked up at Renee. "I need ... to get ... taxi ... I'm done."

"I'm not," said Renee, dropping down to her knees in front of Freya. She held Freya's cheeks in her hands and moved forwards for a kiss.

Freya's reactions were too slow. Renee's lips were on hers, parting her mouth and exploring with her tongue.

She tried to move back but her head was heavy and Renee's hands were supporting her. She let it happen. She could barely keep her eyes open, let alone resist being pounced upon. She eventually got the strength to flick her hand against Renee's wrists, causing Renee to pause.

"Don't you want this?"

Freya shrugged her shoulders. "Scchit ... you ... you're cute ... and ... you've got nice ... lips," it took great effort to wiggle her finger slowly, but she managed it and she tried to sound firm, "but Katss's mine."

"Shut up! Our chemistry is electric, come here!" She reached once again for Freya's sticky neck.

Freya was slow to react, confused by the come on, eventually shaking her head and sniffing. "I want Kat."

"Don't frickin cry on me!" gasped Renee. "I thought you were up for a laugh?"

Freya shook her head and tried to stand. "I want Kat."

"Shit mate, look at you." Renee took Freya's weight on her shoulders and pulled open the door. "Don't worry, I'll get us a taxi."

****

Kat heard the apartment door slam shut and checked her clock. It was before midnight and she breathed a sigh of relief. She had been convinced that Freya wouldn't be crawling in until the early hours of the morning. She was about to jump out of bed when she heard a second voice. She crept out from under her duvet and perched on the end of her bed in the darkness, quickly trying to decipher the mumbles.

CHAPTER ELEVEN

Kat was sitting behind her wooden desk with her classroom door firmly locked. From its position no one peeping through the glass panel would be able to see her, or feel her anguish. She closed her eyes and the screeching of noisy gulls feasting on the littered tennis courts pained her ears. She was in turmoil, cursing her own stupidity. She had waited on the edge of the bed for too long. Trying to make out their voices. Trying to decide. Any normal human being would have jumped up, said hello and asked how their partner's evening had been; but it was Renee's presence in their apartment that had caused her to falter. She was not meant to be staying over, so why was she there? Kat leaned backwards in her padded teacher's chair and replayed the events of the evening, shaking her head and biting her bottom lip at the painful memory. She should have just jumped off the bed and found out, but she didn't. She just sat still and listened to their hushed voices, suddenly hearing Freya's bedroom door close. It was a surreal moment that had caused her heart to quicken and her eyes to widen in the darkness of her own bedroom. What was happening? Why hadn't Freya rushed in? What on earth was she doing alone with Renee?

Kat must have stayed still on the edge of her bed for over an hour, listening and waiting, willing herself to get up and make some noise in the kitchen, show Freya she was awake; but she didn't. She just waited in the darkness as all of her fears came to life.

Kat suddenly froze at the sound of a quiet knock on her classroom door. She felt foolish for hiding away, but desperately wanted to be alone. Maybe it was Ben, she thought. Maybe he wanted to know why she wasn't wasting her free period with him in the staffroom. She eyed the door handle, expecting it to move; but it didn't. She strained her ears over the noisy cawing of gulls and listened for the footsteps to return back down the corridor. What she hadn't been expecting was Freya's small voice.

"Kat? Are you in there? Can I come in?"

Kat jumped up and rushed to the door, quickly twisting the lock and pulling Freya in. She held her so close, so tight and almost started to cry.

Freya looked up and grinned. "Bad day?"

Kat released her grip, flicked the lock closed once more and walked slowly back towards her desk, picking up one of the blue plastic classroom chairs as she went. "Sit down."

"Ooo, I like this! How long until your next lesson?"

Kat could feel herself welling up and tried to take a deep, slow breath, which actually ended up sounding sharp and emotion filled.

"What's wrong?" Freya scraped her chair as close as was possible and held Kat's thighs between her own legs.

"Why are you here?" Kat didn't want to be dramatic or accusing. She just wanted the truth.

Freya took Kat's hand and looked deep into the anxious blue eyes. "You'd gone before I woke up this morning and I missed you. Your timetable at home said you were free lesson four so I thought I'd pop in. My lecture's not until five." Freya paused, unable to read the situation. "That's okay isn't it? You did say it was okay for me to pop into school on the odd occasion didn't you?"

Kat let go of the warm hand and massaged her own temples. There was no easy way to say it. "I saw you. I saw you this morning."

Freya looked confused.

Kat pinned Freya with her piercing blue eyes. "I saw you in bed with Renee."

"What?" Freya's face was a picture of genuine shock. "Well she wasn't there when I got up and I still had all of my filthy clothes on. So I'm not quite sure what you think you saw!"

Kat knew the one thing that Freya hated more than anything was to be accused of something she hadn't done. Now her green eyes were narrow with disbelief.

"I lay awake for most of last night, hoping you'd come in to me-" Freya cut in, her voice was louder and higher pitched. "I was so trashed last night that I didn't want you to see me like that! I thought I was doing you a favour letting you sleep!"

Kat controlled her breathing, desperate to stay calm. "Well I wasn't asleep ... and I heard you two come in."

"What, and then you listened to us shagging all night?"

Kat raised her eyebrows and lifted herself backwards, creating some space with her chair. "No, but I looked in on you this morning as I was about to leave and ... and I saw Renee in your bed ... with her arm over your stomach."

"Are you being serious?" Freya wasn't sure if it was the raging hangover or the absurdity of the situation that was making her cross, but whatever it was she knew she had to keep hold of her fiery temper. The last thing Kat needed to see was her childish side ... but she couldn't help it. "And was she naked? Were her hands down my pants?"

"No, but you were in bed together." Kat lifted her hands in exasperation. "Can you not understand that I'm a bit upset?"

Freya watched as a watery glaze started to show in Kat's emotion filled eyes. She pulled her seat closer and took Kat's hands. "Of course I can. Look, I'm an idiot. I got it wrong. I got so drunk last night that I needed to be carried home. I'm a pathetic, lightweight student and I didn't want my mature, professional, perfect girlfriend seeing me in that state." She bent her head to kiss Kat's hands and lifted her eyes in apology. "I'm so sorry, Kat. She'd gone this morning when I woke up and I won't let her stay again."

Kat was the one who now felt childish. How lucky of Freya to have someone who would bring her home. "It's not about that."

"What's it about then?"

Kat shrugged her shoulders and smiled gently. "I don't know. I guess I read too much into it, seeing her in our bed."

Freya raised her eyebrows. "*In* our bed?"

"Well, no. On our bed."

"Oh right, now we're getting to it." Freya grinned. "And did you see the state of me?"

Kat hadn't really taken her time to study the situation, but now as she thought about it with fresh perspective, Freya had looked rather stained. "Oh, I'm so sorry. I've been sitting in here fretting." She rose to her feet and lifted Freya for a heartfelt hug. "I just love you so much and I guess I was worried that I'd lost you."

Freya shook her head against Kat's warm neck. "You're my one. How many times do I have to tell you?"

Kat felt ridiculous, how much time had she wasted today worrying over her own stupid insecurity. She felt the buzz in Freya's back pocket and reaching down, pulled the phone out of its warm nesting. She passed it to Freya and sat back down on the edge of her wooden desk, feeling as if an enormous weight had been lifted from her shoulders.

Freya read the text and chuckled. "It's Renee." She lifted the phone to Kat. "She says: *Wasn't last night a blast ... We are the girls from the tampax factory! Dreading seeing Martin, please forget about the snog, hope your hangover isn't too bad!* Can you believe she got on a table full of footballers and snogged Martin from our course, who was completely naked and absolutely terrified."

Kat could see the twinkle in Freya's eye, the one that she herself used to get after every uni night out when visions of the raucous events finally came back to her the next morning. "Yes I can." Kat grimaced. "You didn't learn that awful tampax factory song did you?"

"Yes! It's hilarious." She took hold of Kat's slender waist. "I've got so much to tell you. It was such a funny evening. Shall we go out for dinner after my lecture?"

Kat smiled. "I'd like that a lot .... and I'm sorry. I don't want you thinking that I doubt you."

"But you did though, didn't you?" She gently pushed a layer of blonde hair back behind Kat's ear.

"No, I doubted myself. I constantly doubt myself. I doubt whether I'll be enough for you."

Freya rolled her eyes. "Look at you. You're perfect and I don't want anyone else ... ever." She kissed Kat gently on the lips and playfully spanked her bottom before turning to leave. "I'll text you later and I'm sorry for being such a drunken mess."

Kat watched the wavy chestnut hair swaying from side to side as Freya fiddled with the door lock. "As long as it's not you she's kissing, then I don't care how drunk and messy you get."

Freya felt the lock finally ping open as a horrific vision of remembrance flashed into her mind. She couldn't manage a response so she nodded and stepped out into the empty corridor, wide eyed and full of dread.

****

Sitting alone at the table for two, Freya once again rehearsed her speech. She would explain, justify and then reassure. Tearing a strip off the red and white striped napkins she gasped. Kat would never understand. Trying to compose herself she thought about it logically - Kat *would* understand, but she would question. She would question her word, her motives, her version of the story. She would think she wanted it, enjoyed it ... preferred it. She would ask why she hadn't mentioned it at school. How ridiculous to think she'd believe it only occurred to her as she left the classroom. Oh shit! Renee's reference to the snog in the text was meant for her. It was obvious now. Freya rested her elbows on the red and white striped table cloth and supported her head in her hands. The excruciatingly loud music had started again. She looked up and watched as the waiter, who appeared to be dressed as a red and white jester, danced around with a flaming pink birthday cake, in time with the modern Happy Birthday song. The whole restaurant was once again encouraged to shout hip hip hoorah! She rubbed her eyes, trying not to smudge her mascara, having applied more make up than usual in an effort to look slightly less dead than she had for most of the day.

"Howdy, Ma'am. Can I get you any drinks yet?" The waitress had the best American accent and widest smile of the crew; thus earning her the four stripy stars on her shoulder.

Freya looked up at the thirty-something woman with bouncing short pig tails and rosy red cheeks. She managed to shake her head. "No, not yet, thanks."

"Hold your horses, Ma'am, here we go again!" The waitress grabbed Freya's hand and waved it in time above her head as her colleague, who only had two stripy stars due to his atrocious American accent, attempted to rouse the room into song.

Freya looked up at her excitable waitress with bouncing pig tails who was singing loudly, squeezing her hand and nodding for her to join in. "Happy birthday dear..."

The male jester holding the blue sparkling cake tried really hard to put an authentic American twang on it: "Beeeeenny!"

"Happy birthday to you!" finished off the rest of the room.

Freya watched in embarrassment as the stripy jester disappeared around the corner with the flaming blue cake. She looked up at her own stripy, seemingly new best friend, and shook her hand free.

The smile was permanent. "Just give a holler when y'all need me, darling!"

Kat suddenly appeared through a cluster of people, carefully avoiding a bunch of balloons that had been knocked in her direction. She edged into the padded stripy seat at Freya's table and leaned over to kiss her girlfriend. "You look like you're having fun. Thanks for waiting." She dropped her bag onto the table. "Kirsty kept me behind. She wants me to run the school's LGBT history month next year in February. She thinks I'll be perfect for the role."

Freya smiled. "Wow. I read about that the other day. It's the one started by Sue Sanders and the School's Out Project, right?"

Kat nodded as she adjusted herself in her seat.

"That's amazing! From what I read it seems to be a huge thing in most schools."

"It is." Kat lifted herself up and started to unbutton her coat. "We're going to follow the Educate and Celebrate programme devised by Elly Barnes."

Freya moved the workbag from the table and placed it on the floor. "I remember her name from the article. She's the teacher who trains schools on how to be LGBT friendly."

"That's right. She's making a huge difference."

"And so will you," said Freya, smiling at Kat. "You'll be great." She suddenly rolled her eyes at the new party of twelve that had just entered the popular restaurant. "Sorry, I didn't realise it would be this busy. There have been three birthdays already. How was the rest of your day?"

Kat finally hung her black coat on the back of her chair and took a deep smiling breath. "It was great after I saw you." She reached for Freya's hand across the table and looked straight into her pretty green eyes. "I'm so sorry for being all dramatic. I realise how silly I must have looked."

Freya took back her hand and picked up the torn stripy napkin. "You weren't being dramatic and you had every right to be annoyed, but listen," she paused, "something happened ... and I only just remembered it ... and I need you to understand-"

"What the fuck?!" Kat stood out of her seat.

Freya looked up for the first time. Kat never swore and she'd not expected the reaction to be *this* bad.

"That's Ben!" Kat edged quickly out from the table and made her way through the group of people taking it in turns to hit the multicoloured piñata. Ben was standing at the restaurant's exit holding the hand of a small boy and the hand of a very thin blonde woman. Kat was fuming. She pushed a cluster of red and white balloons out of her way and reached him before he made his exit. She tapped him hard on the shoulder. "Ben, hi!"

Ben looked around and immediately released both grips. "Kat!"

She ignored him and crouched down, smiling at the little boy. "Hello, I guess you must be Benny."

"Mmm hmm," he said with a mouthful of complimentary jelly beans. "I'm four." He proudly tapped the large badge on his chest.

"Well happy birthday then, Benny who's four." She smiled, gently rising to her feet and glaring at Ben. She stretched her hand towards the petite blonde lady. "You must be Lisa."

"Mmm hmm," was the nodded response, eyes darting from side to side.

Kat wasn't sure who looked the most shocked, Lisa or Ben. "Ben, could I have a quick word please?"

"Sure, sure," he was frantically rubbing his messy blonde hair. "Lisa, Benny mate, I'll meet you guys in the car."

"Okay Seed Daddy." The voice was angelic.

Freya peered over the crowd of piñata bashing adults and spotted Kat who was now stood hand on hip giving Ben, what looked like, an ear-bashing. Kat was so loyal and so principled that her own inevitable admission was sure to cause hurt. She took a sip of water and watched as the silent show unfolded.

Kat paused for breath. "All I care about is Lucy."

Ben knew how awful the set up looked, but he was telling the truth. "I promise you, Kat. Benny asked us to hold hands on his birthday. Crikey, she was more embarrassed than I was. She's happily married."

"Why didn't you tell me? I mean, how long has this been going on for?"

Ben shrugged his shoulders. "I couldn't. It's all happened so fast and it's completely mind blowing. Kat, I'm a dad. Me, of all people!" He smiled with surprised pride.

"And what about Lucy?" Kat couldn't get her head around what was going on.

"Lucy's the love of my life ... I was going to tell her."

"When?" She realised that it was not her place to judge or bark orders but the poor night's sleep was making her unusually short tempered.

"I wanted to get Jess's wedding out of the way first. You guys are bridesmaids and Lucy's never been a bridesmaid and she's so excited and-"

Kat shook her head. "Oh, so you're doing her a favour by not telling her? Ben, this is huge! You need to speak to her as soon as you can," she paused, "and by that I mean right now. Get home and tell her." She was actually pointing at the door whilst making the order.

"But Jess's wedding, she's so excited."

"You can't seriously be using that as an excuse? This has nothing to do with Jess's wedding. What if Lucy was here now? I was going to invite her, it's a good job I didn't. Can you imagine how upset and humiliated she would feel?"

Ben shrugged his shoulders. "Shit, I'm a knob, I know I am ... I just don't know how to handle this. For fucks sake Kat, I've got a son! Me, with a kid!"

"Yes, and you also have a girlfriend who thinks the world of you. I don't care what you do but don't show her up." She was eye to eye with Ben and wanted him to feel her full force. "Don't make me lie for you. You know I won't do that for anybody."

"Please, Kat. Don't tell her, not yet."

Kat rubbed her forehead. The boisterous noises from the lively restaurant were really starting to grate. "I'm sorry, but my loyalties lie with Lucy. Go home and tell her." She had never said it before and realised it sounded wholeheartedly dramatic, but she had no other choice. "You tell her tonight or I will."

"Come on Kat! Be fair!"

"No, you play fair. Lucy's my friend."

Ben shifted his weight uneasily, thinking about his response. "Lucy's lucky to have you ... and I'm sure you're probably right."

"Aren't I always?" she smiled, bashing him lightly on the chest, hoping he wouldn't hate her.

"I just don't know how to say it."

"Well you better get thinking on the way home then, matey."

"You think I should tell her tonight?"

"Yes, Ben. You tell her at the first possible moment and you pray that she understands."

"That I've got a son?"

"No, that you were confused and that's why you took so long to tell her. Lucy's the most loving, genuine person you could ever hope to meet and you need to give her some more credit. You really should have told her."

He shook his head in realisation. "Oh shit, I'm a knob aren't I?" Pulling her in for a full bodied hug he laughed in defeat. "You bloody women, you're all so perfect!"

Kat pulled away and waved across at Freya who was studying them intently. "Well I know mine is." She smiled and pushed him gently towards the doors. "Off you go then. We won't rush home."

"Good," he said, raising his bushy blonde eyebrows and reaching for another handful of complimentary jelly beans, confident that Benny would have finished his pile already.

Kat watched him edge his way out of the weighted doors and made her way back through the balloon filled area to her table where Freya was sitting rather anxiously. "I need a drink," she sighed, pulling herself back into the stripy table.

"Eugh, don't! The smell will be enough to push me over the edge." Freya pulled a face, the thought making her physically retch. She nodded towards the exit. "What's going on? Who was the blonde lady?"

"That's Lisa. The mother of Ben's child."

"What?"

"Exactly. It's a long story. Let me get the drinks in." She signalled the stripy waitress. "Can I get you a wine or are you okay with that water."

Freya took another slow sip and nodded. "This is all I can manage thank you!"

Kat smiled at the rosy cheeked lady, ordered their drinks and proceeded to tell Freya the full story.

Ten minutes later and Freya was still shaking her head. The revelations had been mind blowing and she was struggling to take stock of the incredible situation. "So you knew he thought he had a son and you didn't tell me?"

Kat put her glass of dry white wine down, slightly puzzled. "It wasn't my place to tell you."

"But I'm your girlfriend."

Both could sense an air of touchiness in the other and understood it was solely from the previous night's escapades, but neither wanted to back down. "I know, and I love that you're my girlfriend, but there are some things that I will not tell you. For example, if something happens at school that is of a sensitive nature, then I'll stick by my professional code of conduct, and I won't tell you."

"What, because I'm just some Tom, Dick or Harry?"

Kat pushed the large shiny menu back into the centre of the table. Embarking on a large three course American-diner type feast was the last thing she felt like doing. "Come on, we're both tired. Let's just forget about everything that's happened today and talk about something else." Kat paused then clicked her fingers. "Like what outfit you're wearing to Jess's wedding." She smiled. "It has to match my peach bridesmaid's gown."

Freya crossed her arms. "Really? You really don't think it's a big deal that you didn't tell me?"

Kat sighed and twisted in her chair, making her crossed legs momentarily more comfortable. "No, I don't. It wasn't a piece of gossip ... it wasn't a fact ... it was a personal worry that Ben told me about, in the strictest of confidence." She reached once again for the shiny menu and scanned the choices, still nothing jumped out. She looked up at Freya and remembered. "Sorry, you were going to tell me something before I saw Ben."

Freya reached across the table for her own menu. "Well, if we don't tell each other everything, then I guess it's not important now."

CHAPTER TWELVE

Lucy heard the apartment door close and raced out of her bedroom before she forgot the words. She jumped up and wrapped her strong legs around Ben's torso, not even giving him time to take off his bomber jacket. "Hiya!" She thought carefully and started to wag her finger. "Can you please stop leaving your lower decker pecker checker on the floor!"

Ben kissed her passionately on the mouth, pausing to think it through. "Okay, do I really do it or are you just saying I do it so you can drop it into the conversation?"

Lucy kissed him back. "No, you don't leave it on the floor. I just wanted to drop it in somehow. My Auntie's tongue twisters get better and better! Have you noticed the difference?" She winked and gave his back a giddy up kick with her bare heels. "Come on, *will you stop leaving your lower decker pecker checker on the floor!*"

He waded into the lounge with Lucy still gripped to his waist. "Lower decker pecker checker? Hmmm." He grinned. "My jockstrap?"

She jumped down and thumped him on the shoulder. "Alright then." She slipped her hand down the front of his trousers. "Shame. Your slick, slimy snake, is still sliding southwards."

Ben pulled her massaging hand back out.

"Ben?" Something must be wrong.

He sighed and collapsed backwards onto the sofa, patting the black leather seat next to his own. "Babe, sit down." He took her hands, pulling her down and held them tightly. "I love your tongue twisters and I love you and I hope my tongue doesn't get all twisted now."

"You can twist your tongue with me anytime!" Humour was the only way she could deal with situations like these; the inevitable break up. She would laugh it off, claim she felt the same and then wallow in self pity for the foreseeable few months. She smiled and waited for it.

"Something huge has happened."

"Oh yeah?" She would be blasé, pretend it was no big deal.

"I've met someone."

Lucy paused and tried to think of a funny tongue twister, but nothing came to mind. "Well fuckity fuck fuck fuck." She couldn't be blasé, she loved him far too much. "You bloody bollockfaced, buggerdy bastard!" She jumped on top of him and started to bash his chest, her anger and upset was overwhelming. "Now get your sorry arsed, shagging shitload out of here and shove the shitterdy shit shit off ... you sodding sod!"

He grabbed her wrists and tried to restrain her, but her strength was incredible.

"And you can get your paws off me!" She collapsed into his chest as her anger quickly turned to sobs. "Please don't go, Ben. I love you."

He lifted her chin. "Lucy, I haven't met another woman."

"Oh great!" She jumped back off the sofa and kicked him in the shins. "So, you're leaving me for a man! Well that's one I've not had yet! Guess that just about completes every dumpable excuse in the book." She stood still, unsure of what to do next.

Ben rubbed his grazed shin and tried not to laugh, none of this was in the slightest bit funny. "Please, just sit down and listen."

"What, to some new age romantic story about how you've met the love of your life and discovered the real you and now you want to settle down with Paul or Steve or Dave or whoever, and get a chinchilla."

"A chinchilla?"

"Yeah, one of those little dogs to carry around in your man-bag!"

Ben smiled. "He is called Benny, and I don't want a chinchilla."

"Ben and Benny ... how sweet."

Ben paused and smiled. "Yeah, he is ... he's my son."

Lucy looked at Ben and waited for the punch line. "Huh?"

"Please just sit down and let me start again." He tapped the black leather sofa with trepidation. "But please, no more man-handling."

She frowned at him. "So you've not been man-handling?"

"No, of course not!"

Lucy plonked herself down. "Did you just say you had a son? Start speaking ... and sorry about your shins ... and the shitload of swearing."

Ben laughed, relieved that her venting seemed to be over for now. What she appeared to be was incredibly confused, and who could blame her, he thought, wondering where on earth to begin. "Remember last year when I thought Jess was going for an abortion and I got mad?"

"How could I forget? You dumped me because of it."

Ben ruffled his short blonde hair. "I know. I was an idiot, but now I need to explain why." He had her attention so he spoke slowly. "Lisa was my girlfriend, and I loved her. I thought she was the one." He offered an apologetic smile. "We'd been together for about two years and suddenly she left me. We had planned to move in and eventually get married and start a family, but she just left me. I had a note posted through my letterbox that said *I'm sorry it's over*, and that was it. She'd gone. I found out from a friend that she had moved back in with her mum in Wales and started a new job there. I tried to contact her and just got stonewalled." He shook his head. "I never understood it until a couple of weeks later when I was out in a club and I bumped into one of her friends, a girl called Terri who never liked me anyway."

"Terri was Lisa's friend?"

Ben nodded. "Yeah. Well anyway, she was pissed out of her face and drunkenly told me that Lisa had had an abortion."

"What?"

"Yeah I know. She said that Lisa didn't want to be tied to me, so got rid of my kid."

Lucy reached for his arm, it all made sense now.

He appreciated the warmth of her support and squeezed her fingers in return. "I've lived for the past four years thinking that she killed my kid and left me for dead."

Lucy was shocked by his admission. "Really?"

"Well, maybe at the start. But then over the years I've calmed down about it all and when we bumped into her at the DVD shop-"

"THAT'S your son? That kid that kept stealing the sweets? And that skinny blonde is the mother of your child?!"

He grinned apologetically. "Yes, that's Lisa and Benny."

She let go of his hand. "That was ages ago!"

Ben looked away in shame. "I know."

"So just how long have you known?" She was not sure if she had any right to get cross. Everything was so confusing. She was thrilled that the woman didn't end up killing Ben's kid, but that meant he was here; that Ben was a dad.

He shrugged and let out a long sigh. "I went back to the DVD shop and found out her address."

"They gave it to you?"

"I lied and pretended to be her husband."

Lucy crossed her arms and nodded her black blunt fringe. "Now we're getting to it!"

"A couple of days later I waited outside her house and pretended to bump into her again, and she had Benny." A smiled washed across Ben's face. "He has my ears, Lucy. I can't believe I didn't spot it before. He has this weird little crunch at the top of his ears like me."

Lucy reached up to the top of Ben's left ear and pulled back the fold of skin, watching it recoil back into place. "That's one of the things I love most about you."

"What? My crunched up ear?"

"Yes," she smiled.

Ben felt heartened so continued. "I just asked her. I said, *'Is he mine?'* and she nodded and burst into tears."

"Why couldn't you tell me?"

Lucy was looking over with real compassion and he felt awful. "I don't know."

She took a deep breath. "Does she want you back?"

Lucy had said it in such an understanding way that he felt overwhelmed with appreciation and spontaneously slid down onto one knee. "No. I want you, Lucy Lovett. I want you forever. I haven't got a ring and I'm not prepared, but I'm kneeling here proposing a proposal. Will you accept this proposition of a proposed proposal in the not too distant future?" He watched as a small tear formed in the corner of her eye. "And no, she doesn't want me. She's been happily married for two years ... and yes, I have met Gerald her husband ... and yes, they definitely both want to meet you ... and so does Benny."

Lucy jumped off the sofa and onto the wooden floor next to him. "What if I'm not ready?"

He grinned. "You, Lucy Lovett, were born ready."

CHAPTER THIRTEEN

Jess looked absolutely gorgeous. She had opted for the *Grace Kelly*. A one piece lace over satin, empire waist, ivory gown. Her huge bump made any other style a definite no no. She had accessorised to the max and taken all of the optional extras: Swarovski encrusted tiara, delicate silk tulle veil and essential white fur bolero. Everything was on loan, but she didn't care. At that precise moment they belonged to her and she was wearing them with style. The baby suddenly kicked and she tried to mask the jolt with a forced smile and shift of weight. She thanked the small mercy of flat shoes, having opted for the white slip on ballet style. No one could see them under the layers of satin and lace, and her priority was comfort. She could barely stand for more than fifteen minutes as it was, let alone trussed up in all of this clobber. She moved an auburn ringlet away from her rosy cheek and turned to nod at Kat.

Kat and Lucy smiled at each other and bent at the knees to pick up the long ivory train. Both had perfected the move having watched Pippa Middleton on repeat, performing her never to be forgotten knee bend and train pick up. Both knew they could give her bottom a run for its money, but their dresses were not quite in the same league. Jess had insisted they wear peach ... puff ball peach. The pastel coloured dresses were strapless and ended just above the knee, so pairing this with their three inch heels, both knew their knee bends had to be executed to perfection. They rose slowly in unison and glanced at one another, discretely performing the planned boob check. Great, still in, thought Lucy, relieved. All she had to do now was try and avoid walking like Tina Turner - a hard feat given her bulging calf muscles, super high heels and out-stretched arms. To be fair they were only walking about five metres to the front of the intimate wedding room, but she still needed to concentrate. The CD of Pachelbel's Cannon in D Major started playing and the short procession began. Jess and Gary had decided to hold their ceremony in the local registry office. It was the cheapest option and both knew they would rather spend their money on the new home and their soon to be arriving baby. The plan was a short service with just one reading from Kat, followed by a quick taxi ride to the sophisticated Paris restaurant in town where they had reserved the balcony table.

Lucy nodded at Kat and they performed the knee bend once again, returning the train to the floor and stepping to the side of the pale blue runway carpet to take their reserved seats at the front. Kat watched as Jess's dad handed his daughter over to Gary. Slow, singular tears were creeping down both of the men's cheeks. Kat lifted her little finger to the corner of her eye, holding back her own warm tears. It was going to be an emotional day.

The service was basic, but beautiful and all twenty in the cosy room had a lump in their throats when Jess and Gary read out their vows. They were so heartfelt and sincere, both staring deeply into each other's eyes and wholeheartedly promising to be together forever. They were a match made in heaven and everyone in the room knew they were one of the few couples who could actually go the distance. Their words had reflected this, promising each other that they would never again have to walk alone. Gary declared that his heart would be her shelter and his arms would be her home, and she had pulled him close as her emotions took over. Jess managed to whisper her final words, offering Gary her hand to hold and her life to keep. It was beautiful, and their love was apparent for all to see.

Kat wiped away a tear, watching for her signal. It was a very hard act to follow. The female registrar nodded in her direction so she rose slowly to her feet and made her way to the wooden lectern, gently placing her reading down and looking up at the intimate group of friends and family. The room had been decorated modestly, with a few pale flowers with peach coloured ties adorning the first and last row of chairs, and a long white ribbon hanging from the lectern. The real beauty however was in the faces of the people within. All smiling and wishing the couple their best. Kat caught Freya's misty eyes and nearly lost her composure. Freya was smiling knowingly, showing her it would be them one day, standing up there, declaring their love for one another. Kat looked down at her paper, took a deep breath, and began. "Love. By Roy Croft." Her tone was soft but the words were powerful. "I love you not only for what you are, but for what I am when I am with you." She lifted her eyes to Freya. "I love you, not only for what you have made of yourself, but for what you are making of me." Her voice cracked and she paused, holding back a tear. "I love you for the part of me that you bring out. I love you for putting your hand into my heaped up heart and passing over all the foolish, weak things, that you can't help dimly seeing in there." She sniffed quietly and looked at Jess and Gary who were both in floods of tears. "And for drawing out into the light all the beautiful belongings that no one else had looked quite far enough to find." She was so aware of the gentle sobs and emotional sniffs coming from the seated guests, that every line took such control to deliver. "I love you because you have done more than any creed could have done to make me good. And more than any fate could have done to make me happy." She connected once again with Freya's glistening green eyes. "You have done it." She paused, returning her eyes to the reading. "Without a touch ... Without a word ... Without a sign." She didn't need to refer to the lectern for the last line; instead she looked straight at her girlfriend. "You have done it, by being yourself."

Jess and Gary started to clap and everyone followed suit, encompassing the small room in a cascade of emotion. The registrar smiled and wholeheartedly announced it was now time to sign the marriage certificate. Kat made her way back to her seat and felt Freya creep in beside her. Jess's parents had stretched to a single violinist who was now playing a beautifully haunting version of Ave Maria. Kat took the outstretched hand and held it tight. People had started to whisper as the register was being signed, complimenting the service, or the way Jess looked glowing, or the perfect choice of reading. Kat and Freya didn't need to speak. They just knew.

A scream suddenly tore through all of the pleasantries. Jess keeled over and clutched her stomach. Gary shot to her side, instantly aware of the pool of liquid creeping out from the layers of skirt, turning the pale blue carpet a slightly darker shade. He had read every single pregnancy book he could get his hands on and this, he knew, was his new wife's waters. "Call an ambulance, NOW!" he yelled.

Jess caught her breath and held onto his knee for support. "It's fine. It was just a big kick."

"Your waters have broken! You need an ambulance NOW!" Gary had been carting around 'The Bag' for over a month now, even though Jess was not due for another two weeks. He had it all planned out. Everything would run smoothly on his watch. He lifted the white cloth and reached under the registrar's table, pulling out the pink holdall. "It's all here! I have The Bag! DON'T PANIC!"

"Gary, let me call one!" Jess's dad was adding to the noise and reaching inside his wife's handbag for his mobile. The damn thing was switched off and he couldn't for the life of him find the correct button.

"NO!" shouted Jess, using the table to pull herself back up. "I don't need an ambulance." She turned to Gary. "Will you please just calm down."

The registrar carefully closed the large book with the signed documents enclosed, concerned about another gush of fluid.

Gary wailed. "But your waters have broken ... that's your amniotic sac! The baby's no longer protected from infection!"

Jess nervously rested on the edge of the padded seat. She turned to her father who was still cursing his modern and incredibly complicated mobile phone. "Dad, could you drive us to the hospital please?"

The whole room was silently watching proceedings with excited tension; no one wanting to add to the kerfuffle, but likewise no one wanting to miss a thing. The violinist started to play *March of the Priests* by Mozart and there was a general hushing sound whispered in her direction. She stopped and placed her bow on the floor.

Jess's dad pulled out the delicately folded peach handkerchief from his breast pocket and wiped his brow. "We came in the wedding cars, darling." His phone finally lit up. "Let me call you an ambulance."

"Kat!" Jess needed some sanity.

Kat quickly rose to her feet and joined the panicking party at the table.

Jess grimaced as another short contraction came and went. "Kat, can we go in your car please?"

Kat crouched at Jess's knee and spoke softly, hoping not to alarm. "I came with you Jess ... in the Jag."

"What's going on with me?!" Jess gasped in exasperation.

"We could go in Freya's car?"

Jess blew warm air up at her even warmer face. "Sorted! This is it then Gary!" She rose to her feet to a rapturous applause from the room. There were shouts of *"Perfect timing,"* and, *"The things Gary will do to get out of a speech!"*

Jess took Kat's arm. "I want you there too."

****

Ben and Lucy were sitting with the other wedding guests enjoying an extravagant meal on the balcony table which overlooked the main bustling restaurant. When the owners of their chosen reception venue had heard that the bride and groom, parents of the bride and groom, and chief bridesmaid, wouldn't be attending, they decided to upgrade the party to the *a la carte* menu, free of charge. Every single person sitting around the huge oblong table had their phones out, hoping to be the first to hear.

But the only ones who could actually hear anything were Kat and Freya. Jess had banished her parents and parents-in-law to the cafeteria, much to the disappointment of the mums and joy of the dads. Gary had fainted on arrival at the hospital and was now sitting in the corner of the private birthing room on the relative's chair, trying to regain his composure. Kat and Freya had been called in from their seats in the calm comfort of the corridor by the midwife, who felt Jess needed some female support since Gary was now incapacitated.

Kat had one hand and Freya had the other; neither having experienced pain quite like it themselves - Jess's grip was incredibly strong. She was lying on her back, wedding dress still on, with the badly bitten gas and air pipe clamped firmly between her teeth. She had been wheeled into the room at breakneck speed by Gary, who was then asked by a very calm midwife to help Jess out of her dress. The dress they were both relieved to have paid the insurance on. Jess had doubled over, grabbing the edge of the bed for support in another long contraction and the midwife thought it best to check her dilation. Popping her head out from under the long white ruffles of lace and satin, the midwife looked up and declared there was no time to take the dress off and would Jess rather deliver standing up or lying down. It was a no brainer for Jess who hoisted herself onto the bed and reached for the pain relief.

"This is it, Jess. Just one more push." The midwife was proud of the effort. All too often the women were shouting and swearing, and demanding epidurals, but this one, this one had just got on with it, in her wedding dress as well. She smiled, just needing that one last big effort. "That's it Jess! That's it. Keep pushing, keep pushing."

Kat and Freya were either side of the bed, involuntarily mimicking each other's furrowed looks of pain, both panting in time with Jess and holding their breath when she was contracting. They were literally pushing with her.

Gary took a gulp of air and stood unsteadily, staring in amazement, no idea it would look quite like this.

The midwife was calm, yet confident, and very clear in her instructions. "Well done, the head's out. Now take a couple of deep breaths. Your baby will be born in this next contraction."

Gary forgot his nerves, fought back the tears and took Freya's place by his new wife's side. "Come on, Jess, you can do this. I love you."

Jess bit down on the plastic pipe and let out what Gary knew was termed as *'the birthing scream.'*

There was a momentary holding of breath from everybody in the room before the midwife shouted: "You've done it!"

The high pitched cry was instantaneous.

The wailing baby was swiftly lifted up to Jess's chest. "Congratulations, you have a beautiful little girl."

Jess was overcome with emotion and started to sob. She looked at the bundle of joy lying on top of her. "This is the best wedding present I could ever have wished for."

The midwife was busily organising the metal dishes, blankets and absorbent cloths. She looked at Gary. "Would you like to cut the cord?"

Gary nodded and followed the quick instructions, cutting the surprisingly tough cord with a firm push on the large hospital scissors.

Kat and Freya stepped to the side, giving the new family some space. They held each other's hands tightly, letting their tears run free. "This will be us one day," managed Freya through soft, warm sobs.

Kat smiled and savoured the moment. "I hope so. I really do."

CHAPTER FOURTEEN

Kat, like all teachers, found the run up to Christmas hectic and exhausting. Students had been missing here there and everywhere, for play rehearsals, concert practices, end of term assembly run-throughs, charity fortnight fundraising events. The list went on. It seemed the only consistent thing at the moment was Chianne Granger's pouty face at the front of her A-Level class. Chianne didn't have a part in the school play, and she wasn't a performer in the Christmas Carole Concert. She hadn't been asked to do a reading in the end of term assembly, and she hadn't offered to take part in any fundraising events. So she sat at the front of the class in every lesson with a perfected look of pouty annoyance. Not annoyance that she wasn't entitled to legitimately skip lessons, but annoyance at snotty nosed Spicer for kicking her best mate, Chantelle Mann, off the course.

Kat had not, in fact, kicked Chantelle off the course. She had actually been giving her extra lessons and was fairly pleased with her progress. Unfortunately, Chantelle had failed to perform in *her and Chianne's* other chosen subjects and the Head of Sixth Form offered her a polite transfer onto the Child Care course instead. Chantelle snapped it up and was thrilled not to have to spend every day sitting at home with her mum, step-dad, two older brothers and older sister. She was always known as the brains of the family and her current dabbling with further education was revered with amazement and scepticism. Amazement that someone from the Mann Clan had scored enough from their GCSEs to progress further in school, and scepticism that her only motive was to qualify and keep for herself the Education Maintenance Allowance; which at thirty pounds a week, was a lot less than she could be getting for them, and the family kitty, on the dole.

Spending time the previous evening with Jess, Gary and baby Daisy - who was coming along nicely - had put Kat in a good mood, so she tried once again. "Come on, Chianne, talk to the class about your best Christmas memory." It was the final A-Level lesson of term, exam papers had been handed back and discussed, numerous students had made their excuses for important places to be and Kat was left with a tiny group who were still, at seventeen and eighteen, excited about the upcoming Christmas break. Everyone, it seemed, apart from Chianne.

"I ain't telling you that, Miss, you perve!"

That was it, enough was enough. Kat could handle a bit of attitude and knew it was never an easy ride with Chianne, but this was crossing the line. A couple of the class members tutted, but none dared face up to Chianne. She had a fierce reputation and no one wanted to get on the wrong side of her. The group had such admiration for the way Miss Spicer managed to channel Chianne's arguments and cut short her outbursts, but this, they knew, was too much. Kat's tone proved them right. "That is completely uncalled for. You will wait after the lesson and I will decide whether to file a language grievance." She shook her head. "And just so you know, I have never, ever, had to file a grievance about a member of my own A-Level class."

Chianne sucked her teeth and pretended not to be bothered. *Shit*, she thought, that didn't work either. Miss Spicer was proving a tough nut to crack. She had dabbled at the start with light flirting and provocative clothes, neither of which seemed to have any effect on straight-laced Spicer. So then she tried the jokes - breaking down the barrier with humour - which failed miserably as well. In fact her gag of: '*What do you call the space between the vagina and the arsehole?*' which she thought would be a sure fire winner, proved disastrous ... even though the lesbian website she got it from guaranteed her that any good lady lover would find the punch line of: '*A chinrest*,' hilarious. Miss Spicer hadn't laughed, so here she was now, trying her final strategy: moody and hard to get. It didn't seem to be turning her teacher on, but at least it got her a private audience at the end of the lesson. Chianne narrowed her tiny eyes and glanced across at Miss Spicer who was now sitting, relaxed and laughing, with a couple of girls on the table to her left. Chianne had no idea what the girls were called as both were far too geeky to be part of her gang. In fact, she was the outsider in this class full of boffins and weirdos. Her only real motive for being here was to finally crack Miss Spicer ... finally get smitten Spicer to admit she fancied her. *Who wouldn't?* thought Chianne, sucking a deep breath through her small piggy nostrils and trying to cross her arms over her protruding stomach.

The bell signalled the end of the lesson and Kat warmly rounded out the remainder of her A-Level students, wishing them a wonderful Christmas and New Year. She loved the class, very different to last year's group of Harley, Big Tom and little Jason Sparrow. That class had been tiny compared to this fully subscribed group. But as she looked over at Chianne, lounging in her plastic chair, she realised that all of her classes would hold a special place in her heart, as would her students ... including this puffing, pouting one in front of her. The cuteness and cuddliness of baby Daisy had definitely lightened her load today. She smiled and approached the front of the classroom. "Chianne, Chianne, Chianne, what am I going to do with you?"

Chianne perked up, she had no idea her moodiness would have worked this well. She sneered sexily. "What do you wanna do with me, Miss?"

"Right." Kat was suddenly firm. "What's all *that* about? You can't talk to me like that. I was thinking about letting you off," she sighed, "but Chianne you infuriate me. You are so clever. I mean really, really clever. You could get a place at Oxbridge if you sorted out your attitude."

"Really?" Chianne had not meant it to sound so earnest.

Kat saw a feint glimmer of the person hiding under the big Chianne charade. "Yes, really." She lifted her hands in exasperation. "What's going on with you?" She was aware she was standing over the desk and wanted to get the balance of strict, yet approachable right so she reached for her padded desk chair and pulled it in front of Chianne's table. If they were ever going to make headway then it would be now. "Tell me why you behave like this?"

"Just being me, Miss."

Kat was unsure if the answer had been surly and indifferent or confused and apologetic. "And who are you?"

"Dur, Chianne Granger." The pout and attempted crossed arms were back.

"Okay, who do you think people see you as?"

Chianne had started to feel a bit uncomfortable. She had only wanted a laugh, only wanted to see how far Miss Spicer would take it. She didn't need the grief of a counselling session; she'd been to enough of those already. She smirked and started to rap. "They see *Chianne, Chianne, you're my biggest fan. I'm a smoking, gun toting-*"

Kat grabbed the hand that was making imaginary pistol shots. "This is what I'm talking about! What's all of that rapping nonsense? And about guns as well? You really should know better, Chianne. You are so much better than this!"

Chianne looked down at the elegant hand wrapped over her large fist and back up with raised eyebrows. "I knew you liked me." She gave a full bucked-tooth smile.

Kat quickly removed her hand and folded her arms.

"It's too late now, Miss. I've seen it in those pretty blue eyes of yours. You'll test me with a bit of hand holding before you make your real play for me."

"Right, Chianne, that's enough." She signalled towards the door. "Out. I'll let you off with a warning. Just please, leave now and have a good Christmas."

The seductive smile continued. "Oh I ain't going anyway now, Miss. Not now I know how you feel."

Kat stood from her seat and pointed once again to the door. "Out."

"But you were just holding my hand. You said you wanted me."

Kat was opened mouthed. "No, I did not!"

Chianne stood up and at almost double the width of Kat, was quite overpowering. She stepped forwards. "So did you, or did you not, just hold my hand?"

Kat started to panic. "No, I moved your hand."

Chianne took a step closer and tried to touch the top of Kat's open-necked white shirt.

Kat instinctively batted the hand away. "What are you doing?"

Chianne looked like she was about to attack. "Nobody turns me down. I ain't even no lesbo like you! I just thought I'd give you a slice of the good stuff! You know you want it."

Kat stepped back and tripped over her workbag, falling clumsily to the floor.

There was a rush of feet. "Miss Spicer, let me help you." Janet Louza had dashed to Kat's side. She looked at Chianne. "What on earth is going on?"

Chianne started to shout. "She touched me! She touched me, Miss! She started it! I didn't want her to touch me! She was touching me and I pushed her and she fell!"

Kat rubbed her trousers and slowly stood back up. "Mrs Louza, I can assure you that's not what-"

"She did! Miss, she touched me! She started it!" The shouts had turned to overdramatic sobs.

Janet had no other choice. "Right, Chianne you come with me. Kat, if I could meet you in the staffroom in a bit?"

"Follow me, Chianne." Janet entered the corridor first and was in no position to see the small eyed wink that Chianne directed back at her teacher as she left the room.

****

Freya felt the buzz in her pocket and reached for her phone.

'Chianne *bleeping* Granger! Need a huge hug when I get home. K xx'

Freya smiled.

"*Kat,* I suppose?" Renee leaned over the cluttered work desk in their private study room and reached for the mobile.

Freya quickly returned it to her jacket pocket and slammed her reference book closed. "Yes, but why do you always call her *Kat?*"

Renee wobbled her head, shaking her latest funky cornrow design which had the effect of clinking the long beaded plaits together around her shoulders. "Because that's her name."

"It's not *Kaaaat*!"

"What's she got anyway?"

The girls were in the university library, supposedly gathering information for a PowerPoint presentation on streaming and whether setting students based on ability was beneficial or detrimental to overall learning progress. Freya knew it was beneficial, but had to back up her argument with quotes and research from the various journals scattered around their study table. She looked up, speaking with definitive meaning. "What has she got? Well let me see. She's the most beautiful woman I've ever met."

Renee huffed with indifference.

"She's the cleverest woman I've ever met."

Renee crossed her arms.

"She's the kindest, most thoughtful woman I've ever met."

Renee rolled her eyes and leaned back in her plastic chair, lifting it onto its two rear legs.

"She cares. I mean, she really cares. Nothing is too much trouble for her."

Renee lifted her arms behind her head and pretended to yawn.

Freya grinned; this was the winner. "And she's mind blowing in bed!"

Renee laughed and tipped her chair forwards, leaning over the table and pinning Freya with a provocative gaze. "Better than me?"

Freya shook her head. "Don't start that again." It had taken a couple of weeks for Renee to mention the kiss in the toilets and subsequent night in bed, but once the subject had been broached, there had been no stopping her. Freya had played it cool and laughed about the drunkenness of the evening, but failed to rise to Renee's odd comments of - '*Can you remember the whole night then?*' or - '*It all got a bit hazy towards the end didn't it?*' Simply saying - '*Yes, great laugh, very drunk, lots of memories.*' She could tell Renee was dying to bring it up, but the more she ignored the probes, the less importance she felt it had. That was until Renee gave up on the tiptoeing and finally came out with - '*You wanna get jiggy again, right?*'

Freya had instantly dismissed the kiss as an *attempted kiss* and clarified that there had not been any participation on her part for her to actually enjoy. She wasn't sure if her response had relieved Renee or disappointed her. All she knew was her light heartedness about the issue seemed to have given Renee a green light to flirt outrageously. Maybe she should have reacted with disgust or abhorrence and made it perfectly clear that she never wanted to go there again, but at the time that had seemed like an overreaction ... and anyway, she liked Renee, she was a laugh, they got on well and the banter was fun.

"You know you want more." Renee closed the lid of her laptop and raised one eyebrow.

"No, actually I don't, thanks." Freya looked at her watch. "I'm going to go home now for some smoking hot sex with my lover."

"We could have some more smoking hot sex in my dorm if you like?"

Freya started to place the mess of journals into one neat pile. "Stop it!"

Renee grinned. "I could give you an early Christmas present as well. I could do that thing you like." She wiggled the tip of her tongue.

Freya dropped her pencil case into her brown leather satchel bag and closed her notebook. "No!"

Renee leaned sexily over the table. "Can I whisper something?"

"Stop it! I'm going home," giggled Freya, "and anyway, what more could I want for Christmas? I've my mother and father gate crashing Kat's parents' Christmas dinner!"

Renee plopped back down into her seat. "Oh shit, yeah you said. Is that what's happened then? They're coming with you?"

Freya had explained to Renee the delicate issue of telling her parents that she would be spending her first Christmas away from home, and with her being an only child it had gone down like a ton of bricks. Her mother had completely overreacted telling Freya her priorities were in the wrong place and asked how on earth she could contemplate doing something so selfish. Her father had looked wounded, but nodded his head in acceptance. It was then that Kat, ever the peace maker, suggested the Eltons also join her family in the Cotswolds, claiming the Spicer saying was *'the more the merrier!*' And actually when Kat had mentioned it to her parents they had indeed said: *'No problem, the more the merrier. That will put us at twenty two this year!'*

Freya placed the final journal back on the old library trolley and sat down on the table next to Renee. "Yes, they're coming too. Kat's parents are so posh and I know my mum will show herself up. I'm dreading it."

Renee slung her arm around her friend's shoulder. "You always have to sit that little bit too close to me don't you?"

"Will you stop it!" laughed Freya, wriggling her shoulders free, "and anyway, why is someone who is *straight*, so intent on instigating an affair with me?!"

Renee had to laugh. "Oh, so that's what it's progressed to now ... an affair! I just thought we were friends with benefits." Renee applied some clear lip gloss to her gorgeous full lips and smiled her dazzling smile. "Well it just goes to show that I'm the dog's bollocks and can get anyone I want!"

For once Freya didn't laugh. "That's actually not funny. I've been with a girl like that before."

"Yeah, good one!"

"Seriously, I was." She grinned at Renee. "She was slightly prettier than you though."

Renee slapped Freya's knee. "You're like one of those children who picks on the person they secretly fancy aren't you."

"Stop it, now!" Freya jumped off the table, grabbed her bag and headed for the door whose sign read Private Study Session in Progress. There hadn't been much studying going on, but it had certainly been private. "Come on, I think the school placement list should be up by now and I can't wait to find out where I'm going. I really hope I get John Taylor's."

Renee followed her to the door and exaggerated her head tilt whilst whistling a slow wolf whistle at Freya's pert bottom.

****

Kat sat down in the empty staffroom going through the exact chain of events. Chianne was right, she had held her hand, only momentarily, but she *had* touched her. Her stomach lurched. Why had she touched her? She thought carefully - it was to stop her toting her finger pistol in the air whilst she was rapping that dreadful song. But Chianne had made it sound like she had touched her inappropriately. Was that inappropriate, she thought, questioning her every movement? She stood up and paced around the kitchenette. Most of the staff had made an early exit home, already on the end of term wind down. She flicked the kettle switch on and then quickly back off again, making her way to her pigeonhole instead. It was empty, as it had been ten minutes ago. She sat back down on her sunken brown chair and exhaled, jumping at the click of the staffroom door. A very flustered Janet Louza walked in. Kat stood up and pulled her blonde hair back behind her ears. "Janet, I can assure you that I-"

Janet flopped into her chair. "I know. Don't worry, Kat, it's all sorted."

Kat edged back down, sitting opposite her Head of Department.

"I took her to the pastoral facility and talked her through the process of recording her allegation, which would obviously include lots of form filling and a statement to the police." Janet fingered her wiry cloud of grey hair. "She then told me not to worry about it, which obviously I said I had to. She had made an allegation against one of my members of staff and therefore it would need to be dealt with." Janet looked up with tired dark eyes, this term had been long and hard. "So once I said that, she started to back track, and told me you had held her hand and that she didn't mind you holding her hand as long as it didn't lead to anything else." Janet had to ask the question. "Did you hold her hand, Kat?"

"Yes."

Janet moved uncomfortably in her seat. "Right, well I'll have to file an incident report ... you know how it is ... we have to file a file about the files we've filed don't we?!" She was getting a bit flustered.

"Janet, I took her hand and placed it back on the table. She had been waving it around like a pistol and I was simply trying to calm her down."

"Oh right, okay, like I said, it's fine. She doesn't want to take it any further."

Kat frowned. "And what if she did? Would I be suspended for *that*?"

Janet didn't know how to put this delicately. "Well, your *situation*, might raise extra questions."

Kat straightened in her seat, unsure of what Janet was insinuating.

"Sorry, that came out wrong. Look it's been a long day, she doesn't want to take it any further." She paused. "But I'll make a note of what you've said about her waving her hands around like a gun - you know how it is - just to cover both of our backs, but anyway, I'm sure it will come to nothing." She fingered her wiry hair once more. "No, I mean, it *has* come to nothing. Look, we all know Chianne, and you're not the first member of staff she's accused of one misdemeanour or another." She took a deep breath. "Anyway, talking about your *situation* ... I needed to show you this."

Kat watched her walk over to her pigeonhole and pull something out. She tried to mentally formulate a response to Janet's handling of the situation, not content with how it had been approached or consequently left; but any planned reply was about to be forgotten.

Janet handed over the envelope headed 'Teacher Training Programme.'

Kat pulled out the letter.

Janet smiled nervously. "That won't be a problem, will it?"

****

Freya and Renee scanned the Teacher Training notice board in the corridor of the modern education building searching for their names. "Yes!" Renee pulled a fist with her fingers and did her own unique burst of the running man. "I've got John Taylor's! I've got John Taylor's!"

Freya followed her finger across to her allocated school. "Holy Mother of Fuck!" she said in disbelief.

CHAPTER FIFTEEN

Freya had never experienced a feeling quite like it. Ten o'clock, Christmas morning, lying in the Spicer's festive front lounge in their glorious Georgian house in the Cotswolds, surrounded by selection boxes, new books, perfume, scarves, novelty toys and several still unopened presents. She lifted her feet towards the warm glow of the crackling log fire. They were lying on an exquisitely old fashioned oriental rug that lay in front of the red and black diamond hearth. Freya had noticed the odd burn mark from where the smouldering embers had jumped out of the fire and simmered to a rest. That's what she loved about Kat and her family, they were not precious. The rug was probably a family heirloom of great value, but instead of displaying it with pride in an area of safety, they chose instead to lay it out for everyone's enjoyment. The section where they were lying, both flicking through their new Christmas novels, was clearly worn more than the rest. Freya pictured the number of people who may have rested there and enjoyed the warmth of a fire like this. It was crackling with heart, and Freya felt the love. She turned to Kat and whispered gently. "This morning's been perfect. I feel so at home here."

Kat smiled, leaned to the side and tenderly kissed Freya's cheek. "Good, because my family love you."

Freya felt her heart grow and knew it was true. The very first time she met Jeremy and Gloria she had felt instantly at ease. They had come up to the apartment to take them both into town for a posh meal. Jeremy had embraced her with a whole hearted hug, and Gloria had pulled her close with a two handed hand shake and kissed her cheek warmly, saying: "I feel like I know you already, Freya." The relationship between Kat and her mother was one she could only dream of. They seemed to speak almost every other day and shared a connection of mutual admiration and respect, both clearly very proud of the other. Yes, thought Freya, wrapping her arm around Kat's waist, I am very happy here.

The morning so far, of just Jeremy, Gloria, Kat, and herself, had been very relaxed and enjoyable, but in the last half hour she had noticed an increase in Kat's parents' activity. It would have to be a military procedure to put on a successful Christmas dinner for twenty two guests.

A red faced Jeremy bounded back into the festive room, rubbing his hands in anticipation. "Sorry about that, I just needed to turn the bird. Come on, girls, you still have our stockings to open!"

Freya smiled at the apron just about fastened around his middle, it read: *'I'm dreaming of a White Christmas ... and when all the White is gone I will drink all the Red.'* They had already got through one bottle of sparkly so far this morning.

"Smells good, Dad," smiled Kat, sitting up and reaching for the two bulging pillow cases. "Really, I told you, you shouldn't have!"

Jeremy wiped his forehead, the kitchen was hot, the log fire was burning and he had also put the radiators on to ensure there wouldn't be any complaints about the cold. "Well, we can't have Freya spending her first Christmas away from home without a stocking."

"I wasn't expecting one stocking, let alone two." She smiled at Kat, understanding where her generosity came from; clearly a family trait.

"Wait for me!" Gloria dashed back into the room, potato peeler still in hand. Her complimenting apron read: *'One wise woman beats three wise men any day!'*

Freya was in awe of the way she had been multi-tasking with the cooking, the table arrangements, and the final bits of straightening. All done in her full Christmas outfit, complete with high heels and antique pearl necklace.

"Please, is there anything we can do to help?" Freya felt embarrassed still lounging around in her pyjamas and pink pom pom slippers. It was the third time she had asked, but their response was always the same.

Jeremy jokingly wagged his finger. "How many times do we have to tell you girls!? Just relax and enjoy your morning ... all hell's going to break loose in about an hour when the rabble arrive!"

"Tell me about it!" laughed Kat, opening the neck of the yellow pillow case and realising it was stuffed with screwed up balls of newspaper.

"Keep looking," encouraged Jeremy.

Kat and Freya made it to the bottom of their pillow cases and both pulled out a small rectangular box. It was a gold colour, with a loose silver ribbon tied neatly at the top.

"Open them together," smiled Gloria, taking hold of her husband's chunky hand.

Freya looked at Kat with apprehension and untied the silver ribbon, slowly lifting the lid of her box. Kat did the same. Freya wasn't sure who gasped first, but she knew that she had never before seen a cheque in her name for that amount of money.

Kat jumped up and wrapped her arms around her parents' necks. "You shouldn't have! You two are so naughty!"

Jeremy's eyes welled up with pride. "You deserve it. Go away on a nice holiday, or save it for something important." He smiled at his daughter who was also welling up. "Just make sure you enjoy it!"

Freya stood nervously behind the party of hugs. "Umm, I don't think I should really be getting one too. I feel a bit uncomf-"

Jeremy stretched out his arms and pulled both girls back in for another Christmas morning cuddle. "Of course you should! You're part of the family now. Students always need money don't they?! And it's not like teachers make much, so you girls enjoy it!"

Freya was lost for words.

Kat took Freya's hand. "They do this every year and we tell them not to, but if you don't cash the cheque in he'll transfer it into your bank account."

"And so he should," confirmed Gloria, picking her potato peeler back up. "We are from the baby boomer generation and it's our duty to help you girls out." Gloria patted Jeremy's ample behind. "Come on, my husband, we need to make the stuffing and prepare the hors d'oeuvres."

Jeremy tightened his apron and looked at Kat and Freya. "Ladies, relax and enjoy."

Freya remained in shock as the pair made their way back into the steaming kitchen, shutting the latch on the panelled mahogany door and disappearing from view. She lifted her cheque to Kat and wiggled it open mouthed. "I can't accept this."

Kat took her hand and guided her back to their warm spot on the oriental rug. "It's their gift to you. They love to help, what more can I say?"

"O.M.G." Freya lifted the check once more to within an inch of her eyes, double checking the amount. "O.M. bloody G."

****

"I really think we should stop somewhere for a coffee." Patrick Elton glanced across at his wife who was sitting bolt upright in the passenger's seat of their reliable Volvo Estate.

"No, Patrick! It is always good to be early." Sue Elton pulled down her visor and checked the reflection once more. She adjusted her fake pearl necklace and used her little finger to dab some pink lipstick that had gone astray at the corner of her mouth. She glared at him out of the corner of her eye. "Will you sit up straight! Your new shirt's going to be creased. That's a Matalan best!"

"Sue, I'm driving. This is how I sit when I'm driving." He held the steering wheel even tighter. They didn't frequently go out in the car together, but when they did it was often marred with tit for tat bickering, most of the titting and tattering coming from his wife who insisted on reminding him when a roundabout was approaching, or gasping in shock and clutching at the sides of her seats when his braking was not up to her standards.

"Well don't sit like that!" She pointed at a car in the distance whose brake lights had been momentarily touched. "Watch, watch, watch - that car is braking." She glanced back at her husband's slightly creased shirt. "You look a real mess. What will Jeremy think?" She paused, and looked at the beautiful scenery flashing past the window, not quite wanting to admit how special it actually looked on this slightly frosty Christmas morning. She asked her husband the question once more. "What should we call him?"

Patrick sighed, checked his rear view mirror and flicked the indicator. "I'm going to call him Jeremy." They must have had this conversation three times already.

Sue pushed up her freshly curled brown hair. "I think it should be Doctor." She checked herself in the mirror. "Doctor Spicer."

Patrick kept his indicators on and edged past the slow moving car. The traffic had actually been surprisingly quiet this morning and the few cars they did pass seemed to be full of presents, or piled high with bedding. Clearly people making their obligatory trip home to their extended families for the Christmas break. Patrick sighed. "I'm not calling him Doctor Spicer." He had been trying to drive slowly to avoid their inevitable early arrival, but had now decided an early arrival would be better than further excruciating time spent in the car with his wife.

"Or is it Jeremy G.P.?"

Patrick hit the accelerator. "Yes Sue, call him Jeremy G.P. When they open the door say, 'Merry Christmas Jeremy G.P.'"

Sue slammed the mirror shut. "Just drive, Patrick!" She had to have the final word. "And for goodness sake will you sit up straight!"

****

"I'm a bit nervous," said Kat, rolling onto her side on the worn rug. The pair were still lounging in front of the warm log fire having quickly become engrossed in their new Christmas novels.

Freya lifted her head from her book. "About my parents coming?" It was the only thing spoiling her heavenly Christmas morning, the slight nagging, nervous anticipation lurking in the back of her mind.

Kat rolled back over and lifted her bare feet to the fire. "No, I mean about what your parents will think of my family."

Freya frowned. "Are you serious? I'm worried about what your family will think of my parents!"

"But you haven't met Uncle Bart yet, or Pam," laughed Kat, pulling Freya on top of her. "And I know you've met Kelly, but you haven't seen her in all of her glory, surrounded by the wonder kids."

"I'm sure everyone will be lovely." Freya pecked her playfully. "But I do want to get changed before people arrive."

Kat tilted her head. "Hang on, that sounds like a car now."

Freya laughed and squeezed her shoulder. "Don't tease."

Kat sat up swiftly and lifted Freya with her. "No, seriously, it does."

****

"This is it!" Sue checked her reflection in the mirror for one final time. "Patrick, stop the engine!"

Patrick looked up at the handsome Georgian country house. "Are you sure?"

Sue flicked the mirror shut. "Yes of course I am." She paused and looked pleased with herself. "I came here yesterday."

Patrick unfastened his seatbelt and tried to tuck in the back of his shirt. "You came to the Cotswolds yesterday did you?" He knew she hadn't been anywhere as she had spent the whole day complaining about how miserable Christmas Eve was without Freya.

"Yes, on Google Earth. I zoomed right in on those lovely sash windows over there," she pointed at the house, "and I think I saw a shadow."

Patrick tried not to laugh, he knew it would be taken the wrong way. "Oh right."

"Yes, and I researched the house. It's not a listed building but it's built in the Georgian style." She reached into her handbag and pulled out the neatly folded piece of paper, reading it she continued. "It has five main bedrooms and four bathrooms, with three further bedrooms, a bathroom and games room on the second floor. It has a swimming pool, a tennis court and a large party barn. It has planning permission for a four bedroom house. It has paddocks and it is set in a total of fourteen acres." She folded the piece of paper and tucked it back into her handbag. She glanced up and registered Patrick's look of dismay. "It is always important to be prepared."

"For what?" He checked the clock on the dashboard, they were over an hour early. "Come on, Sue, let's go for a little drive. We can find out a bit more about the area."

"No need," she reached back into her old fashioned handbag and pulled out a selection of pamphlets. "I had the Cotswold Tourist Information Office send me some guides." She looked up with pride. "It is the most quintessentially English area of the UK." That was the bit she had memorised, she had to refer to the pamphlet for the next bit. "The Cotswolds is characterised by picturesque villages built of warm coloured limestone, sitting besides clear, fast flowing streams, set in a stunning landscape."

Patrick tried to look impressed, but failed. "Are you planning on quoting that at the dinner table?"

"At least I won't mumble around trying to make conversation."

"Is that what I do, mumble around?"

Sue flapped her hands furiously. "Patrick! Someone's coming down that big drive! Look, he's waving at us. He wants us to pull in." She smiled profusely at the jolly looking man in the red apron and growled at her husband like a ventriloquist. "For goodness sake, Patrick, start the Volvo."

Patrick nodded at the signalling arm and turned the ignition. "That must be Jeremy."

Sue continued the smile and whispered between clamped teeth. "Well, I looked on Genes Reunited and found the Spicer's family tree, but there were no photos."

Patrick was now the one to speak through a forced smile. "You had better be joking."

There was no response as Sue was already half way out of the car almost curtseying at Doctor Jeremy Spicer G.P.

****

Freya straightened her pyjama top and looked out of the huge sash windows. "I specifically told them not to be early. What are they doing?" She frowned. "And what is my mother doing?"

Kat peeped over Freya's shoulder. "Oh dear, your mum has gone for the double kiss."

"She never double kisses!"

"Oops, well she has now ... yep, Dad was not expecting that."

"Shit, she just kissed his nose!" Freya stepped back from the embarrassment visible through the window. "I knew this would be a disaster."

Kat pulled her in for a huge cuddle and laughed. "Everyone will be on the sherry soon. It will be fine!"

"This whole thing is just going to be so cringe worthy."

Kat looked into Freya's green eyes. "At least we get to spend Christmas together."

Freya smiled and kissed her softly. "You know what? ... I want to spend every occasion together ... forever."

"That can be arranged," whispered Kat, holding Freya's cheeks and kissing her gently.

CHAPTER SIXTEEN

"Hey! Is my company that bad?" Lucy elbowed Ben's ribs, hoping for a smile.

Ben didn't flinch. He simply returned his broken poppadom to the plate that was splattered with mango chutney. Both had agreed that a return to the local Indian for Christmas lunch was a definite must. Last year's celebration had been amazing, crammed side by side with strangers who quickly became lifelong friends until the effects of the local Indian beer wore off the following morning. This year it felt different. The music was still rousing and the atmosphere was still lively, but Ben couldn't seem to get into the swing of it. He looked around at the bright orange walls and complimenting red curtain drapes, noticing yet another small statue of a bejewelled elephant sitting lazily on the window ledge. All of the pictures hanging from the walls were bright and bold, mostly of elephants or obscure female faces encrusted with more jewels. He turned to Lucy and stared into her eager brown eyes. "No, your company's not bad. It's not you ... it's me. I just-"

Lucy choked back some of the fizzy beer and laughed. "Did you really just say that?"

The fact she was already slightly tipsy annoyed him but he wasn't sure why. "Yes, I did and if you let me finish-"

"Look at you with your knickers in a twist! What's up? This time last year we'd already done that yard of ale." She pointed to the yard long glass that was shaped like a huge test tube, hanging above the bar, she checked her watch. "And we'd sneaked off to the loos ... twice! Remember?" She was expecting a naughty smile to wash across his face, but it didn't. Last year they had made it their mission to have a shag on the hour, every hour, no matter their surroundings. This year there had been no such action, and their one early morning kiss had been cut short by Ben and his desire to immediately phone Lisa and Benny.

He paused. "It just feels wrong that I'm here."

"Cheers, thanks for that," huffed Lucy, grabbing her tall glass and taking a hearty swig of beer.

"Oh, you know what I mean, Luce."

Lucy placed the glass back down and turned her body to face him. No one else was paying any real attention to their domestic, but she did not want to make a scene all the same. "No, actually, I don't!"

He turned to her and hushed his voice. "It's Christmas Day. I should be with my son."

Lucy was starting to get fed up. The game of smash the poppadom that had just started on the table opposite looked like much more fun than this. "But he already has a family and they'll be having a wonderful day and spoiling him rotten. We have him for the whole day on Thursday."

"Yeah, and what's Thursday?"

Lucy buzzed her head with her index finger. "Durr, it's the day after boxing day."

"Exactly, it's just a normal day."

"Oh Ben, grow up, would you." Lucy spun back around and reached once again for her glass.

Ben raised his voice. "Sorry, did *you* just tell *me* to grow up?!"

She turned her body to the left and chinked glasses with Mr and Mrs Walker, quickly involving herself in their animated conversation about the spicy, yet succulent starters, and joining their marvel at how much fun an alternative Christmas dinner could be. When she turned back around, she realised Ben had gone.

****

Kat and Freya had nipped upstairs and watched the Elton's arrival and subsequent awkward greeting from the huge sash window in Kat's bedroom. Freya instantly wondered how on earth they would make it through the day. Her mum and dad only mixed with people in their comfort zone and this consisted of individuals of a similar perceived social standing and a home within a five mile radius of their own. She knew her mother had only dreamed of hobnobbing with people like the Spicers in a country pile in the Cotswolds. Now she was here, Freya had no idea what to expect. With a burst of adrenaline she gave Kat an apologetic kiss of good luck, threw on her Christmas outfit, swept the blusher brush across her cheeks and flicked her eyelashes with mascara. There would be chance to touch up her hair and make-up later, but no chance to rectify her parents' inevitable entrance faux pas. She dashed back down the stairs into the lounge in time to see her mother handing over a bottle of cooking sherry. Freya had explained to her mother all about the Christmas traditions in the Spicer household, which included the sampling of the latest sweet and dry sherries and the tasting of Uncle Bart's revolutionary hors d'oeuvres.

Sue looked across at the antique silver wall mirror and saw Freya racing down the mahogany staircase. She stopped fawning over Gloria's matching pearl beads, unaware that her own beads were clearly cheap imitations when viewed in such close proximity to the Real McCoy, and turned around to Freya. "Happy Christmas, my darling!"

Freya had absolutely no idea where the new accent had come from. She raced to her father and gave him a huge hug. "Happy Christmas, Dad .... Mum." She lightly hugged her mother and nodded at the baby grandfather clock nestled in the corner of the room between the two large Christmas wreaths. "You're a bit early."

Sue nodded approvingly. "I was just saying to Gloria how your father and I like to follow good social etiquette and arrive on time for events."

Gloria smiled kindly. "Well it's lovely to finally meet you and so wonderful that you could come." She placed her arm around Freya's shoulder. "Your daughter has been a delight."

Sue coughed lightly and raised her eyebrows. "I hope she's been brushing her hair. Really, Freya, it does look a mess!"

Jeremy caught the comment as he bounded back into the room, armed with a fresh bottle of bubbly. "She looks great! The girls have been lounging around all morning and so they should! Cheers everyone. Happy Christmas! Who'd like a drink?" He aimed the cork at the crackling fireplace and started his countdown. "Three, two, one!" The swollen cork blasted across the room and hit the brick chimney breast. "There she blows!" He caught the bubbling liquid in a tall champagne glass and proceeded to pour the drinks. "Sue," he passed her the first glass, "you don't mind if I call you Sue?"

Sue lowered her chin and pretended to blush. "You can call me anything you want to, Doctor."

"Mum!" scowled Freya, flicking her mother's arm.

"I can tell that your mum's going to be great fun!" grinned Jeremy, raising his glass. "Cheers everyone, Happy Christmas! Good health and good happiness! Gloria, turn the Christmas music on would you please?"

Bing Crosby joyously filled the room.

Freya lifted her glass half heartedly. No one had ever described her mother as great fun. "Cheers" she said, aware that everyone else had turned towards the corner of the room. The traditional mahogany staircase was in itself a real eye catcher, but as Freya turned she realised it wasn't the bespoke wooden spindles that everyone was admiring, or the fresh holly and ivy that had been lovingly hung by Gloria from the banister. Instead, all eyes were on Kat. She was elegantly descending into the warm room with real grace and beauty. Freya even thought she heard her mother gasp.

Sue gasped again in case people hadn't heard, and walked over to the bottom step. She wrapped her arms around Kat and flattered. "Oh Katherine, you look wonderful." She gave her an over the top double kiss. "Happy Christmas!"

Freya was embarrassed by her mother's display of over familiarity, but had to admit that Kat's choice of Christmas outfit was indeed sensational. She was wearing a deep red crepe dress with a plunging v neck, pleated wrap front and diamante brooch, and her blonde hair was impeccable.

Kat managed to edge away from Sue and greeted Patrick with a sincere warmth. "Happy Christmas. Thank you for coming." She looked towards Freya. "Doesn't your daughter look beautiful?"

Sue glanced across to Freya before returning her eyes back to Kat. "Not as beautiful as you, Katherine."

Freya had to laugh. "Thanks Mum!"

Sue spoke with a forced smile. "Well you could have brushed your hair. Really, what will the Spicers think of us?"

Jeremy raised his glass once again, keen to keep this Christmas on track. "Happy Christmas, one and all! Please, you four relax in here and I hope you don't mind, but Gloria and I have a few jobs to finish in the kitchen."

Gloria tapped the second unopened bottle of bubbly that was sitting on Jeremy's antique mahogany desk. "Please help yourselves when your glasses are empty."

Freya watched as both Gloria and Jeremy made their apologies and rushed back into the steaming kitchen. Her parents' early arrival must have put them behind schedule. She waited for the latch to click closed on the door, then spun back around to her mother. "What are you doing?"

Sue leisurely waltzed around the room, examining the set of large pewter plates hanging from the wall and nodding in approval like she knew what they were. "What do you mean?" she said with nonchalance.

"The voice?! What's with your voice?"

Sue came to a rest at the beautiful Georgian sofa which had been upholstered in a gold leaf fabric. She looked at the thin tapered mahogany legs, patted the seat, and nodded in approval.

"Mum?! What are you doing?"

Sue sat down. "Making myself comfortable, like the good doctor said."

"Dad! What is she doing?"

Patrick took a seat on the mustard coloured high back wing chair and tried to relax. "Your mother's just pleased to be here."

Freya turned to her ally. "Kat! Mum doesn't usually talk like this does she?!"

Kat took a seat next to Sue and smiled warmly. "Did it take you long to get here?"

Sue sipped some of the champagne, eager to show off her correct glass holding position. She had done an intensive search on the internet about the protocol when it came to eating and drinking in a posh establishment and the results made it clear - you should hold the glass around the stem. "Just over an hour." She tapped Kat's knee. "I didn't realise we were so close."

"Well don't think you'll be popping in whenever you feel like it!" Freya plonked herself down in front of the fire and took a swig of champagne.

Sue tutted. "Don't hold the bowl of the glass, Freya. You will heat up the champagne and change its flavour."

Freya encased the glass in both hands and downed the remaining mouthful. "Cheers!"

Sue turned to Kat for confirmation. "I'm right aren't I? You should hold the stem of the champagne glass."

Kat sipped her fizzing drink. "To be honest, I don't really know." She looked at Freya whose cheeks were starting to burn and was unsure if this was from the heat of the fire, or an effect of her mother's presence. She slid off the seat and took a place next to her in front of the hearth. "Shall we remind your mum and dad who's coming?"

Freya shrugged her shoulders. Kat had to be on her side if she was to make it through the day.

Kat decided to ignore the obvious tension and began her spiel. "Okay, so we have us four. My parents. My sister Kelly, her husband, Richard, and their two children, Ava and Bobby." She smiled trying to lighten the mood. "You'll know when they arrive because the noise will quadruple."

Patrick adjusted himself on the buttoned high back chair. "Are they young children?"

"Three and four, but the noise will be from my sister. Poor Richard doesn't seem to get a word in."

Patrick made a mental note to seek solace in Richard's company.

"Then there's Auntie June and Uncle Steven, her three children, James, Jilly and Greg." She signalled to Freya. "They're all about our age."

Freya watched as her mother reached into her handbag and started to make notes on a piece of paper.

"Then there will be Grandpa Ed, his new girlfriend Audrey - they met at the whist drive about six months ago. Uncle Bart is coming-"

Sue lifted her head and jumped in. "Yes, he is the one making the whores curves."

Freya shook her head. "For goodness sake, Mother! It's *hors d'oeuvres!*" She couldn't help herself. "...and I don't know why you brought cooking sherry!"

"That's what I said." Sue rolled her eyes, embarrassed by the correction. "We brought the Tesco finest sherry to drink with the *whore durves.*"

"Tesco finest *cooking* sherry!"

Kat gently squeezed Freya's thigh. "It will be wonderful." She smiled. "So yes ... we also have Uncle Bart and Aunty Jean. The neighbours, Bill and Janet, are coming this year and so is Pam."

Sue paused her pen on the piece of paper. "Who is Pam?"

Kat laughed and stood up, making her way to the desk and unopened bottle of fizz. "To be honest, I'm not quite sure. She's been coming here for Christmas since I can remember and she's a distant cousin twice removed of dad's ... no mum's ... no, I don't really know, but she's great and she's the queen of the Christmas party games."

Sue straightened in her seat. "You play games?"

Kat opened the bottle, keeping hold of the lid and expertly stopping any precious spillage. "Yes, we always play after dinner games."

Sue turned to Freya. "You didn't say they played games."

"Yes I did, Mum. They always play after dinner games and from what Kat tells me the Spicer Christmas games are infamous!"

Sue pictured Gloria in her elegant black jacket, high heels and pearls. "I'll sit and watch with Gloria."

"Mum's the first one involved," smiled Kat, carefully refilling Patrick's empty glass.

Sue stiffened in her seat and took another sip of champagne trying to recall an episode of Downton Abbey where the toffs played any sort of parlour games. She suddenly felt unprepared.

Kat continued to do the rounds, topping up the glasses as she did a mental count. "So that is ... mmm ... twenty. We also have Katie and Bob, who are our relatives from America." She smiled. "Again, don't ask me how they're related. I just know they're relations from America who always come over for Christmas! Mum will be able to talk you through the family tree."

Sue nodded, she actually had a copy of the Spicer family tree in her handbag but didn't want to appear too eager. She lifted her glass and let Kat fill it back up to the brim.

Kat returned the empty bottle to the desk and lifted her own fizzing glass.

Freya cut in. "Right, before we do any more cheers, can we just sort one thing out?" She turned to her mum. "Mother, can you please lose the ridiculous voice?!"

Sue lifted her hand. "Ood yaouw rather I terked loike yaw fairther an' 'ad them all loff at us?"

Freya and Patrick chastised in unison. "Mum!" "Sue!"

Kat frowned. "What did she say?"

Freya shook her head. "She said: would you rather I talked like your father and had them all laugh at us?"

"Nobody will be laughing at you." Kat placed her hand on Sue's knee. "And anyway your accent is hardly noticeable," she lied.

"It's not now she's talking like the Queen Mother!" Freya gulped another mouthful of champagne, but had to smile. "But if I had a choice then I'd rather you avoided sounding like the broadest Brummie in the world please."

Sue nodded. "Thank you. Now kindly paaarse me my glaaarse and I will have my laaarst sip of champagne."

Freya, Patrick and Kat couldn't help but laugh, and lifted their glasses in what was to be one of many Christmas toasts throughout the day.

****

Lucy checked the restaurant clock once again. Ben had been gone for over half an hour. Mr and Mrs Walker were busy tucking into the Indian equivalent of vol-au-vents and she had completed the small ball maze from her cracker three times already. She reached into her bag for her phone. No messages. Sitting in a restaurant bustling with people, most of whom were merry before midday, she had never felt so alone. She dialled Kat's number. It went straight to answer phone, and she suddenly remembered how no one could ever get a signal at the Spicer mansion. She rang the home number picturing the Spicer clan mid way through present opening, or cheering as another bottle of bubbly got popped open. She had joined Kat down there for a couple of previous Christmases and they were some of her fondest memories.

After several long rings, Jeremy answered in his usual jovial fashion, wishing her the very merriest of Christmases and a Happy New Year. She could hear the sound of laughter and a shout of *"We're here!"* from what must have been Kelly and the kids. She almost burst into tears as Kat eventually came on the line. She tried to pull herself together. "Happy Christmas, Kat."

"Oh Happy Christmas, Lucy! Thanks for ringing!" Kat could hear the Indian music and loud noise reminiscent of a pub atmosphere. "How's the Indian? Have you had your starters yet?" Kat found herself shouting over the clamour at both ends.

A lump caught in Lucy's throat and she nodded, unable to speak.

"I can't hear you. Hang on." Kat shut the heavy wooden door and silenced the noise of her sister taking control of events in the front lounge. "That's better. How was your morning?"

"Okay," she managed, "...and you?"

Jeremy opened the door. "Kelly's ready to do the presents."

Kat nodded at him, she knew if Kelly had said it was present time then present time was about to start. "Sorry Lucy, I've got to go. I'll give you a call after lunch."

"Yep ... okay," she was close to tears.

"Happy Christmas, I'll ring you later." Kat wasn't sure if she heard, but the picture Lucy had painted of last year's Indian, complete with hourly hook ups, left her in no doubt that her very best friend would once again be having the time of her life.

****

Kat returned the old fashioned black circular dial phone back onto the receiver and re-opened the door to the front lounge. Kelly was sitting at the head of the circle that she had requested everyone formed, explaining how the present giving would work. Great Grandpa Ed and Audrey had arrived exactly on schedule, weighed down with bags of presents for the children. Everyone knew that Ava and Bobby were the most important part of the day and everything would now be centred on them and their mother. Kat smiled to herself, she didn't really mind and she knew it would be her one day, surrounded by little ones. She suddenly wondered how Kelly would feel about it. Smiling, she crept up behind her niece and nephew. "Boo! Happy Christmas, you terrors!"

Ava and Bobby jumped up and down. "Auntie Kat! Auntie Kat! Father Christmas came!"

Kat knelt down in the centre of the circle and pulled them both in for a cuddle. "What did he bring-"

"Kat, if you could sit on the desk chair next to Audrey please. We're going to give presents in a circle."

Kat rose back to her feet. "Right, okay. Happy Christmas, Kelly." She leaned down and kissed her sister on the cheek.

"Yep great, right, let's go. We want to get these presents given before the rest of them arrive and then we can do the other presents after lunch." Kelly looked up and scanned the room, fixing her eyes on the newcomers. "Okay, Sue and Patrick, do you have anything to give?"

Ava and Bobby raced up to their knees and looked at the new adults with eager eyes.

Sue tried to playfully tap one of the sticky hands resting on her new Marks and Spencer skirt. "Maybe later."

"Sorry Sue, it's just that there are so many people coming that we like to do presents with the immediate family first then we have lunch and then the others give theirs later. Now that you're here, you might as well give yours now."

Sue coughed and glared at her husband. "Patrick, are they in the car?"

Patrick shifted in the upright chair that was becoming more uncomfortable by the minute. "I think I left them in that bag in our hall at home."

Ava and Bobby sulked back away from the new adults who weren't going to be any fun at all and plopped back down into the middle of the circle.

Kelly clapped her hands. "Not to worry. Great Grandpa Ed!"

Ava and Bobby jumped up and raced to the old man's knees. His wrinkles and thin sticky up hair were a bit scary, but he had a very big bag of presents, so they would try and be brave.

Sue was fuming. How dare Freya not tell her they were expected to bring gifts? She reached for her wine glass and emptied its contents in one long swig. The only good thing to come from Freya's lesbianism was this chance to up the family's social status and she was not going to fall at the first hurdle. She stood to make an announcement. "Don't worry, children. We'll pop back down tomorrow with your huge presents."

Ava and Bobby didn't hear. They were head first in a supersized bag full of goodies.

Kat and Freya heard and squeezed each other's hands in unison, as did Jeremy and Gloria.

CHAPTER SEVENTEEN

Ben felt his heart quicken as he pressed the small black bell at number 16 Winterton Lane. It had all been so clear on the long walk over. It was Christmas Day and he needed to see his son. The past three months had been such a mind fuck. Benny now knew him as *'Ben The Seed Daddy'* and had absorbed the news with significant interest - that was until his next question arose about where the sun went at night. Lisa had insisted it was her plan all along, having moved back to the area, to find Ben and explain everything. Gerald, Lisa's much older husband confirmed this on their first meeting and had been overwhelmingly supportive. Something that Ben still couldn't understand. He pressed the black doorbell twice more and asked himself once again - what sort of man, who has raised a child as his own from the age of one, allows his wife to relocate to the area where her ex boyfriend lives, with the plan to fess up to the said ex boyfriend that he is her child's biological father? Lisa had explained it as guilt and a desire to ensure Benny got to know his real dad, but Ben didn't buy it. He had to be missing something.

The white door swung open and revealed a dishevelled looking Lisa. Ben almost stepped back at the sight. She looked odd, like something was missing.

Lisa was instantly aware of his shocked stare and attempted to straighten her hair, pulling her fringe down towards her eyes. She took a deep breath and tried to collect herself. "What are you doing here?"

Ben couldn't work out if she had done something different with her bobbed blonde hair or her eye make-up. Whatever it was, it didn't suit her. He was suddenly lost for words. "I ... umm ... Happy Christmas!"

"Happy Christmas. Where's Lucy?"

He felt a pang of concern. "Lucy's at the Indian. I just ... I just thought maybe I should pop in and say Happy Christmas to Benny."

Lisa made one final attempt to adjust her hair. "You and Lucy are with him all day on Thursday."

"I know, I just thought it was important to see him today."

She shook her head and closed the door slightly. "He's four. Christmas lasts for days when you're four. It makes no difference to him which day you wish him a Happy Christmas. Now get back to Lucy and enjoy yourself."

"It makes a difference to me."

Lisa leaned against the door for support. "Well I'm sorry, but that's selfish. He's spending today with Mummy and Daddy. Tomorrow he knows we're going to Nana Pearl's and on Thursday he knows he's seeing Seed Daddy and Lu Lu." She took a slow breath and held onto the door handle. "You can't confuse a child, Ben."

Ben was about to respond with a smart remark about how this two dads situation might be confusing, but he actually knew that Benny wasn't confused at all. He crossed his arms and looked down at the damp paved step, kicking a small pebble back onto the modern flower bed. "I guess I just wanted to see him."

"And you will, on Thursday." She took another deep breath. "Now tell me why you're here without Lucy."

Ben tilted his head and eyed her sunken cheeks. "Are you okay?"

"Yes fine. Where's Lucy?"

He immediately dropped his head in shame. "At the Indian."

"On her own? On Christmas Day?"

Ben nodded.

This was the last thing she needed. "What are you doing? I thought you two were great? I thought you had promised to propose?"

It hit him like a ton of bricks. The image of Lucy sitting alone in the restaurant. "I did, and we are, and I don't know what I'm doing." He ruffled his already messy blonde hair. "Being a knob as per usual."

He tapped his finger on his chunky brown watch. "Shit, I've got to go. I am such a dick. Sorry Lisa. I'll see you on Thursday."

"He'll be ready for you at ten. Don't be late!" She watched him race away down the path, and took a step back inside her hallway, slowly closing the door and pulling the itchy wig from her head. She hurled it to the floor and started to sob.

****

The present giving had been wonderful and Bobby and Ava's little faces had been a picture as they excitedly ripped open the shiny red and silver wrapping paper from Auntie Kat and Auntie Freya's gigantic present. The motorised jeep, large enough for them both to sit in, had been the hit of the morning, with Bobby immediately jumping into the driver's seat, calling for his sister to strap herself into the passenger's seat, and hitting the pedal. The noisy vehicle, which could actually reach speeds of five miles per hour, crashed straight into Sue Elton's shins.

Sue's mood had failed to improve as the day progressed and now she was squashed into the huge dining room table with Uncle Bart on her left, who had polished off the gravy by drinking from the jug, and Grandpa Ed opposite, whose constant coughing fits due to poorly chewed food did nothing to make all of this posh nosh any more appetising. Everyone had been complimenting the hosts on how delicious the meal was and marvelling at the way Jeremy and Gloria had outdone themselves this year with four different types of stuffing, a perfectly cooked three bird roast consisting of a pheasant, in a chicken, in a goose, and every possible vegetable you could think of. Sue reached for her glass and had to admit that the plonk was very good indeed. They had started the day with champagne, followed quickly by sherry and hors d'oeuvres and now it was a lovely white wine that had topped the Guardian's twenty best Christmas white wines list, or so Gloria had informed them.

Sue wanted to add to the buzzing conversation, so she raised her glass. Everyone had been making little toasts throughout the noisy meal, so she thought she would have a go. She tapped the crystal wine glass with her fork, and watched in horror as a small crack suddenly appeared and began to spread down the glass to the stem. She quickly gulped the wine in case the glass shattered completely.

To everyone who sat at the table, it looked as if Sue Elton was announcing the fact that she could down almost a full glass of expensive white wine. "Mum! What are you doing?" Freya was aghast.

One of Auntie June's grown up children gave a whoop of respect and let off another party popper, only to realise that a fellow grown up child had replaced the contents of the popper with squirty cream. The subsequent mess of exploded froth offered a momentary distraction.

Sue realised the crack hadn't been noticed, so decided to continue. She leaned forward so that everyone from all ends of the oblong table could see her. "I just wanted to make a toast. To Kat and Freya ... and the joining of two distinguished families." She raised her glass with her hand covering the bowl.

"I thought you were meant to hold a glass by its stem?" shouted Freya, unable to resist the dig.

Sue felt the thin crystal give way between her clenched fingers. Everyone heard the crack. "Now look what you've made me do!"

Gloria jumped out of her seat and raced to Sue's side with her red Christmas napkin. "Just drop it in here. These pesky glasses are so thin. Are you okay? It hasn't cut you has it?" Gloria collected the remains of her treasured wedding present. "Don't worry, it happens all of the time," she lied.

"I'm fine. I'll replace it."

Jeremy had dashed to the kitchen and was now returning with a new glass. He refilled it with the incredibly expensive white wine.

Sue looked up at Gloria with a smile. "We picked up a lovely set of twelve wine glasses from IKEA, didn't we Patrick, and I think we only paid a couple of pounds." She took the topped up glass from Jeremy. "I'll let you have one when you come up and visit us."

"Is that an official invite?" flirted Jeremy, keen to distract from the incident.

Sue smiled. The man was a real charmer, unlike the monotone husband sat next to her. "Of course it is." She bashed Patrick's arm. "Maybe we could host a New Year's Eve Party?"

Freya huffed again. She had deliberately chosen a seat at the opposite end of the table to her mother, but could hear every word of the embarrassing encounter. "You've never hosted a New Year's Eve Party!"

Sue leaned forward and looked past the six other people sat to her right. She eyed her daughter. "Yes we have, darling, and this year I think we should invite everyone that's here. Like I said in my toast..." She raised her new glass and increased her volume. "...To the joining of two distinguished families."

Grandpa Ed and Audrey hadn't the foggiest idea who this woman with the annoying accent was, but the chance of another free knees up sounded great. "Count us in," spluttered Ed, as a piece of chestnut from the chestnut and mushroom stuffing went down the wrong way.

Jeremy and Gloria returned to their seats and lifted their glasses. "To Kat and Freya."

Everyone followed in unison and Sue wondered why no one had repeated her offering. "...And two great families," she tried again.

"Yes okay, Mum! We get it!" Freya wanted the ground to swallow her up.

Kat was aware of the simmering tension and aware of the strong Birmingham accent that was slowly returning to Sue's slightly slurred speech. She decided to make the final toast that everyone had been waiting for. "I would just like to say thank you again for having us. Mum and Dad, you're the best!"

"Here, here!" shouted Kelly rather too noisily, as another dud party popper exploded.

Jeremy and Gloria's Christmas's were complete. It was all they needed to hear - their daughters were home and their daughters were happy. A small tear formed in the corner of Jeremy's eye. "I'm a sentimental old fool, but this is what's important to me. Thank you everyone for coming and please, help yourself to seconds!"

Sue was the first to reach across the table - for the expensive bottle of white wine.

****

Ben flung open the door and was hit with the strong aroma of spices and beer. He scanned the Indian restaurant. Lucy wasn't in her seat, or at the bar. He paced to all corners of the room checking the other tables. Last year's impromptu game of musical chairs saw them all switching seats and forgetting where they were originally meant to be, but it didn't look like that frivolity had happened yet.

The stern Indian waiter approached him with a look of disapproval. "Missy, Missy gone home."

Ben sank against the bar stool at the small bar. "She's gone?"

"Yes, she go. Missy not happy. She cry."

Ben quickly stood back up. "She was crying?"

"Yes. You be bad man to Missy. You be ashamed. It's Christmas, what you be bad man for?"

Ben reached into his back pocket for his leather wallet, took out a tip and gave it to the waiter. "Thanks for all of your efforts today. I'm sure it would have been great."

The waiter snatched the ten pound note. "Yes, but you spoil it, bad man!"

Ben shrugged, what could he say? "I'll learn one day."

"Make sure you do. Missy very very lovely lady. You be lucky."

"I know, I'll go home and make it up to her."

"Don't be doing no jiggy jiggy, Mister!" He pushed Ben back down onto the bar stool. "Wait here, you make it up to Missy with this." He returned from the kitchen a couple of minutes later with a bulging white bag full of takeaway food. "Say it from Pritpal. Missy like Pritpal."

Ben smiled. "Thanks, Pritpal, I will."

"Hey, you tell her she beautiful."

Ben felt crushed. "I will."

****

Lucy had returned to the apartment and deliberately chosen to re-enact her favourite scene from Bridget Jones's Diary. Celine Dion's *'All by myself'* was playing and she was basking in her new found depression with a tub of Ben and Jerry's chocolate ice cream and her favourite pink fleece pyjamas. She pictured Ben, Lisa and Benny dancing around the Christmas tree singing *'here we go round the mulberry bush'*, declaring their love for one another and running off into a snowy sunset. The click of the heavy apartment door snapped her out of it and the instant enticing smell of Indian food was too hard to ignore. She lifted her head from the black leather sofa and felt her heart melt. Ben was standing in the hallway with his brown bomber jacket zipped up to his lips, a bulging bag of takeaway food in one hand and a pitiful bunch of handpicked flowers in the other. He raised his eyebrows and apologised with a loveable puppy dog look of sorrow.

Lucy was torn. Usually one widening of his beautiful brown eyes was enough to have her forgiving his minor misdemeanours, jumping up to his waist and hauling him into the bedroom for make-up sex. This was different, this time she was going to hold her ground.

Ben saw her flop back onto the sofa and realised it would take more than some crappy flowers and his puppy dog eyes to sort this one out. He tiptoed across the laminate wood floor with his boots still on and knelt at the bottom of the sofa. He lifted the steaming bag to the black ash coffee table and unzipped his jacket, revealing a downturned mouth and even wider eyes.

"You know we always leave shoes at the door. Take them off." Lucy was sharp.

Ben didn't know how to play it. They never rowed and he knew he was in the wrong, but he just didn't know where to start. He swivelled onto his bottom and untied his laces. Lifting his boots he rose to his feet and crept back to the hall, placing them neatly on the shoe rack. He took off his jacket and hung it from the spare peg. Celine Dion finally tailed off and silence filled the room. He tiptoed back to the sofa and opened his mouth to speak. Celine Dion started up again.

Lucy had to smile. "It's on repeat."

Ben paused not knowing what to do.

Celine Dion sang loud and clear. '*All by myself...*'

He knelt at her knees. "I don't want you to be all by yourself."

Celine continued. '*Don't wanna be, all by myself...*'

"And I know it's my fault that you're all by yourself."

'*Hard to be sure, sometimes I feel so insecure...*'

"I'm the one who's being insecure. I'm insecure about everything at the moment."

Lucy pressed the red button on her iPod remote, cutting Celine Dion in full flow. "I'm not having you base your entire apology around this song, no matter how fabulous it is."

"Oh, I wanted to get to that '*Don't wanna live by myself, by myself, anymorrrrrrrrrrrrrrrrrrrrrrrrrrrre*' bit."

Lucy hurled a red bobbly cushion his way and laughed. "Why do I put up with you, Ben?"

Ben jumped up next to her, relieved by the slight break in frostiness. "Because you love me and I love you and we're going to get married and have children of our own and live happily ever after."

"Are we?"

He took her hand. "Yes we are ... and you put up with me because you can see what a life changing event I'm going through and you understand how my head might get a bit messed up with it all sometimes. I'm not making excuses for myself but I guess I'm just struggling with my role." He paused ruffling his messy hair. "I felt like I should have been there with him today."

"But he already has a mummy and a daddy for that."

"I know, I know, that's what Lisa said and it makes sense now. I'm just confused."

Lucy dropped the hand. "So you did go round to see her then?"

"No, I went round to see Benny. Listen Luce, Lisa and Gerald are the perfect couple-"

"No they're not. He's about eighty and works abroad for most of the week. You suddenly come back into her life and start showing up on her doorstep and she thinks way-hey!"

"You're worth a million Lisa's and a million Tanya's and a million Tracey's ... shall I list all of my ex-girlfriends?"

Her lips started to turn at the corners. "No, don't flatter yourself with your long list of conquests."

"Is that a smile?"

"No."

He laid his head in her lap and made a tiny little yapping sound. "Puppy dog sorry."

She couldn't help but laugh. "What would your students think if they could see you now?"

"Way-hey probably!" He sat back up and looked at her with sincerity. "I'm so sorry, Lucy. I should have talked to you and explained how I was feeling. Please forgive me."

She smiled. "I forgave you the moment you walked through the door with that steaming bag of food and those crappy flowers from the neighbour's garden. I might act daft sometimes, but I know what you're going through and I want to go through it with you."

Ben held her close and whispered in her ear. "I love you, Lucy Lovett."

Lucy spanked his muscular thigh. "Well go and get some plates and turn Celine back on." Her grin was wide. "Let's see who can hit that high note for the longest."

Ben smiled to himself, what a perfect woman.

CHAPTER EIGHTEEN

Kat and Freya walked hand in hand up the steep winding path out of the picturesque Cotswold village, sucking in the crisp winter air and laughing with shock and horror at how they had managed to make it through the Christmas meal. Sue had continued to get steadily drunk, increasingly loud, and her politically incorrect comments became progressively outrageous. She had put the world to rights in one sitting. Slamming the migrants that were coming into the country and taking all of the jobs, reminiscing about the time when men were not afraid to be men. Criticising the way society had gone downhill now that women were putting careers ahead of family life. Her pièce de résistance was when she announced it was in fact the toffs and the thieving Tory government that were to blame for the whole global economic meltdown. Gloria had quickly folded the blue tea towel that she'd been using to wipe the children's table; it read *Proud Conservative* and was a free gift that arrived after their membership to the party had been renewed for the twelfth consecutive year. Luckily, most of the extended family had already left the table and moved into a room of choice.

The lounge was where Grandpa Ed, Audrey, Uncle Steve, Uncle Bart and Pam were all sat open mouthed, competing for the title of loudest snorer. Aunty June and her grown up children were all in the conservatory deliberately avoiding the cleanup, and Kelly was noisily dealing with the latest battery drama involving Bobby and Ava's new electronic toys. Jeremy had received an ear bashing from his eldest daughter for failing to stock up on all of the different types of battery, but at ten different sorts, Jeremy had thought he had it covered. How wrong he had been.

Kat and Freya had offered to help with the washing up, but had been ushered out of the cluttered kitchen and into the soft winter sun, with the explicit instructions to: *'get out of the mad house and enjoy the village.'* Gloria was about to put the suggestion to the rest of the guests but Freya asked her for a ten minute head start. The last thing she needed was her mother tagging along and finding fault in the beautiful scenery, or the idyllic houses.

Freya looked at the picture perfect postcard landscape and enjoyed the feeling of the cool crisp air filling her lungs. She squeezed Kat's hand. "I'm so sorry about my mum."

Kat smiled. "Oh she fitted in perfectly. Did you see Uncle Bart swigging from that two litre bottle of White Lightening Cider that he had stashed under the table?"

"Actually I did."

"And did you notice the way Kelly's Steve managed to get through the whole meal without saying a word?"

Freya chuckled. "No, I think I was too busy listening to Kelly."

Kat pointed at a robin redbreast hopping along a naked branch. She loved this time of year, especially now she had her soul mate to share it with. "Did I tell you about that time at Brownies? That time with Kelly?"

"No. I never even knew you went to Brownies. Mum wouldn't let me go. She said things like Brownies and Scouts were run by paedophiles. I was only eight."

Kat could picture the way Sue would have said it, and was more and more understanding of Freya's struggle. She watched the robin fly away and returned her focus to the story. "When you start Brownies, you have to go to the front of the Brownie circle and recite the *Brownie Guide Law.*"

Freya frowned. "Okay." It was difficult to imagine Kat as anything other than the smart, sophisticated, grown woman that she had become.

"Well, when we were all making a circle ready to start the ceremony I chose to stand next to Brown Owl, who's the leader and runs the ceremony, and Kelly, who had already been at Brownies for two years, took my hand and escorted me to the far edge of the large circle opposite Brown Owl instead."

"Why?"

"Well exactly. She told me to stand there so that when my name was called everyone would watch me as I crossed the circle."

"Oh bless!"

"Obviously I was really embarrassed and had only wanted to shuffle to the side and mumble my words." Kat smiled in remembrance. "So basically yes, she's always liked the attention."

"At least your family have got some life about them."

Kat slowed her walk and pulled Freya close. "Well you and your parents are part of that family now."

"Oh no, don't tell my mother that. She'll be moving in before you know it."

Kat swept a piece of long chestnut brown hair back behind Freya's cold ear. "You're the most beautiful woman in the world and I love everything about you ... even your mother."

"Don't tell her that either!" she joked.

"I mean it. You make me so happy."

Freya looked deep into those piercing blue eyes. "And you make me so aware. So aware of the person I want to become - the person that you deserve."

Kat softly kissed her lips. "You already are that person."

Freya returned the kiss with passion and felt the familiar surge of desire engulfing her body. "Why do I want you so much?" she moaned.

Kat glanced up at the entrance to the hedged thicket. It was the area where villagers would come with their wheelbarrows full of hedge trimmings and garden prunings to dump on the natural compost. If you followed the path deep enough, you came to a dense wooded area where people occasionally walked their dogs. Kat used to play there as a child and had once found some old rusty bikes with two metre high baby sycamore trees that had actually grown through the spokes of the wheels. Her favourite time to come and seek solace in the secret hideout was in April, when the area was carpeted with beautiful fragrant bluebells. She took Freya's hand and pulled her towards the thicket's entrance.

"What are you doing?"

"I want you too." She did a final reccy up and down the country road. "Follow me."

Freya's pace quickened to a run and she giggled with the naughtiness of it all. They had not passed a single person on their walk and her desire to feel Kat's hands on her body far outweighed her worry of being spotted. Kat pulled her deeper and deeper into the wooded area and Freya realised that no one was around. She stumbled over a large fallen tree branch and laughed at her sudden wobbliness. "Look at me, I can't get here quick enough!"

"Good, because we're here," gasped Kat, pushing her against the thick trunk of an old oak tree.

Freya enjoyed the roughness of Kat's embrace and the impatience of the searching fingers that reached under her thick Christmas jumper and immediately squeezed her hard nipples. She moaned at the force at which the other hand pushed straight down the back of her trousers and deep inside. She gasped at the intrusion.

"Too hard?"

Freya pulled Kat's head back to her neck. "No, give me more."

Kat bit Freya's neck again and added another finger.

"Oh, yes." Freya moaned as she was stretched further. "Yes, Kat!"

Kat continued to squeeze the rock hard nipple as she thrust her wet fingers in and out. She knew she would have to move her hand round to the front in order to use her thumb to stimulate Freya properly, but she wanted to get her as close to orgasm as possible.

"I think I'm coming!"

Kat's response was muffled; she had moved her teasing bites to the base of Freya's hairline. "But I'm not even touching you."

Freya gasped. "You're pulling on the back of my trousers and the front seam is rubbing against me." She moaned in heated arousal. "Oh yeah, keep fucking me, keep going ... fuuuuuck!"

Kat felt Freya clamp around her fingers, easing momentarily before clamping once again. This pattern continued at least ten times before the muscles slowly relaxed and allowed Kat to slide her fingers out. She smiled, herself also slightly out of breath. "That was quick!"

Freya panted. "My orgasm wasn't! You make it last for so long!" She smiled, slightly embarrassed. "How did it feel to you?"

"Powerful."

Freya nodded. "It was! Sorry about the swearing, but you are just so fucking good!" She switched places with Kat and pushed her back against the tree. "Now come here." Kat had changed from her long red dress into more appropriate walking gear and Freya had no trouble popping open the buttons on her old rambling jeans. She sank to her knees and pulled the jeans down past Kat's bottom.

Kat felt the cold bark pressing against her bare behind and smiled in anticipation. Freya was already great in bed and she very rarely had to guide her fingers or alter her pace. She closed her eyes and felt her stomach lurch as Freya's lips fixed around her. She was expecting to feel her tongue gently licking and stroking, but instead she felt Freya's mouth moving in fast circles. The sensation was intense and took Kat by complete surprise. Freya's actions were indirectly stimulating her and it felt amazing. She looked down at Freya's head making the circular route and moaned in satisfaction. The whole area was moving and she could feel the tension building.

Freya continued her pattern making sure her tongue didn't touch Kat directly. She could hear the groans of pleasure and feel her wet arousal. She was almost ready for the grand finale.

Kat thought she was about to come. The tension was unbelievable and she was holding her breath, then suddenly it happened. Freya sucked her with such a force that she was almost drawn forwards. The orgasm was immediate and wild and she cried out loudly.

Freya plunged two fingers deep inside and felt the power of Kat's orgasm.

Kat finally gasped. "No one has done it like that before!" She literally felt weak at the knees.

"Good," smiled Freya, lifting to her feet with her fingers still in place, forcing Kat back against the tree with a rough embrace. She started to gently rub her thumb in small circles. "I have something else for you too," she grinned.

****

The cool air hit Sue Elton like a brick wall. "Are we going far?" she asked, wondering why on earth Gloria and Jeremy thought an afternoon Christmas walk would be good for the digestion. The other members of the extended family clearly knew better, choosing to stay and snooze in the warmth of the house.

Gloria rubbed her suede mittens together. "No, I just thought we could show you the church and the duck pond."

"Sounds wonderful," said Sue with a forced smile. Who did these people think they were with their posh dinners and Christmas rituals? She would take her two up two down and Christmas TV dinner over this any day.

"So, how does this compare to your usual Christmas festivities?" quizzed Jeremy, trussed up in his beloved wax jacket, wrapping a solid arm around Sue's thin shoulder.

Sue looked up at him and fluttered her eyelashes. "Simply marvellous, I would take this over our standard Christmas any day!"

"I don't believe that! I bet you Brummie lot know how to have a good shin dig!"

Sue playfully tapped his chest and smiled through gritted teeth. "We don't live anywhere near Birmingham! We actually have a South Staffordshire postcode, don't we, Patrick."

Patrick was enjoying the fresh air. Lunch had been wonderful, but it was weighing rather heavily on his stomach. "Yes, Sue, we do, but both our families are from The Black Country." He rolled his eyes at her. "I'm sure people can tell from our accents."

"*I'm frum Burminum*," laughed Jeremy. "That's what they say isn't it? And, *am ya alrooight me babby*?"

"Jeremy!" Gloria immediately scolded him.

Sue lifted her nose into the air. "*Var, var good, thank one for asking one.*"

"Sue!" Patrick immediately scolded her.

"He started it!" said Sue, folding her arms and cursing her husband for spoiling the flirtatious, if slightly too close to the bone, banter.

Jeremy removed his arm and coughed, unsure of who was in the wrong. It was only a bit of friendly teasing and Sue had looked like she needed livening up. "So, Patrick, tell us what it was like when Freya told you she was a lesbian."

Patrick spluttered. Sue had banned the word lesbian from his vocabulary. "Ahem, excuse me. Right, erm, Freya told us she liked girls quite recently actually."

"Oh right."

"Yes, and I think we're finally getting used to it, aren't we Sue?"

Sue had started to puff, Jeremy and Gloria were obviously keen walkers and she was struggling to keep up. "Can we stop for a minute?"

"Of course," said Gloria, frowning at her husband for marching off so briskly. She indicated to the side of the road that had been empty enough for them to walk along. "Let's have a seat in the bus shelter."

Sue looked to her left and noticed an old wooden shelter nestled a good five metres back from the open road. It certainly didn't look like any of the modern vandalised plastic monstrosities from round by them; and she hadn't seen an original red telephone box for years. "This will do. Thank you." She had started to sober up. Her head was pounding and she was unsure of how much longer she would be able to keep up the pleasantries. She took a seat and looked across at Gloria, who was incidentally looking magnificent in a pair of pink Hunter wellies and a sky blue Barbour wax jacket. She was still fuming at Freya for not telling them a change of clothing would be required. It seemed like the whole family had relaxed into afternoon wear once the meal had finally finished. She thought for a second about how to phrase it. "I have to admit that I still think it's odd."

Gloria frowned. "The fact Kat used to teach her?"

"No, I'll come onto that in a minute..."

Patrick glanced up at Jeremy, who had chosen to stand against the wooden pillar, and shared an apologetic smile.

"...No, I think being a lesbian is rather odd. I mean, let's all be honest with one another while the girls aren't around. It's not normal is it?"

Gloria tried to be tactful. "It depends on what you class as normal. I think that being gay is just a genetic difference. Similar to being left handed."

"My point exactly! Lefties were always the weird ones at school!"

Jeremy had to turn away to smother his laugh. Sue had clearly not noticed which hand he'd used to carve the three bird roast.

"...and coming onto the matter of the student and teacher issue. I'm appalled that both the university and the school are going to allow it all to happen all over again!"

"Sorry, I'm not following you." Gloria would always try and be diplomatic, but there was a line and that line involved her daughters.

"Well, putting Freya back at Coldfield for her first teaching placement ... and with Kat as her mentor!"

Jeremy clapped his hands and exhaled a large foggy breath. "Shall we carry on to the church?" It was his mission in life to avoid all possible conflict, even if it had meant a quick trip out to the only local garage that was open on Christmas Day to find the correct batteries for his demanding daughter. Or likewise a sharp exit from the bus stop and a potential ruffling of female feathers.

"Give us a minute," said Gloria and Sue in unison. Gloria continued. "It's only a four week January placement to see if the trainees do indeed want to spend the next three years working to become a qualified teacher. And I'm aware, from what Kat has told me, that it's common practice to place any local students in their old schools to make the experience less daunting." Gloria felt she had made her point, but decided to continue. "Freya's only nineteen and she'll be expected, amongst other things, to teach an introduction to an A-Level lesson. Imagine if one of those A-Level students took a year out after their GCSEs, they could in fact be older than she is."

"The whole thing's preposterous then!"

Gloria coughed lightly. "Well not really. Kat said that the numbers on her course shrank dramatically after the first school placement, with people quickly realising teaching wasn't for them. And I have to admit, even Kat had a few jitters."

"Actually, Gloria, my main point is that it's unethical to have the two of them who are in a - well you know - in a..." she mouthed the word, "...*lesbian* relationship, to have them working so closely together, and dare I say it ... around children."

Gloria leaned further forward on the soft wooden bench. "I'm not quite sure I understand." She understood perfectly, but the Eltons were their guests, and one day Sue might become Kat's mother-in-law. "There are many, many, married couples teaching in the same schools across the country and there are also many, many, partnered couples teaching in the same schools across the country, and yes, a proportion of those will be same sex couples."

Sue was unsure whether she could detect a sharp note in Gloria's tone. "I just think it's unprofessional."

"Well they'll hardly be having their wicked way with one another in the classroom, Sue!" The sharp tone was definitely there.

Sue looked aghast. "Of course they won't! They're not even married yet!"

"Civil partnered, and I don't think that matters!"

"That's what I meant, and of course it matters!"

"Right, shall we carry on?" said Gloria, annoyed to have risen to the bait.

"I think we should," said Sue, secretly pleased to have eroded Gloria's saintly veneer.

****

"So, are you going to have your wicked way with me in your classroom?" puffed Freya, pleased to be nearing the brow of the hill. The walk had been exhilarating in more ways than one.

"Of course, and in the staffroom, and the store cupboard, and the teacher's toilets, and while we're making plans, I'm doing a Year Ten assembly on Tuesday, why don't you pop down and we can put on a show!"

Freya grinned. "I'm only teasing. I know you're Miss Professional, and I know you'll be my mentor, and I know I'll have to obey you, yada yada yada!"

Kat took the final step to the summit, the view of the village would be magnificent from up here. "Well, I might give you a quick kiss while my classroom door is locked."

Freya took her hand. "I look forward to it, Miss!" She paused, the view was breathtaking. "Wow, what a lovely part of the world." The limestone village looked honey-coloured and the odd scattering of Christmas lights had started to twinkle in the dying afternoon sun. "You are very lucky-"

Bleep Bleep

"You are lucky-"

Bleep Bleep

Freya frowned as the message tone beeped again. "Have you got your phone?"

Bleep Bleep

Kat shook her head. "No, it sounds like yours."

Bleep Bleep
Bleep Bleep

Freya thought for a second and padded her pockets; she hadn't used her phone at all over the past few days because of the low signal in the village.

Bleep Bleep

"It's in here," said Kat, reaching into the internal zip pocket of the jacket she was wearing. "I looked after it at the carol service."

Bleep Bleep

Kat pulled out the phone and looked at the screen. "How many messages have you got?!"

Bleep Bleep
Bleep Bleep

"It must have just got a signal," said Freya anxiously.

Bleep Bleep

"Eleven and counting..."

Bleep Bleep
Bleep Bleep

Bleep Bleep
"Pass it here then," said Freya.
"Hang on a minute, that's..."
Bleep Bleep
Bleep Bleep
"...Sixteen."
"What can I say? I'm popular." Freya's laugh was nervous. She kept her hand outstretched.
Bleep Bleep
"Can I see who they're from?" asked Kat, genuinely intrigued.
Bleep Bleep
"Are you being serious?" The response was defensive.
Kat looked back down at the screen at the flashing envelope with eighteen messages. "If you're going to look guilty like that, then yes!"
Bleep Beep
Bleep Bleep
Freya snatched the phone.
"Hey!" Kat rubbed her hand. "What are you doing?" She had been joking and was about to tease Freya for receiving so many of those awful Christmas round robin poems.
Freya switched the phone to silent and shoved it into her back pocket. "I never ask to look at your phone."
"You don't have to! It's always just lying around, and anyway you use it all the time to search the internet."
"But I don't go nosing through your messages."
Kat crossed her arms. "You can look at my messages whenever you want."
"But I don't want to look at your messages."
"That's fine, but why aren't you looking at yours?"
"Because you've made this into such a big deal. Come on, it's getting dark."
"Me?" Kat had absolutely no idea what was going on.
"Yes, you." The wind had started to bite and Freya turned away. "Let's just go back."
Kat stood still. "I don't care what they say, just show me who they're from."

Freya turned back around and raised her eyebrows. "No."

"Why not?"

"Because they're *my* messages."

"I don't want to read your messages, just show me your inbox so I can see who they're from."

"Listen to yourself, Kat! I know you said you were insecure, but I didn't realise it was this bad." It was a low blow and she knew it.

"Ouch, that hurt." Kat paused and spoke slowly, hugging herself with her jacket. "Show me then. Show me I'm being ridiculous." She could feel her eyes misting up. "Show me I have no reason to feel insecure."

Freya could sense the sorrow in her tone and felt her own heart shrink in shame. "I don't want to."

"Why not?"

Freya reached into her pocket for the phone. There was no other option. She walked back to Kat, stood shoulder to shoulder and unlocked the screen. She clicked on the inbox.

Renee
Renee
Renee
Renee
Renee
Renee
Renee
Renee
Renee
Renee
Renee
Renee
Renee

CHAPTER NINETEEN

"Good morning and welcome back." Kirsty Spaulding was standing at the front of the staffroom commanding her troops. "New year, new slog. Get your teaching hats back on and show me the goods." She tapped the scrap of paper she had been clutching. "On one final point..." There had been three final points already and could possibly be two more, but this was an important final point so Kirsty raised her pitch even higher. "...I would like to welcome the four trainee teachers that we have with us from Birmingham University. They are all on a four week placement here at Coldfield and I would like you all to treat them like full members of staff. If you could please wave or stand or do a little curtsey for us when I call your name so we all know who you are." It was more for her own benefit as she had no idea who the four new faces in the staffroom actually were. She could recognise the good and bad teachers, but there were a whole bunch of mediocre ones that she had hardly ever spoken to - she had James Dapper, her Deputy, for all of that. "Right," she lifted the scrap of paper up to her eyes and squinted. "Tracy Tubbs in Maths."

A very podgy girl tried to stand, but struggled to make it out of her low staffroom chair.

"Yes, yes, I see you." Kirsty waved her back down. "Kelly Craptree in Science."

A modern looking girl with a short spiky haircut raised her hand. "It's Crabtree."

Kirsty lowered her moon shaped glasses. "I know."

"You said Crap."

"I did not. Let me continue." Kirsty made a second mental note, hoping this third trainee might be in with a chance of lasting more than a week. "Freya Elton in History. Ah yes, Freya, welcome back." She nodded to herself, *good - one potential teacher in the making.*

Freya waved, unsure whether the rush of blood to her cheeks was due to nerves or embarrassment.

"Finally we have, Fiona Butts in Business Studies."

A tall, confident girl stood up and nodded. "Thank you, Mrs Spaulding. May I just say it's a pleasure to be here at Coldfield and share this staffroom with such-"

"Yes thank you," Kirsty cut her off. This was no place for show offs.

Ben whispered into Kat's ear. "So we have Tubby in Maths, Crapper in Science and Butt-licker in Business. Looks like you got lucky."

Kat glanced across the small round table at Freya, who was sitting confidently as if this was a run of the mill morning. She questioned once again if she had indeed got lucky.

Freya felt the eyes from the other side of the table and turned just in time to see Kat drop her gaze.

Kat stared at the tiled blue carpet and wondered if she was, in fact, a fool. The noise of shuffling staff members snapped her out of it. She focused and smiled at Ben. "See you in here at four?"

"Shit, no. We've got Benny again tonight. I'm not saying shit that we have Benny, I'm saying shit that we can't do our usual start of term debrief at the pub."

Kat frowned. "You have him again?"

"I know. We had him four times last week. I just don't get it. She asks us to have him and I'm assuming it's because Gerald is working somewhere abroad again and she wants some peace, but each time it has been Gerald who's dropped him off." Ben grinned. "I'm not complaining though. Benny's even promoted me from Seed Daddy to Daddy Number Two."

Diane had been hovering and decided to hiss. "An instant family. Just what you've always wanted ... not!"

Ben ignored the remark, gathered his register and books and winked at Kat. "Don't be too tough on the newbie!" He smiled at Freya. "You're learning from the best there, kiddo!"

Freya nodded in acknowledgement and stayed seated, deliberately trying to ignore Miss Pity's dirty stare.

Diane felt content that she had given Freya a thorough enough up and down so turned her attention and affection towards Kat. She slid into Ben's recently vacated seat and oozed passion with a flick of bleach blonde hair and wiggle of thinly plucked eyebrows. She leaned into Kat's personal space and took a breathy gasp as she plunged her breasts forwards. "Can we do it one last time, for old time's sake?"

Freya straightened in the uncomfortable fabric seat, but Kat stayed still, unaffected by the onslaught.

Kat stared straight into Diane's eyes. "I assume you're talking about a lesson plan?"

Diane leaned back and huffed, what was she doing wrong? Why hadn't Kat even once given her tits a quick glance? They were cracking tits and everyone knew it. Everyone apart from Keep 'Em Closed Kat! She tried again. "If that's what you like to call it."

Freya tried to joke. "Should I be worried?"

Kat pinned Freya with her piercing blue eyes. "No, should I?" The regret was instant and she cursed herself immediately.

"Ooo, lovers tiff! This is the reason that you shouldn't be here!" She spat the words at Freya as if she were a lifelong enemy.

"Yes she should, and no it's not, and yes I will see you period two." Kat just wasn't in the mood for any of this.

Diane smiled. Every lesson plan that Kat had helped her with had secured a good, if not excellent, observation and if today's went well then she would be back off probation. "Thank you," she couldn't help it, "and don't worry, Kat, I'm here if you need to talk about any personal issues."

"Thank you, Diane, but I'm just fine."

The silence was deafening as the final few teachers trailed out of the staffroom. Freya lifted her eyes to Kat's. "Should we go up to your form room?"

"I don't know if I can do this." Kat leaned forwards and rubbed her hands together between her knees. "I've never brought my personal life into school and now I am suddenly doing it in front of Diane Pity of all people." Kat was fuming with herself more than anything.

"What have I done now?" Freya's tone was one of exhaustion. They had been through everything a million times. They had sorted it out. Kat had said she understood.

"You got a message."

Freya folded her arms. "Did I? When?"

"This morning, when you were in the shower."

"So you've actually started checking my phone then? Cheers!"

Kat gathered her register and room keys and started to stand. "Yes ... and I'm glad that I did."

The march down the pale blue corridor was quick and uncomfortable and neither wanted to break first.

"Giddy up Spicer!" shouted Ben from his doorway as he ushered his last pupil in. "The responsibility of a trainee teacher and your timing has all gone to pot!"

Kat knew he was teasing, but ignored the remark. She was always so in control, so calm, so confident, and suddenly she felt unsure of herself. Unsure of herself in her one safe domain.

They were hurrying up the second set of stairs when Freya finally spoke. "What did it say?"

"I didn't delete it. It was obviously for you." Kat could feel herself getting drawn in, making smart remarks that just weren't her style. They were almost at her door, she needed to focus.

Freya reached into her bag and drew out her mobile. She clicked on the inbox and saw the new message. *"Wish I was with you. Don't get sucked in. R xxx."* Freya caught up with Kat. "I can explain."

"Don't bother."

"Happy New Year!" came the giggling chant from the impeccably straight line outside Kat's classroom. The Year Eights had been planning the surprise and looked chuffed to bits that their favourite all time form teacher looked like she was close to tears.

"You lot are adorable," whispered Kat as she unlocked her door and tried to stop her bottom lip from quivering. She took a deep breath and turned to welcome each child with a personal smile and word of greeting. Nothing had ever got in the way of her professionalism and nothing ever would. She told Freya to sit at the back.

****

The day had been a real eye opener for Freya. She knew Kat was good, but she had never fully understood how good until now. Last year she would experience one of Kat's wonderful lessons and then move on to a boring biology class, worthless English session, or wasted free period. Kat seemed to go from exceptional lesson, to exceptional lesson, to break time chat with some eager Year Eight girls, back to another exceptional lesson, followed by a lunch time on duty and then two further exceptional lessons. Freya was exhausted and in awe of Kat's kindness in devoting her one free period of the day to Miss Pity and her quest to try and teach a half decent lesson. Freya had watched from the back as Kat guided Diane through the complicated planning sheet, making the most confusing syllabus statements sound simple and clear. Diane had tried to flirt, but Kat had carried on unabashed, dissecting the syllabus criteria and transferring it into fun filled, thought provoking lesson tasks. Diane had nodded in all of the right places, but Freya knew the truth; her lessons were shit because she failed to give a shit. The only thing Miss Pity cared about was herself. Once Diane had left the room, following numerous innuendos about repaying the favour, Freya had asked Kat why she bothered. Kat's answer was simple - *'I care about the kids.'* Freya had hoped for a momentary break in frostiness, but Kat had dropped her gaze and turned her attentions to the lost boy in the corridor who was looking for room 220.

Freya had had the whole day to watch and admire ... and solidify her story. Here was her chance.

Kat closed the classroom door and collapsed on her padded teacher's seat. "So there you have it, a day in the life of a teacher."

Freya stood from her lonely plastic chair at the back and walked slowly to the front. "You're incredible."

Kat pulled her blonde hair back behind her ears. "No, I'm just doing my job."

"I hope you can show me how to be as good as you?" The request was deliberately timid.

Kat stood up and raced around to the other side of the desk. She threw her arms around her girlfriend and held her tight. "I'm sorry."

Freya was taken aback, she had no idea it would be this easy. "*You're* sorry?"

Kat looked into Freya's wide eyes. "Yes, me. I shouldn't have read your message. I shouldn't have kept it to myself until this morning and I shouldn't have snapped at you in school. I love you."

Freya tightened the hug. "I love you too. I had my speech prepared. I knew I had to convince you."

"Of what?"

"That nothing's going on."

Kat ran her fingers down Freya's arms and took her hands. "You told me at Christmas that nothing was going on. That Renee was just a flirt." She looked away for a moment. "That she instigated it." Her eyes were back. "I believed you then and I believe you now."

"Really?"

Kat maintained the connection. "Yes, really." Her gaze suddenly dropped to the floor.

"What?"

"I don't want you thinking I'm controlling, or demanding, or keeping tabs on your texts ... but ..." she trailed off.

"But what? You want to know what she meant?"

Kat nodded.

Freya was prepared. She reached for her phone. "The text said: *Wish I was with you.* Well apparently John Taylor's were having problems in their history department at the end of last term and Renee's mentor has changed and she's worried they won't be any good. She knows you'll be fab and she was meaning *wish I was with you* in the sense of being here mentored by you."

Kat frowned, not entirely convinced. "Okay, and the thing about *getting sucked in?*" Kat paused, unsure whether her next admission would be a positive or negative move, she decided to continue. "Don't laugh, but at 7.45 a.m. this morning, I assumed she was talking about getting sucked in by me and scuppering your plans to do a runner back into her arms."

Freya released the grip. "I've never been in her arms."

"I know, I know. See, now I'm sorry I said it." She had never been any good in relationships and was desperately trying not to make the same mistakes. Concerns about previous partners' indiscretions had actually been confirmed on two out of three occasions, but she was desperately trying to ignore this fact. *No*, she thought. Freya was different. Kat pushed the unwanted alarm bells to the back of her mind.

Freya saw the conflict in Kat's eyes. Her response was hasty. "She meant sucked in by the kids. We had a lecture last term on the ability to maintain a higher moral ground when it comes to provocation by the people in your class. Like you this morning with Chianne, when she told the whole class that you tried to hold hands with her until she set you straight and told you she-" Freya wobbled her head in imitation, "-*ain't in the butch brigade.*"

Kat had to laugh as the impression was really good.

Freya smiled and reached once again for Kat's soft hands. "She meant don't get sucked in like that. How you manage to keep your cool with her though I will never know." She grinned. "And please don't make me take an A-Level class as I won't stand a chance. Did I ever tell you about the time she sprayed a can of Impulse body spray in my face?"

Kat nodded.

"Look, I can see how the message might have appeared, but I'm telling the truth. That was all Renee meant."

Kat took a deep breath and pulled her girlfriend close.

The classroom door creaked open.

"Knockedy, knock knock." Janet caught the tender moment and was unsure of an appropriate comment. She opted for: "Will you two get a room!"

"Janet!" Kat stepped backwards. "It's not what it looks like!"

"It's okay, I'm all new age now it comes to these similar sex relationships."

She turned to Freya. "Your mentor has taught me a lot too!"

Freya didn't know where to look. "I've had a great observation day today, Mrs Louza, and I'm looking forward to getting stuck in tomorrow."

"Please, call me Janet. You're one of us now, my dear."

Freya smiled. When she was at school everyone thought Mrs Louza was a boring old spinster who slept in the store cupboard.

Janet scratched her fuzzy cloud of grey hair. "Sorry to be the old party pooper, but as Head of Department, I do need to add that you really ought not to be getting too up close and personal in school."

Kat knew Janet was trying to get the balance right and felt incredibly guilty. "No Janet, you are absolutely right. What you saw was not appropriate and it won't happen again."

"Right, ahem. Well you know what I mean. I mean..." she swung her fist in the air, "...*go girlfriends* and all of that. I like the equality movement, but I also have to mention the code of conduct with teacher behaviour on school property." She was starting to get flustered. "Oh you know what I'm trying to say, Kat."

"I do, and I'm sorry. A lapse of judgement. Anyone could have come in."

Janet felt guilty. "Well no, it's four o' clock and every bugger has scarpered, but anyhow, what did I come up for?" She tapped her grey cloud. "Ah, that's it. Trouble at John Taylor's. Can we take on their trainee teacher?" She reached into her long grey cardigan for the piece of paper. "A, Miss Renee Eves."

Kat and Freya's eyes both widened in horror.

CHAPTER TWENTY

"Look, Daddy Two's a monkey!" Benny was beaming from ear to ear. "Again, again, again!"

Ben held on to the small red bars and lifted his knees. He swung one arm forward and started his journey across the play park's apparatus. "Ooh ooh, ahh ahh!"

Benny squealed with laughter. "Again, again, again!"

Ben twisted himself back around. "Ooh ooh, ooh, ooh, ahh, ahh, ahh, ahh, ahhhhhhhh!"

"Again, again, again!"

Ben straightened his legs and stood up carefully, ducking back out from under the worn monkey bars. "Daddy Two needs to sit down with Lu Lu for a moment." He crouched down at his son's side. "Why don't you show us how good you are on that slide." He pointed at the small slide attached to the climbing apparatus.

Benny had no fear and would often impress his audience by sliding in a variety of different fashions - his favourite being on his tummy, head first. He nodded eagerly, excited about his plan.

Attending parks had been a real eye opener, as had so many other things on Ben's journey as an instant dad. All parks were different on so many different levels. This time last year he would walk past them, not noticing a thing. But nowadays, he stopped and judged them on their apparatus, their security, their cleanliness, their graffiti, their level of excitement - yet appropriateness, and their proximity to a sheltered area where Benny could nip for the inevitable wee wee. This particular park was not one of his favourites, but Benny had seen it from the car window on the way home and insisted they stopped. It was very old fashioned, with slightly rusty equipment and lots of teenage graffiti. The flooring was not padded and there were no wood chippings, or cushions of sand. It was just plain old metal equipment stuck into the concrete floor. Just like parks from the old days, thought Ben, remembering how his friends would spin each other around on the dangerous metal roundabouts, until someone fell off and got injured.

"Watch this!" Benny giggled with anticipation and raced off to the old metal slide. "I'm the best! Watch me go bumpy bumpy bumpy!"

Ben joined Lucy on the paint chipped park bench and rubbed his palms together. "I need to work on my upper body! Those monkey bars are a killer!"

Lucy looked across at his solid chest and large arm muscles bulging out of his rolled up school shirt. "Shut up, you show off."

Ben winced at the sharp jab directed to his side. "Careful! You don't want to damage super dad!"

Lucy watched the way Benny waved from the bottom of the slide with such pride and accomplishment. "Well he certainly thinks you're a super dad."

"Do you think so?"

Lucy nodded. "Yes! Look at him. He's checking you're watching each time he gets to the top."

"I am watching."

"Exactly. See, you are a super dad." She ruffled his messy blonde hair. "How was school anyway?"

"Great actually. You know what it's like; once you're back it seems like you've never been away."

"Was Kat okay?"

He turned his attention to Lucy. "Yeah she seemed to be, why?"

"I may be completely wrong here, you know me-"

He nodded.

"But things have just seemed a bit frosty between Kat and Freya recently."

Ben twisted his body towards Lucy, he loved a good gossip and this was the first he'd heard of it. "Well *you* know *me*, and I'm very good on picking up body language and I haven't noticed anything. Come on, Mystic Meg, what have you seen?" He shook her blunt black fringe.

"Kat's quieter."

"That's it?"

"Yes, but I saw what her ex put her through and she was quiet through all of that."

Ben had been sucked in. "So what exactly went on between her and this ex? I've never heard the whole story."

The shout was one of excited achievement: "Look Daddy, me monkey too!"

Ben and Lucy both swivelled round in time to see Benny perched at the edge of the two metre high metal monkey bar ledge. He suddenly lunged forwards with his hands outstretched.

"Noooooooooo!" Lucy and Ben cried out in echoed unison.

It was too late. Benny was falling forwards. His short arms missed the first rung and sent him plunging, face first, towards the concrete floor.

For Lucy and Ben, the fall happened in slow motion. Both launched themselves off the bench, but it was too late. They couldn't get there in time. The thud was hollow.

"Noooooooooooo!" screamed Ben.

Lucy reached Benny's side and fell to her knees.

Benny lifted his head and opened his mouth with the loudest piercing wail.

"He's okay, he's okay. He's crying. At least he's crying." Lucy had scooped him up into her arms, shielding him against her warm chest.

"His face, check his face!" Ben was panicking. "Check his teeth, shit his teeth!"

The wailing was ear-splitting.

"Give him a second."

"Shhhitttttt! Something's bleeding!"

"Ben, will you just calm down. You need to stay calm for him."

"I'm calling an ambulance. You saw him fall." The vision raced through his head once more. He knew in that moment that he would never forget the image of his son thudding face first onto the park's concrete floor. "Shit, I'm calling an ambulance."

Benny wiped away a wailing tear and immediately screamed with frantic panic as he saw the blood which now covered his tiny hand. "Benny's bleeding! Ahhhhhhhhh!"

The cries were piercing and Ben had no idea what to do. "Shit! Look at the fucking state of his face!"

Lucy burrowed him back between her breasts to shield his ears and offer some calm. "It's okay, big man. You're going to be okay."

"Of course he's not going to be fucking okay! He fell fucking face first off that stupid fucking ledge!" Ben was fumbling with his phone. "Shit, let's just drive him, it will be quicker."

Lucy peeped down and offered a reassuring smile. The wails were slowly turning to sobs as Benny tried to be brave. "I think he's okay." Lucy leaned backwards revealing Benny's swollen bottom lip and gashed chin. "I think he has been a very brave boy."

Benny gave Lucy the same puppy dog look as his father. "Did I do the monkey?" he managed to sniff.

Lucy smiled. "Almost."

Ben wasn't listening. "He fell fucking face first onto the floor! We're taking him to hospital."

"Okay, that's fine. Let's just try and do it calmly shall we?" She spoke with a forced smile.

Ben helped the pair of them stand and reached for his son. "I'll carry him, we'll get to the car quicker." He started to jog.

"Ben! Will you just calm down!" Lucy had to shout as nothing else was working. She kept a steady pace besides them as they crossed the open field towards the car park. "Benny, we're going to go and see the doctor so he can check your chin. You might get a sticker if you're really brave."

"Giddy up, horsey!" Benny had momentarily forgotten about the fall and was enjoying the fast bumpy journey in daddy two's arms.

"I'm sure he's not bothered about a fucking sticker!"

"Ben!!"

Benny grinned. This had started to become very exciting. "Benny gets stickers when he goes to hospital with Mummy. When Mummy is sick." He stuck out his tongue and made a sicky sound.

Lucy frowned. "Is Mummy having a baby?"

Benny wrinkled his scuffed nose. "No! Mummy goes to find her hair."

Ben increased his pace, worried that concussion would be setting in. "Good, so you won't be scared of the doctors then."

"Ben! Did you hear what he just said?"

"Not really, no. Now hurry up! I think I can feel him getting hotter."

Lucy was nearly at a full sprint by now. "That's probably all of the friction you're creating by bouncing him up and down like that."

Ben glanced down at his son, who was now grinning like a Cheshire cat.

****

Lucy had somehow managed to talk Ben into attending the Minor Injury's Unit instead of the full blown A and E department. Both were in the same hospital, but one wouldn't take kindly to a little boy who was now racing around, excitedly demanding a Spiderman sticker. Lucy held the tiny blood stained hand. "Right, let's just wait here, Benny, so Daddy Two can find out where we have to go."

Ben was busy with the hospital receptionist, describing the treacherous fall in minute detail, when in fact her job was simply to give directions to the various departments.

"Mummy, Mummy, Mummy!" Benny jumped up and down. "Look! Mummy's here!" He suddenly slipped his hand out of Lucy's and darted off down the main corridor.

Lucy exhaled loudly and shook her head, *what was Ben playing at?* There was no need to call Lisa. It would just cause unnecessary panic. She squinted to the far end of the corridor. *Oh shit!* Benny was shaking the arm of some old woman's wheelchair and the old man who was pushing her seemed to be telling him off. She started to run. "Benny, come away!" She looked up. "I'm so sorr-" and did a double take, "Gerald?"

"Told you, Mummy here!" Benny was now on the old woman's lap.

Lucy looked down. "Lisa?" She was almost unrecognisable.

A slow tear slid down Lisa's gaunt cheek.

CHAPTER TWENTY ONE

Freya pushed a piece of cold tortellini around her dinner plate and looked incredibly sulky. "You could have said no."

"To what?" Kat knew exactly what Freya was talking about.

"To Mrs Louza."

Kat shifted in her chair, put her fork back down and pushed away her plate. She had hardly touched the evening meal either. Janet's news about Renee joining Coldfield had caused a wave of instant unease to wash across the pair of them, leaving them both decidedly queasy. "Why would I say no?"

"Because of everything that's been going on."

"But that's just it, Freya. You said nothing's been going on, so why would I, as a teacher trainer, say no to training an additional student?"

"Because it's Renee."

"Well that's actually even better. I've met her and you said she works very hard, and I think, from what I've seen of her, that she has the natural charisma that every good teacher needs."

"So she'll get all of your attention then?"

Kat frowned. "What's going on? Why are you so edgy?"

Freya pushed her plate into the middle of the glass table next to Kat's and folded her arms. "I just don't want her nestling in on us."

"Is that what this is about?"

Freya nodded.

Smiling, Kat slid out from her kitchen chair. "Well you don't have to worry about that." She stood up and extended her hand.

Freya took the peace offering and let herself be pulled up into the reassuring arms.

Kat whispered into her girlfriend's ear. "I love you, and nothing, and no one - especially not Renee - will ever change that."

Freya kept her eyes open and watched the large red hand on the oversized kitchen clock tick slowly round in a never ending circle.

Kat kept her eyes closed and hugged Freya even tighter. Neither of them noticed the heavy apartment door as it slowly creaked opened. The voice was subdued. "Hi girls. Oh, sorry to interrupt."

Kat swivelled round. "Lucy! Hi, you're not interrupting." She smiled. "We have some Tortellini if you fancy it? It's a bit cold, but that doesn't usually bother you."

Ben followed Lucy into the warm apartment and kindly took her coat, hanging it on the one spare hook and hoping his heavy bomber jacket would squash onto the top. It didn't. It fell to the ground, pulling hers down with it. He swore and kicked both coats, sending them skidding across the polished laminate floorboards.

No one spoke.

Ben walked into the lounge and bent for the jackets, grabbing them and shaking them with unnecessary force. "For fuck's sake!"

"Is everything okay?" Kat didn't know what else to say.

Lucy looked at their plates in the middle of the table, still full of food. "Have you finished?"

Kat and Freya both nodded at each other. Their enjoyment of the meal had never really begun.

"We need to talk to you guys."

Kat had only seen Lucy serious on two occasions. One was last year when Jess had her miscarriage and the other was when Ben had left her. She nodded in worried acknowledgement and made her way into the lounge, taking a seat on the black leather sofa, hoping they were not about to split up. They were such a wonderful couple, both able to take life in their stride and always see the positive in any situation. Lucy made him laugh and he made her happy. They were a perfect fit and as Kat watched them now, both with sorrow in their eyes, she feared the worst. Freya slid in beside her and the feeling of her warm hand squeezing her own gave a much needed sense of reassurance. Kat turned to Freya and smiled.

Lucy sat down opposite them on the single seat and Ben joined her on the arm.

"We've got some really bad news." Ben's voice had started to crack. He looked to the floor and willed himself to continue. "Lisa's really poorly."

Kat looked to Lucy who was desperately trying to hold back the tears.

Ben coughed and tried to compose himself. "She has..." His voice cracked again. "...she has got cancer."

"Oh no." Kat and Freya both gasped, leaned forwards, and lifted their hands to their mouths in utter shock. "Is it treatable?" It was Kat's first thought.

Lucy shook her head as a small tear dropped onto her pale cheek.

Ben put his arm around her shoulder. "I don't know where to start really. She's been having, umm, treatment..." He paused, trying to control his breathing. "...for umm, for the past six months..." He started to sob. "They have tried everything." He shook his head. "Umm, she is ... she is going to die."

Lucy buried her face into his chest and started to cry.

Freya quickly wiped away a tear and looked to Kat who stood up and walked around the coffee table to kneel gently at Lucy's side. She hugged her softly and looked up at Ben. He wouldn't look back.

"How long has she got?" Freya was hardly audible.

Ben wiped his eyes and shrugged his shoulders. "One month, maybe two."

Lucy re-emerged with puffy red eyes. She sniffed back a tear and tried to speak. "They want us..." The tears came thick and fast. "...they want us ... to have Benny."

Kat felt a surge of despair, *poor Benny*.

Lucy was crying hard. "He's only four and his mummy ... his mummy is dying."

Ben pulled her back into his chest. "It's okay, it's okay Luce. She wants you to be his mummy now."

Kat held her hands together in front of her mouth. "They want you to have him?"

Ben nodded.

Freya beckoned Kat back over to the sofa. She needed to feel close to her. As Kat sat slowly back down she whispered in her ear. "I'm so sorry."

Kat held her tight and understood. Times like these made you realise what was important. Life was precious. Life was short. Life could be snatched away in the quickest of moments.

Ben coughed again and took another deep breath, blinking quickly and trying to clear his damp eyes. There were things that needed to be discussed. Arrangements needed to be made. He spoke slowly and clearly, reaffirming the facts for himself as well as the others. "They decided that we should have joint custody with Gerald. Benny will live with us full time and Gerald will see him at the weekends, or in the week, or whenever he needs to really." He squeezed Lucy's shoulder. "But Lisa wants Benny's home to be with us."

Lucy rubbed her face and shook her head. "They said it had been planned for months. Imagine planning what's going to happen to your baby after you die. Imagine deciding who will look after it, who will care for it, who will love it like you would."

Kat smiled gently. "She imagined you."

The tears were back. "She hardly knows me."

Ben inhaled loudly and tried to sound composed. "They just felt Benny would be better off with me being his biological father, and the fact that Gerald works abroad so much," he paused, "and without being rude to the man, the fact that he's slightly older. Lisa said she would rather have Benny growing up with us and the possibility of having brothers and sisters." He looked at Lucy and smiled with his eyes. "And I'm sure Benny will have brothers and sisters one day."

"Is Gerald okay with all of this?" Kat could hardly take in the enormity of the situation.

Ben nodded. "He was the one who suggested it. It turns out that Lisa *had* been telling the truth. She *was* planning on finding me and telling me about Benny, only I bumped into her first." He needed to make it clear. "Gerald will still see Benny as much as he does now. It's just that Benny's home will be with us."

"What about grandparents?" Kat didn't want to appear judgemental or questioning but the questions kept coming.

"Gerald's parents have died, and Lisa only has her mum and, as Benny says, Nana Pearl is crazy!" The picture of Benny doing a crazy Nana Pearl impression raced across his mind, quickly followed by the image of Benny plummeting face first into the concrete floor. He shuddered. It was the tenth time he had re-lived it since it happened. He shook his head. "Shit, we can't look after a kid."

Lucy rubbed his knee, it was her turn to be strong. "Yes we can, and yes we will. He's not just any kid. He's your son. If this is what Lisa wants, then this is what's going to happen. We're going to be the best mummy and daddy that wonderful little boy could ever imagine."

Ben started to cry. "I hope so ... for his sake."

CHAPTER TWENTY TWO

Ben and Kat waited silently as the final few teachers shuffled out of the staffroom. It was the second week in and Christmas seemed like a distant memory. Carole the Cleaner was busying herself with the pile of brown stained mugs in the overflowing sink. The bearded supply guy had picked up a copy of the TES, made himself comfortable in the far corner of the staffroom, and smiled with relief that all the teachers, for once, seemed to be accounted for.

Kathy from Cover immediately popped her head around the door. "Sorry, Geoff, Hannah Phag's not turned up for her class."

The bearded supply guy put his paper down, huffed, and rose to his feet, wondering how so many teachers were able to misplace, or forget about, their classes. It seemed to happen almost every day. "Room twelve?" he questioned knowingly, scratching his beard and trundling past Kat and Ben, out into the quiet corridor. He knew room twelve very well.

Kat waited for the door to shut and turned to Ben. "Hannah's gone AWOL again?" She shook her head. "I really thought she was on the up."

Ben would usually have responded with a quick witted remark, but today he simply nodded in acceptance.

"Oh, Ben. How are things?" It had been a week since that shockingly awful evening in the apartment and everyone had been so busy.

He leaned forwards and heavily rested his elbows onto his knees. "Not great. Benny's fine though. He seems so together for a four year old. He knows that Mummy's going to heaven soon to see the angels and live with her daddy and the puppy."

Kat frowned. "The puppy?"

"Yeah, they got a puppy last year but it died. Benny still talks about the puppy in heaven. I think Lisa got him one of those shitty Disney films about dogs that go to heaven or something." He shook his head. "There's still so much I don't know about him ... and I fucking hate Disney films."

Kat tried to connect. "You're not trying to talk yourself out of this are you?"

Ben immediately twisted round, looking at her properly for the first time. "Oh god no!" He paused, pulling at a loose thread from his brown fabric chair. "I just don't want to fail."

Kat looked him straight in the eye. "There are two types of people, Ben. Those who need to achieve, and those who need to avoid failure. The ones who need to avoid failure always set themselves easy tasks. They never push themselves, they never let themselves be put in a situation in which they might fail. They therefore never know what it is like to truly succeed. You're not one of those people, Ben." She spoke with fierce determination, trying to snap him out of this momentary self pity. "You're someone who needs to achieve. You embrace challenges, you thrive in situations where the outcome is unknown ... and Ben, you nearly always succeed."

Ben smiled. "Where do you get this bullshit from?"

"Sport psychology."

"Just how many strings are there to your never ending bow, Miss Spicer?!" he laughed, teasingly squeezing her knee.

"At least it's put a smile on your face." Kat studied his chin, usually home to some short sprouts of trendy blonde stubble, but now currently teetering on the brink of an actual beard. "Seriously, Ben, what do you need us to do?"

Ben took a deep breath and scratched his chin. "I need you to move out of the apartment."

Carole the Cleaner accidentally dropped a mug onto the wet draining board. A result of her not so accidental ear wigging.

Kat jumped at the clatter, but was more shocked by Ben's request. It was the first she'd heard of it. "Right?"

He smiled apologetically. "I'm a complete dick-head I know, and I'm so sorry. Lucy wanted to be the one to talk to you, but I've gone over and over it in my head and I just can't think of any other solution. You did just ask if there was anything you could do to help."

"Right..." Kat was waiting for the punch line.

"Benny's okay for the moment staying at Lisa's. Nana Pearl has moved in to help, but Lisa has said she wants to see him settled before she goes and she doesn't want him around her near the end. She wants him to remember her full of life."

Kat rubbed her temples. "So why our apartment?"

"Well my flat's hardly appropriate and he knows the apartment and he actually thinks that's where I live. I just want to do this properly, Kat. I want to give him a home with me and Lucy that he feels is his."

"Couldn't you look for somewhere new for the three of you?" Kat was trying to be delicate; she loved where she lived.

"It'll take too long, and he knows the place. He's happy staying there."

"Ben, he's only stayed over twice and both of those times it was in Freya's room." She thought for a moment. "Could I suggest that Freya and I share a room?"

"Well, we were going to suggest that."

"Oh right, were you?"

"Yes and I ... umm ... I was hoping to decorate Freya's room this weekend." He leaned forwards in earnest. "I just want everything to be perfect for him. I know this is completely crazy, but I have to do something. I have to put Lisa at ease, show her that I can do this."

Kat straightened in her seat, unsure of her feelings. "Is Lucy okay with all of this?"

"Yes. She was dreading asking you and she'll no doubt tell me off for mentioning it without her ... but she agrees. She thinks the apartment would be a great first family home for the three of us. Shit Kat, we've only had a week to think things through. I know it's hasty and I know it's asking a lot." He was pleading now and knew he was sounding like a complete cock. "Of course you two can stay in your room for as long as you need to."

"Thanks for that!"

"You're cross aren't you?" Ben noticed a nod of *'of course she is'* coming from the kitchenette where Carole the Cleaner had given up on the mugs. "I know I have no right, and I know I have no say in what goes on in your apartment, but I have no other solution."

Kat thought about it for a moment. "No, I'm not cross. I'm just shocked. What sort of time frame are we talking about?"

Ben shrugged. "I don't know. Lisa wants him staying at home for as long as she feels fit. The doctors have given her a couple of months, maybe three. But hey, you hear those stories where people defy the doctors and go on to live for years with a terminal diagnosis."

Kat nodded, she didn't want to burst his bubble.

"But I want to be prepared ... just in case."

Kat shrugged; what could she say? "Okay. I'll talk to Freya."

****

Kat's walk up to her classroom was long and thought filled, with her attention drawn momentarily to the glass topped door of room twelve and the bearded supply guy who was trying to make himself heard above the din. She thought about going in. Doing so would quieten the class, but it would also completely undermine the little authority that Geoff, the bearded supply guy, managed to retain. She continued her walk. It was the same with Freya and Renee. The guidance suggested you should only step in if there was a serious breach of student behaviour which the trainee teacher had not dealt with. For example, a child swears at a trainee, the trainee fails to follow the correct protocol, the mentor should step in. So far Kat had enjoyed her new role, watching the girls grow in confidence with the odd lesson introduction or conclusion being taught. She had eased them in gently, giving them the nicest of Year Seven classes. Today was different though. Today was bottom set Year Nine history and they had the task of starting the lesson and leading the first activity. She had given them this free period to make the final lesson preparations, but as she made her way up the B Block staircase and reached her classroom door, this was the last thing that she expected to see.

Renee was at the white board, dressed in a smart black two piece suit, with a red marker pen in hand. She was crossing out the letter U and drawing a noose.

Freya was sitting on a blue plastic chair with her feet up on the table. "Give me a clue," she said.

Renee licked her lips. "It's what you are."

Kat looked at the board H _ _ / _ I S S E _

Freya smiled. "O."

Both were oblivious to Kat's presence in the doorway.

Renee put an O in the second gap.

Freya grinned. "T."

Renee wiggled her head, swishing her long beaded braids. "You so good, girlfriend!" She put a T in the third gap.

Kat pushed the door fully open sending it clattering against the battered grey filing cabinet. "I think you're missing a K and an R."

Freya swung her feet off the desk. "She's just pissing around!"

Renee quickly grabbed the dry cloth and wiped the board clean. "Sorry, we had finished and were just passing the time."

"Yes, by pissing around."

Freya knew Kat must be cross if she was swearing. She stood quickly and presented their lesson plan. "Is this okay? We finished about ten minutes ago." She pointed hastily at the pile of textbooks. "Everything's sorted."

Kat scanned the piece of paper. "You're missing your objectives. Where is the class size? Where is the time frame? How do you know how many resources to have if you don't know the size of the class?" She was nit picking, but she was flustered, *what was going on?*

Freya reached for Kat's arms, looked up into her fragile blue eyes, and spoke slowly. "Renee was just messing around."

Kat immediately shook her off. "Don't do that in school please, Freya." She slapped the lesson plan back onto the table and turned to leave. "You've got ten minutes before the class arrives. I expect you to bring them in, introduce the lesson and start the first activity. I will be watching from the back." She walked out into the empty corridor, pulling the classroom door with her. She hadn't meant to slam it, but that was the effect it had.

"You fucking idiot," mouthed Freya to Renee.

****

School could be eerie when all the children were in lessons. The corridors seemed longer and strangely silent. Kat had nowhere in particular to go, so she headed towards the pristine staff toilets. Carole the Cleaner took real pride in ensuring the staff had the softest toilet roll, the nicest smelling hand wash, and even a fresh bunch of flowers at the edge of the sinks each Monday morning. It was also Carole's job to maintain the numerous student toilets scattered around the school and she had absolutely no qualms about providing them with the cheapest blue tracing paper on which to wipe their sorry little arses. Some of the sights she had seen at the end of a break time absolutely beggared belief.

Kat pushed open the weighted door and entered a cubicle. Dropping the lid she took a seat and sunk her face into her hands. She tried not to cry. *What was going on? Why was everything changing? Who had her girlfriend become? How ridiculous would it be to suggest setting up home together? Freya clearly had other plans.* She heard the toilet door creak open and listened to Freya calling her name.

She coughed, stood up, flushed the toilet, and opened the door. She headed straight to the sinks and kept her eyes fixed on her own reflection.

"Kat?"

"I thought I asked you to correct that plan? The bell will be going soon."

Freya grabbed Kat's wrists, pulling them from under the taps and wrapping them around her own waist. "Will you listen to me. Nothing's going on. Renee's just a flirt."

Kat felt heartened by the connection, by the perseverance, by the warm green eyes on her own; but she couldn't help it. "I just don't know what to believe anymore."

Freya's eyes narrowed and she flung the arms away, pointing her finger directly at Kat. "Fine, but I can't do, or say, anymore. I explained what happened at Christmas. I just told you what happened in there. Yes, it was a bit unprofessional, but there were no kids around." She shook her head. "This is you, Kat. This is your insecurity, not my infidelity. You either trust me or you don't. It's your choice," and with that she walked straight back out of the ladies.

Kat looked at herself in the mirror. Freya was right, *who would want someone as insecure as her anyway?*

****

It had taken a couple of minutes to pull herself together and focus on the task in hand, but she had and she was. Kat strode out of the staff toilets and headed back along the corridor to her room. She arrived at exactly the same time as a very colourful Elaine Springer.

"Hi there! That wonderful student receptionist brought me up!" Elaine was signalling to the tiny Year Seven boy who was hurrying back to the front desk to continue the most exciting day of school to date.

Kat smiled, disguising her immediate concern. "Yes, the Year Sevens take it in turns to help out in Reception. It's meant to act as a confidence builder."

Elaine was almost bouncing and her lime green skirt and bright pink ruffled shirt were causing a haze of distracting colour. "Yes, great scheme! Great scheme!" She tilted her funky triangle shaped glasses and peeped over the top of the rim towards the classroom door. "Are the girls in here? Thank you once again for taking on Renee. We really were in a pickle and I'm telling you now, that's the last time we'll be using John Taylor's as a link school!"

"Yes they are. I've asked them to start my Year Nine lesson next." There was no easy way to ask. "Umm sorry ... is this a planned visit?" As far as Kat was aware the first observation wasn't until Friday.

Elaine nodded quickly. "Yes, yes! I was due to go to John Taylor's today to observe Renee. I saw her last week at university and told her the observation would obviously now be here. I might as well observe them both. She did tell you didn't she?"

Kat tapped her teeth together and shook her head.

Elaine hopped up and fanned Kat's face. "Don't worry, don't worry! Crikey you are tall aren't you! It's all very informal at this stage. I just like to get a rough idea of whether they're up to the job! Listen to me trying to teach you to suck eggs! You went through this not long ago. You know how it works. Such a shame our paths didn't cross. You were quite the star, or so university legend has me believe!"

Kat was sucked in by the animated spiel, not quite sure on when to cut in. "They'll be fine. I'm really pleased with them both."

"Great, great!" The shrill bell sent Elaine into an involuntary jump. "Saved by the bell, shall we go in?"

Kat nodded, unsure if she had ever met anyone with more bubbling energy before. "They'll be fine," she said, mostly to herself.

Renee was the first to notice them enter and simply waved a welcoming greeting to Elaine before heading to the door. She waited for the Year Nines to congregate and loudly asked them to: "Line up quietly," and much to Elaine's, tick box approval, they did.

Freya however, remained at the front of the classroom with a look of apprehensive confusion on her face.

Renee instructed the class to take a seat in their usual places and get out their exercise books and pens. Elaine added another tick to her sheet.

Kat suddenly felt a surge of panic, Freya had yet to speak and her sheet was currently blank. She leaned back in her plastic classroom chair and squinted down. It looked like Elaine had a series of simple statements that required a tick or a cross. Renee had already achieved points one and two – 1: Show authority with the class. 2: Speak in a clear and coherent manner. She looked up at Freya to offer a reassuring smile, but was met with her back. She was busy scribbling objectives onto the board.

Elaine whispered into Kat's ear. "I always encourage them to have the objectives on the board ready for when the class arrives. Obviously I know this isn't do-able on all occasions, for example between lessons one and two, or four and five where there are no breaks, but you know what I mean." She tapped Kat's knee. "Of course you know what I mean! Please stop me from rattling on!" She continued. "I just find some of the trainee mentors need a whole lot of mentoring themselves, like that one from John Taylor's, but I don't have to worry about her now, thank goodness! Oh look, they're about to start!" Elaine hushed herself.

"Okay, today I'll be leading the class along with Miss Eves." Freya was clear and calm. Kat waited for a tick in the box; but it didn't come. Elaine was too busy watching the loud, late arrival of a rather scruffy looking lad.

The lad slammed the classroom door and sidled up to Kat at the back. "Soz Miss, Faggy wasn't in the last lesson and we had that bloke with the beard again and he kept me behind."

"It's Miss Phag, but thank you for the apology, now go and sit down. Miss Elton and Miss Eves are taking the start of the lesson today."

"Ai ai!" The late boy jeered and winked at Freya.

Freya snapped back. "Sit down and shut up."

He immediately spun back around to Kat. "You can't let her talk to me like that, Miss!"

Kat stood up and spoke loudly. "Right, now that we're all here, can I just make it clear that it will be Miss Elton and Miss Eves taking the lesson. Ignore the fact that we're here at the back."

"Who's that?" The late boy was scrunching his nose up at Elaine and her multi-coloured outfit.

"This is Miss Springer."

The boy jeered at Freya. "Ooo, she's watching you!"

Kat cut back in. "All eyes to the front. Sorry Miss Elton, please continue."

Freya leaned back against the board smudging her slightly wonky writing. "Okay, the first thing we're going to do…" She paused, noticing the red pen on the sleeve of her shirt. "…the first objective we're going to achieve is to establish the effect of the Industrial Revolution."

The late boy spun back around. "Miss, she does know we're bottom set, don't she?!"

Renee cut in. "We're just going to find out how the Industrial Revolution changed people's lives."

Elaine added another tick to Renee's sheet.

"Exactly, thank you, Miss Eves." Freya turned back to the board. "So we need to consider the impact on, jobs-"

"Ha! Miss you have red pen on your shirt!"

Freya held out the board marker. "Right, it's Danny, isn't it?"

The late boy nodded.

"Okay, Danny, could you come up here and write the following words on the board?"

Kat nodded to herself. She had taught the girls to get the trouble makers involved, make them feel part of the lesson so they weren't so intent on disrupting it. She waited for Elaine to make a tick; she didn't.

Freya had started to sweat, but carried on. "Okay, so we need to look at how the Industrial Revolution impacted on *jobs*. Danny, write jobs please."

Danny rolled up his sleeves and wrote jobs in large capital letters.

Freya relaxed slightly and continued. "How it affected health. Danny if you could add *health* to the list." She turned to see that a hand in the wanking position had been drawn in front of the word JOBS.

The class burst out laughing.

Renee calmly stepped forward and handed him the cloth. "Clever, now wipe it off."

Freya raised her voice. "Write *health* please, Danny."

Danny slowly formed his letters - HELF.

The class started to laugh again and Freya looked at the board. "Not so clever now are we, Danny?" She regretted it the moment she said it.

"Fuck this, I don't have to listen to this." He threw the red marker pen onto the floor and stormed back to his desk. "Who are you anyway? Sorry Spicer, but I'm out of here." He reached for his scrappy backpack. "I'm not having her speak to me like that. Tell me when you're teaching and I'll come back. You never talk to me like that, Miss, do you?" He slammed the classroom door shut and stalked off into the corridor.

Kat calmly nodded at Freya to continue.

Freya knew she was drowning, but turned back towards the board and corrected the spelling. "We also need to see how it affected transport." She added TRANSPORT to the list.

"We ain't all as good at spelling as you, Miss." A usually timid girl felt she had to speak up. Danny was always getting into trouble and it wasn't always his fault.

"I know. I made a mistake." Freya's voice had started to wobble. "That's why we're called trainee teachers."

"Fair play, Miss." The girl nodded in approval, not many teachers admitted when they were wrong. "So, what are we doin' now?"

Freya clapped her hands together and tried to get back into her stride. "Well, if you would turn to page thirteen of your textbooks." She waited for the moaning and flicking to subside and signalled to the same girl. "Could you read the first paragraph out loud for us?"

"No chance, Miss, I can't read." The girl spun round to the back. "Tell her, Miss Spicer, you never make me read. I'm on that *speedy reader's* scheme."

Another boy laughed. "Stupid name. Everyone knows you lot who skive off to speedy readers are really the slowest readers ever!" He pointed at some text in his book. "W-eee ...... arrr-e .... llll-ur-ning ... a-bbbb-out .... the ... in-in-duuuus-tt-rr-eal ... rrrr-evvv-"

Renee literally stepped in and took control. "Right guys, not to worry. Let's just have a quick quiz round instead. It's fun, I promise!"

Freya admitted defeat and sank back down onto the padded teacher's chair.

CHAPTER TWENTY THREE

Their lovemaking had been slow and tender, but neither had spoken. Both knew what the other wanted and they easily pleased. Kat lay quietly in the darkness of her bedroom, with Freya under her arm. She felt fulfilled, but somehow not content. Freya's long and drawn out breaths were sending a flow of warm air across her chest, but it wasn't the warmth that she so badly craved. Freya had been distant, evasive, and her eyes had seemed sad. She clearly had a lot on her mind, and in so many respects Kat wanted to hear it, dissect it and put it all right; but in so many others, she didn't.

Freya wriggled back onto her pillow and was the first one to break. "I'm shit aren't I?" She sighed into the darkness. "Just admit it, I'm shit. I know you're thinking it and I know I've disappointed you. I can see it in your eyes."

Kat touched the bedside switch and the room gently lit up in a warm, soft glow. She pulled a long chestnut curl away from Freya's face and studied her. She looked beautiful. "You're not shit. You're not shit at anything. Now if you're talking about today's lesson again, then Renee is the shit." Kat looked up at the ceiling and the small stars that had started to twinkle in the light. "I can't believe she lied. Why didn't she tell us Elaine was coming?" Kat frowned. "Who does that?"

Freya moved further away from Kat and adjusted her pillow. "She said she did. She said she texted me."

Kat rolled her eyes. She had met girls like Renee before, always looking for the glory, always stepping over others for personal success. In a way she was pleased. It had brought them closer together and put that silly game of hang man into perspective. How could Renee be trying to steal her girlfriend if she was willing to set her up like that? Freya had been visibly knocked by the experience and she had been able to empathise. There was nothing worse than the feeling of sinking in front of a class; letting them get on top of you and letting them drag you down, until you were drowning with no way back up. She had told Freya about her very first teaching placement where she had experienced a similar thing with a bottom set Year Ten class who got completely out of control. She had lost it and didn't know whether to scream at them or cry. Her mentor at the time had put things into perspective, as she had just done for Freya, asking her to name exactly who it was that caused the lesson to fall apart. Kat had given the names of three pupils, as had Freya - Danny the late boy, Josie the slow reader, and Chris the mocker of Josie. She had then asked Freya to tell her how many others were in the class. There had been twenty four other pupils sitting quietly, politely, waiting for instruction, and it was these pupils that Kat reminded Freya to think about. They were the majority, and the majority were well behaved. She leaned forwards, kissed Freya's bare shoulder and decided to broach the subject of the apartment; but Freya cut in first.

"Are you sure you didn't delete the text?"

"Which text?"

"The one Renee said she sent about Elaine coming."

Kat lifted her eyes from Freya's shoulder. "What?"

"The text from Renee, about Elaine coming to observe me."

Kat lifted herself onto one arm. "Yes, I heard the first time, but I can't believe you're asking me. Why would I delete a text from Renee about your first observation?"

Freya pulled the covers up to her chin. "She said she sent one and you *have* started to read my messages."

Kat frowned. "Are you being serious? I read *one* message last week. What would be my motive for deleting a text? Don't forget that I'm also judged on how you pair perform."

"What would be *her* motivation?" Freya's reply was too quick.

Kat no longer knew what to do. She felt lost, once again in a situation that felt uneasy. It was like she was at the bottom of a huge uphill struggle, unsure if she had the strength to make the effort. She decided her only option was to bare her soul. She sat up in bed and took Freya's hand. "Will you listen to me please? I love you. I want to spend the rest of my life with you-"

Freya shrugged her shoulders and cut in. "What's the point if you don't trust me?"

Kat took a deep breath. "I was about to say, I love you, I want to spend the rest of my life with you and I want us to think about getting a place of our own."

Freya turned to face her. "Really?"

"Yes really. It's a long story, but I feel ready. All I want is you."

Freya couldn't reply.

CHAPTER TWENTY FOUR

It was one of those days that Kat would remember forever. The music was soothing, the atmosphere calm, and everyone had pitched in together to achieve Ben's dream. It had taken the whole day, but now Freya's bedroom looked like a scene from the Jungle Book. Ben had ordered two sets of gigantic Disney room stickers and Mowgli and Baloo were hopping from wall to wall in a never ending game of chase. Gerald had come around with the latest state of the art paint roller system, saying he would love to help and was glad of the change of scenery. It was the first time that Kat had actually met the man, and it all finally made sense. Lucy had said he was old, but Lucy was often prone to exaggeration. However on this occasion, she had been pretty close to the mark. He was the wrong side of fifty and struggled to catch his breath as they made their way back up the apartment stairs after lunch out and a much needed break from the painting. He had insisted on paying and spent most of the mealtime yet again explaining their decision for Benny. It was exactly as Ben and Lucy had described it, but his constant comments of *'what's best for Benny,'* made Kat wonder if he was in fact trying to ease his own conscience. He clearly loved the little boy, but it became obvious with the way he spoke about his job and the constant long calls he took throughout the day that work was in fact his first true love.

Lisa had been a stay at home mum for the past four years and if Gerald was really honest then he had to admit he knew very little about raising a four year old boy. Their marriage had worked in the traditional way - she was the homebuilder and he paid the bills. Kat didn't doubt that he would spend as much free time as he could with Benny, but she understood that he could not provide the stable and secure home that Benny would so desperately need. Yes, if push would have come to shove, then Benny could have stayed at home with Gerald, but he would have needed nannys, babysitters, pre-school and afterschool clubs, and various different travel arrangements. All at a time when the one thing he would truly want would not be there; his mummy. *Yes*, announced Gerald once more on his way out of the apartment, *this was for the best*.

Ben shook the man's hand and offered a heartfelt word of thanks, not only for his help with the room, but for his trust in their abilities; their abilities as parents. The thought sent a shiver down his spine as he shut the apartment door and walked back into the brightly coloured new room. He reached out, pulled Kat and Lucy close and nodded at their efforts. "I don't know what I'd do without you guys." A tiny tear formed in the corner of his eye. "I just want everything to be perfect for Benny."

Kat smiled. "It will be," she banged his broad chest, "but the amount of stuff in my room just isn't do-able, and I'm sure it'll be the same when you move your stuff in too."

Ben nodded. "I know, but it might not be for ages yet. Lisa seems to be picking up."

Kat nodded encouragingly. "Is she?"

Lucy shook her head. "She's stopped her treatment."

Kat understood. There would be a momentary reprieve before a rapid downhill struggle, with an almost undeniable ending. "We'll get out of here as soon as we can."

"Don't say it like that." Lucy hugged her very best friend. "I love you, Katherine Spicer, and I can't believe you're doing this for us."

"What else would I do? You and your new little family will need all of the help you can get."

It was now Lucy's turn to wipe away a small tear. "Are you guys going to be okay?"

Kat knew who she was referring too. "I think so, yes. Freya's just a bit on edge at the moment. She has an observation tomorrow with her tutor. Remember me telling you that her last one didn't go very well?"

Lucy nodded, she had heard all about that bitch Renee stealing the limelight and taking the glory.

"Freya's tutor thinks she should transfer onto the pure history course instead."

Lucy shook her blunt fringe. "Oh no! Freya's a natural teacher! Crikey, she's taught me loads over the past few months."

Kat rubbed her forehead. "I know, I think she's just started to doubt herself. But hey, if everything goes okay tomorrow then I'm sure she'll be back on track." She checked her watch.

"Is she still on the phone?"

Kat shrugged her shoulders. "I guess so."

"Are you sure that's all it is? A worry about her work?"

Kat frowned at her non-perceptive friend. "Yes, why?"

"Oh nothing. She's just been a bit distant today."

"Haven't we all?" suggested Kat, thinking back to the mellow tunes and quiet, determined teamwork. All for a rather depressing cause.

"Yeah, I'm sure everything will be fine." Lucy flicked her black fringe, eager to change the subject. "Have you started to look for places yet?"

Kat shook her head and reached down to the carpet to pick up a stray piece of plastic wrapping from the Disney stickers. "No, Freya's said she doesn't want to think about that yet. She wants to get this observation out of the way first ... and I totally agree." Kat felt the need to add the last bit.

"Well go and get her. I think it's about time we cracked open this bottle of bubbly. I know we're not celebrating, but we've worked damn hard today and we all need a good wind down."

Kat popped her head out into the lounge, but Freya wasn't there. "Oh, she must have taken the call outside. I'll give her a shout."

Lucy felt a pang of worry. Kat was the one person in this life who deserved true happiness. She looked at the slight anxiety in her telling blue eyes and prayed that Freya was the one to give it to her.

****

The apartment door was ajar and Kat paused. She didn't know why she paused, but she did. Maybe it was Freya's hushed voice; hushed, but audible. Kat willed herself to make a noise and call her in, but she didn't. She simply stood still and listened.

Freya was pacing the corridor. "No, it's been awful ..."
"Yes of course I'm trying ..."
"No ... No ... I'm not telling her ..."
"No, not yet ...."
"The timing's not right ..."
"You'd better not tell her ..."
"Yes of course I do ..."
"In my own time ..."
"Yes ..."
"Yes ..."
"I do ..."
"I do ..."
"I love you too."

Kat heard the approaching footsteps and rushed away from the door, skidding into the kitchen area. She flicked the switch on the oversized red kettle and froze, transfixed by the shining metal cooker hood.

Freya shut the apartment door and crept up behind her. "Any chance of a cup of tea and a chat? I'm so nervous about the observation tomorrow. I just don't want to muck it up." She rubbed Kat's back. "I can't imagine not being a teacher. I need your help, Kat. Could you talk me through it just once more?" She spun Kat around. "Please?"

Kat smiled gently, *what choice did she have?* "Of course I'll help. You'll be a wonderful teacher." She nodded towards Benny's new room. "I think they're finished with us now. So if you get the plan, we can go through it once again."

Freya smiled and turned towards their new double bedroom that was now completely overcrowded with their joint belongings. "What would I do without you?"

Kat caught her breath and held onto a tiny tear. *Only you know the answer to that one, Freya.*

CHAPTER TWENTY FIVE

The walk to school had been cold and quiet, but both blamed the other for nerves. The priority had to be the morning's observation, and both Kat and Freya understood its importance. Kat had accepted her duty and managed to put it first. Thoughts of the overheard conversation pushed far away to the back of her mind.

Now sitting at the back of her classroom, which was home to twenty eight Year Eight students, she peeped down at Elaine Springer's observation sheet. It appeared to be far more detailed than before. She glanced up at Freya who was now standing confidently at the front of the classroom, with a look of steely determination. Kat breathed a sigh of relief. The welcome and introduction had been calm, clear and in control.

Freya continued to address the class. "So, next month is..." She looked around and nodded.

A flurry of hands shot up. Freya signalled an eager looking girl sitting at the front.

"February, Miss."

"Yes, perfect. Next month is February and I'm not sure how many of you will know this, but February is LGBT history month." She tapped the red board marker against her bottom lip, this time she had ensured the lid was on securely. "Now, can anyone tell me what LGBT stands for?"

A flurry of hand shot back up.

Freya started to walk around the room. "Okay, Gracie, give me the L."

Gracie puffed up even further in her seat, thrilled that the new teacher already knew her name. "Lesbian, Miss."

"Great! And David, give me the G."

"Gay, Miss."

"Spot on! Who wants to try the B?" Freya craned her neck around the waving hands to the small boy sat at the back. "John, what does the B stand for?"

"Bisexual, Miss."

"Yep, and the T?" Freya looked around the classroom. "Jessie?"

"Trans, Miss, like transsexual, transgender or transvestite, Miss."

Elaine whispered to Kat. "How times have changed. Did you see there wasn't a single giggle."

Kat nodded, but then again, she hadn't been expecting one.

Freya clapped her hands. "Fantastic guys. Well, LGBT history month takes place in February and it celebrates the lives and achievements of the lesbian, gay, bisexual and trans community. Miss Spicer will be leading a whole school event that focuses on celebrating diversity, and you will be looking at this topic in many of your other subjects over the next few weeks." She paused. "But I wanted to start a couple of weeks early and give you guys a lesson on how LGBT people have contributed to our history."

A girl at the front tilted her head and spoke politely. "But why are we doing it in January, Miss, if LGBT history month is in February?"

Freya smiled. "Well unfortunately, I won't be here in February. I'm only on a four week placement and I have to go back to university to carry on with my course."

Nearly everyone in the class moaned. They had enjoyed having the enthusiastic new teacher starting their lessons, or finishing them, or even just crouching down at their tables and helping them with their work. She was very kind and always seemed to be smiling. "Gutted, Miss!" said the same girl, with a downturned mouth.

Freya paused. Their general reaction of disappointment had warmed her, but she didn't want to dwell. She needed to grab their attention, to get them excited. She addressed the whole class. "Well, let's start in the modern day. As a starter activity can anyone think of a famous person who will be looked back on by people in the future as someone who has made a difference to our LGBT history?"

The flurry of hands were back. "Lady Gaga," said an enthusiastic girl in the middle of the room.

"Okay, what has Lady Gaga done?"

The same girl answered. "Well she has started the Born This Way Foundation and she wants everyone to be confident in their own skin and she encourages people to accept others for who they are." The girl adjusted her bright pink glasses. "Her motto is to embrace difference and celebrate individuality."

"That's wonderful. Hasn't she got the most Twitter followers on the planet or something like that?" questioned Freya.

"Over twenty eight million." The girl was clearly a fan.

"Well isn't it wonderful that she's spreading such a fantastic message of support for people in the LGBT community." She could feel the connection with the class and they were all clamouring to speak. "Has anyone got anymore?"

A small boy near the front pushed his hand even higher. "Ellen DeGeneres."

"So, tell me what you know about Ellen then," said Freya, surprised.

He rolled his eyes. "My mum watches her every afternoon just before tea time and she always gets up from the sofa and does that silly dancing thing that Ellen does when the show starts." He paused. "Ellen's a much better dancer than my mum though!"

Freya laughed. "I know what you mean about the dancing. But tell me why people in the next generation may regard her as a person in history who has made a difference to LGBT rights."

He scratched his head. "I think I heard my mum say she was one of the first famous women in Hollywood to be open about her sexuality, and I think she's given other people the courage to do the same." He paused and clicked his fingers remembering the comment. "You can be gay *and* great at your job."

Elaine was scribbling away. She turned to Kat and whispered. "This is incredible. I really think some teachers fail to give kids enough credit. They're so aware and accepting of all of these issues nowadays, that soon this will be a complete non issue."

Kat smiled and whispered back. "I believe we're almost already there, Elaine."

"Well we will be if we have great teachers like Freya who deal with this in such a fantastic way."

Kat kept to a whisper. "The LGBT history month looks set to be a great success. I ran a preparation session with the staff last week and I think they grasped the two main aims."

"What are you focusing on?"

"One: that we have to be inclusive of diversity, and two: that we have to educate out prejudice."

Elaine shoved her pen into Kat's hand. "Write that down for me! That's great! I'll use that in my lectures!"

Kat smiled to herself, her beliefs once again confirmed. Times were changing and they were changing for the best. LGBT people were fast becoming a 'regular' part of lessons and the new wave of teachers and trainers were all singing from the same hymn sheet, to a tune of inclusion, diversity, tolerance and acceptance; and most of the older teachers were also joining in with heartfelt voices. She looked back up at Freya, who was glowing with confidence.

Freya was scanning the classroom and smiling. "Fab, who else?"

A girl from the back started talking. "Chaz Bono. Did you see him on Dancing With The Stars, Miss?"

Freya laughed. "I certainly did, and yes, he's made a difference. But tell me why."

The girl started to reel off the facts. "Chaz Bono is the son of that old singer, Cher. My Dad loves her, but she's old enough to be his granny. Anyway, he was born into a girl's body and a few years ago he put it all right again by having gender transition surgery. So now his body matches the person he really is. So I guess he's the first really famous person to be so open about it. That's why he'll be remembered."

Another boy piped up. "And there was that woman Nadia who won Big Brother. She was born in the wrong body too. People like that are role models for others going through the same thing."

Freya was nodding and questioning further and as Kat watched her animated expressions, she was filled with such pride. Freya had the class eating out of the palm of her hand.

Freya leaned against the solid wooden teacher's desk and lifted a stack of paperwork. "Now tell me, who's heard of Harvey Milk?"

A tall boy's hand shot up. "I saw the film, Miss."

Freya exaggerated a puzzled expression. "Hmm, I'm sure that was a fifteen, but shh, I won't tell anyone."

The tall boy smiled shyly. "It was a good film about the first openly gay man who got into politics."

"I'm impressed! So come on, how about Oscar Wilde?"

There were a couple of nods.

"Sappho?"

The class shook their heads.

Freya pointed at the objectives written clearly on the board. "Well it's our aim to look back through the ages and familiarise ourselves with the people who have made a difference to LGBT history."

A little girl put her hand up.

"Yes Molly?"

"Then at the end can we say who we think has made the biggest difference?"

Freya laughed. "You're a mind reader Molly! That's exactly what I want you to do."

The little girl spoke quietly. "Can I tell you mine now?"

Freya waved the pile of brightly coloured sheets with photos and jumbled biographies that the class had to match. "You might change your mind when you hear about all of these wonderful people."

The little girl smiled. "No I won't. Mine is the most wonderful."

Freya laughed warmly. "Come on then, Molly, who is it? Who do you think has made the biggest difference?"

The little girl turned to the back of the classroom. "It's Miss Spicer, of course."

****

Elaine waited for the final student to leave the classroom and watched as they got swallowed up by the steady stream of bodies flowing down the busy corridor. She called Freya to join them at the back. "You have a free period next don't you?"

Freya nodded, still slightly flushed from the exuberant throws of teaching.

"Great! Well, not that it really matters because this is going to be short and succinct."

Freya pulled up a plastic chair and caught Kat's smiling eye. "Okay."

Elaine wiggled her triangle shaped glasses and began. "You are clearly a natural teacher and that first observation must have been a blip."

Kat nodded, still worried that she had been to blame.

Elaine continued. "The lesson has been engaging, informative and well structured and *you*, the teacher, have made an exceptional impact on learning." She presented the evaluation sheet to Freya with a large tick in the Outstanding Lesson box.

Freya re-read the main points. She hadn't realised how much this would mean until now. "Thank you."

Elaine waved her away dismissively. "Don't thank me, you dafty! Thank your mentor."

Kat smiled kindly. "This was all her."

Freya grinned and placed the piece of paper back on the table. "I think we all know that's not true."

Elaine took both of their hands. "Well the bottom line is that you two are a great team. Ooo, could you imagine if you got a job here? Your department would be a force to be reckoned with!" She laughed loudly at Kat. "Not that I mean it's not now! I've seen the county statistics and you're off the scale." She squeezed their hands and sniggered. "But if you two were running the place, then who knows where you could take it." She laughed again, getting carried away with herself. "The stratosphere I expect. You pair really would be great here!"

Kat was unsure how long the hand holding would last, but for once she decided to just lose her inhibitions and go with it. "We sure would," she said, holding Freya's eyes.

Elaine picked up on the moment and gave one final hand squeeze. "Right, got to dash. I'm off to see Gaynor Newman next and good god that woman's a bore! She teaches like it's the Middle Ages!" She scraped her papers and pens with one swift swoop off the table and into her large open workbag, adjusted her triangle shaped glasses, and made a final leaving statement. "There should be a rule that teachers automatically fail to qualify if they insist on wearing ankle length floral skirts and high buttoned shirts that are sealed at the neck with a brooch."

Freya laughed out loud. She had never seen Gaynor Newman in anything other than an ankle length floral skirt, high buttoned shirt and neck brooch. "Good luck!" she shouted, as Elaine almost skipped out of the door.

"I'll need it," came the echoed reply.

Kat was bursting with pride. The lesson really had been sensational. She turned to Freya. "You were brillia-"

"Knock, knock!" Renee miraculously appeared in the open doorway, looking incredibly chic. She seemed to have a never ending supply of funky work clothes and today's offering was a fitted pinstripe trouser suit. Her long braided hair was tied up in a neat bun and no one could deny that she certainly looked the part. Kat looked away as she waltzed into the classroom. "I've just passed Elaine Springer. She did a thumbs up! How did you get on?"

Freya pushed her chair back away from the table. "You're not the only outstanding trainee in this school now, *biatch*!"

It was in times like these when Kat felt old. Since when had *biatch* been an acceptable form of address?

Renee plopped herself on a spare table. "I knew you would, that's why I got you..." She reached into her jacket pocket and withdrew a small pink card. "...this! Here you go, sweetie."

Freya stood up and leaned forwards to give her a hug. "Ah! Thank you." She opened it carefully and read the handwritten prose, pausing with a private smile. "Oh thanks, Renee. That means a lot."

Kat coughed. "Sorry, Renee, but we're not quite finished with the debrief."

Freya spun back around. "We are, aren't we?"

"Come on! She deserves the rest of this lesson off. She's just pulled it back from the brink of course dismissal!"

Kat looked at the pair of them and admitted defeat. If there was somewhere else that Freya would rather be, then she would rather she went. "Fine, off you go then."

Freya looked thrilled. "Really?"

"Yes, Freya. It's fine. I need to catch up with Diane anyway."

Renee wiggled her head. "Now *that* shows what a super mentor you are! Pulling *her* back from the brink!"

Kat stood up and frowned at Renee. "You know what? I think it's about time we had a little chat about the appropriate way in which you should speak to senior members of staff."

Renee burst out laughing and put her arm around Freya's shoulder, pulling her in close. "Hey, you're my best friend's missus! Of course I'm going to tease you!"

Kat watched in disbelief as the pair of them giggled off into the corridor. She didn't know what to do. *Was she being a stickler? Did she need to relax?* Freya's words shot back into her mind. *'The timing's not right ... I love you too.'* A wave of realisation came crashing down and she struggled to catch her breath. It had happened again. She had failed to see what was going on right in front of her nose. Why hadn't she reacted yesterday? Why had she ignored the obvious? Why had she tried to believe? She already knew the answer. She had wanted the fairy-tale.

She gently closed her classroom door and felt a numbness slowly cascade down her body. She walked into the store cupboard in the corner of the room and grabbed hold of a wooden shelf. A slow tear crept down her cheek and she bent her head into her arms. The old wooden door creaked closed and she stopped herself from pulling the frayed string light. The darkness was a comfort and the musty smell of shelves and worn text books served to calm her senses. She inhaled deeply and wanted to disappear. She lifted herself up with a long drawn breath and leaned back against a wooden pillar. As pain engulfed all of her senses she slid slowly down to the floor. She hugged her knees and bowed her head in the darkness. *This was it, her dream was over.*

The classroom door hit the metal filing cabinet and clattered loudly, jolting her back into consciousness. She heard their giggled laughter and pulled herself into a tighter ball on the dusty floor. The voices were clear. The voices were unafraid. The voices didn't care who might be listening.

Renee spoke first. "She's not here. Don't you mind that she spends so much of her time with Pouty Pity?"

Freya was clearly animated. "Do I get jealous? Of Miss Pity? No, of course not!"

Renee was laughing. "No you're right. It's true what they say. A jealous girlfriend is a faithful girlfriend. If you don't get jealous when someone has her attention, it's because someone has yours."

Kat heard the sound of Freya hitting Renee's shoulder. "Shhh! Will you be quiet!"

It sounded like Renee was doing the running man. "And I got your attention, baby!"

Freya was laughing again. "Will you pack it in! I've never met anyone quite like you!"

The sound of a chair being scraped across the floor sent shivers down Kat's spine. Someone had just sat down.

Renee was loud. "I know! I'm one of a kind. Tell me more. Tell me more! What have I got that others haven't?"

Kat put her hands over her ears, but the voices were too clear.

Renee was probing. "What do you love the best?"

Freya was giggling and Kat could picture Renee striking a pose. "I have to give you a point for sense of humour."

Renee was huffing and feigning outrage. "What about my kissing skills? You said I was the best person you had ever kissed."

Kat's heart shattered completely and she gasped out in pain.

The chair scraped again. Renee must now be standing, edging closer to Freya no doubt.

"Come on. Kiss me here. On her desk. You promised, remember?"

Kat hugged herself tightly, aching from the hurt, feeling like she was sinking, deeper and deeper.

Freya was still laughing. "I'm not kissing you on her desk."

Renee was getting closer. "Okay, let's go to the toilets again."

"No!" The laughed response wasn't convincing.

"Come on, you know you love it in the toilets. We could christen the ones next to Block A."

Freya had paused. "Hang on a minute."

"What are you afraid of? You seem pretty adventurous to me! Wink, wink, nudge nudge!"

Freya's volume was raised. "Whoa, whoa, whoa. Listen up, Missy!"

"I love it when you talk dirty!"

"Seriously now. Listen to me. I'm not kissing you in the toilets again-"

Kat was shaking with tears.

"You know you want to."

Freya's tone changed completely. "I'm not kissing you in the toilets again, because I have never kissed you in the toilets! You tried to snog me *once* in the toilets when I was drunk beyond belief and I can't believe you're still going on about it now!"

"Alright! Alright!"

Freya was getting louder. "No, it's not alright. I'm going to say this once more. You started this, and now I'm asking you to stop it. You need to pack it in right away!"

"Alright!"

"Seriously. You shouldn't have done it in the first place and you shouldn't have turned it into this joke, which is quite frankly really starting to bore me."

"Kat's not around."

"I don't care if she's around or not. I want you to stop it." She paused. "And anyway, Kat knows everything."

Renee quietened her tone. "She knows?"

"Of course she does! She's my girlfriend and I love her and I don't keep anything from her."

"What, even the toilets?"

"Yes, that one, easily forgettable moment in the toilets ... and all of your stupid messages over Christmas."

Renee seemed bruised. "What did you do that for?"

Freya was loud, clear and sure of herself. "Because I love her and guess what, she loves me ... and she trusts me."

Renee was suddenly quiet. "And she took me on, knowing that I made a pass at you?"

"Yes, she fucking did! Because she's the nicest, kindest, most caring woman there is, and she puts a little shit like you to shame!"

"Alright! No need for that!"

Something had snapped inside and there was no stopping her. "Well there is if it gets the message through! You're a laugh, but pack it in now. I'm fed up with your innuendos and smart remarks. You could never, ever, compete with someone like Kat."

"Seriously?"

"Yes, seriously."

Kat heard the chair being lifted back into place under the table. "Fine then. Point taken. You could have broken it to me gently though."

"I have! Numerous times, but you just keep going on, and yes, I admit it was funny maybe the first time, but not anymore. Seriously, Renee, just get over it will you?"

"I'm over it! I apologise and I'll catch you later ... but just so you know I was only pissing around." The footsteps headed away towards the classroom door. "Don't go flattering yourself."

"I won't," shouted Freya as the classroom door slammed shut.

Kat heard the bang and held her breath. She waited. Freya didn't appear to be moving. Five minutes passed, but there was still no movement. The tears had stopped and the shaking had calmed, but the emotional turmoil was far from over. Kat slowly rose to her feet and pushed open the store cupboard door. Freya was sitting at her teacher's desk, tightly holding a bundle of leaflets.

Kat coughed quietly.

Freya spun around and looked at her in confusion. "Kat? What are you doing? You're filthy!"

Kat looked down at her black trousers now covered with dust and shrugged her shoulders. "I don't care."

Freya stood up quickly and walked towards her. "How long have you been in there?"

"Long enough."

"What's going on?" She looked at Kat's blue eyes, surrounded by puffy red skin. "Shit! Have you been crying?"

Kat stood still. "I thought we were over. I heard you. I heard you on the phone."

"On the phone? When?"

"Yesterday, when you were in the hall."

Freya pulled her by the hand back over to the wooden desk. "Well the time wasn't right yesterday. But it is today. I wasn't being rude earlier. I just wanted to get away so I could nip to the staffroom and grab these." She lifted up the leaflets. "I came straight back up and you weren't here."

Kat stood still.

Freya bent down and dusted Kat's trousers. "It seems like you were doing some tidying in the store cupboard! I'm so sorry if I've been a bit distant. I was just so worried about that observation. But now it's all done, I wanted to show you these." She smiled and pushed the leaflets into Kat's hands.

Kat still didn't move. "I thought I'd lost you. I thought you were leaving me." She shook her head. "You don't want me, Freya. I'm damaged. I'm so insecure that the smallest thing knocks me completely off balance." Tears were forming once again in her eyes. "Seeing you up here with Renee, flirting and laughing at the hot kisses you shared-"

"She tried to kiss me, once!"

"It doesn't matter. I can't handle it. Look at you. You're perfect. You're going to have so many people trying to kiss you." She looked at the floor. "You can do so much better than me."

Freya pushed the leaflets harder into Kat's hands. "Will you just look at these!"

Kat slowly lifted the bundle and read the bold writing. *'Modern two bedroom house, views of Sutton park, perfect for first time buyers.'* She looked back up into Freya's expectant green eyes. "But these are homes to buy."

Freya's green eyes twinkled. "I know."

Kat could hardly talk. "But that's such a huge commitment." She swallowed deeply. "You're ... You're ready to buy? With me?"

Freya nodded in earnest. "Of course I am! Listen to me will you? You're the most sensational woman I have ever met. Maybe I just assumed that you knew! How can anyone like you ever feel insecure? I'm constantly wondering what you see in me!" She sighed lightly. "You *must* open up though. You must tell me about your ex."

Kat shrugged. "But that's just it. I don't want it to change how you treat me. I'm the one with the problem here-"

Freya cut in. "No. I've been insensitive. I didn't realise how this stupid bit of nonsense with Renee was getting to you. I should have been more thoughtful."

"You were just having a laugh I guess."

"But I can see now, it's not funny at all." She grinned. "I'm a quick learner though." She squeezed the leaflets in Kat's hands. "Will you look at them again? Dad's been pushing me to tell you, but the timing's not been quite right. He was on the phone yesterday going on about it, insisting I tell you. They want to pay our deposit. You won't believe how much they've given us."

"You really want us to buy a place together?" Kat still couldn't believe what she was saying.

"Well that's first on the list, yes," she grinned, "before marriage and children and-"

Kat dropped the leaflets and reached for Freya's face, holding it gently, and kissing her with passion.

Freya pulled back and looked into those deep blue eyes. "I love you, Miss Spicer, and I promise I'll love you forever."

Kat paused. She had no words, so she simply kissed her right back.

"Gotcha!" The hulk of Chianne Granger filled the doorway. "You might have got away with touching me up, Miss Spicer, but you ain't getting away with this. I don't care how good a teacher you are."

Kat turned around to see the little red light flashing on top of Chianne Granger's state of the art mobile phone.

"Molesting a trainee teacher. Tut, tut, tut, who's been a bad girl!"

Kat held Freya even closer. "You know what, Chianne, right at this moment I couldn't give a flying fuck what happened to my teaching career."

"Ai, ai, and I've got you swearing at a pupil as well!"

Kat turned back to Freya. "All that matters is what's right here in front of me."

Freya looked anxious. "She's got that shitty site. She'll upload the video."

"Let her," said Kat holding her tight.

Freya gazed across in amazement. "You'd give up your teaching career for me?"

Kat smiled. "Every, single, day."

Chianne kept the camera still. This footage was priceless.

"What are you doing, Chianne?" sneered Diane Pity, popping her head into the classroom and nosing at the commotion.

"Nice one, Miss!" barked Chianne. "Glad you're here. You hate this pair of weirdos as much as I do."

Diane looked up at Kat and Freya now standing in front of the board, staring into each other's eyes like it was the first time they'd met. She looked back at the phone. "What have you got, Chianne?"

Chianne lifted the mobile and played back the footage. "You're watching the end of Super Teacher Spicer."

Diane cackled, amazed at the clip. "Great footage!" She paused. "But won't you need Miss Spicer to help you pass your exams?"

Chianne whistled through her big buck teeth. "Ha! I could get an A if I had Miss fucking Fag teaching me."

Diane pulled the phone closer and laughed. "You're right. So long Spicer!" She turned to Chianne and touched her tongue against her bright red lipstick. "Show me once more. I want to relish every moment."

Chianne had had enough of Miss *I want to save your soul* Spicer and her constant quest to discover the real her. She knew exactly who she was and she was proud of it; she was rotten, spoilt, a bad egg, one of those little shits that would never be saved because they were deliberately trying to drown. That was her, that was Chianne and she just didn't give a fuck. She proudly passed the phone to Miss Pity. "Just press play there." She pointed again. "No, there." She tried to grab the phone. "No! .... Shit! ... What are you doing? No ... give it back ... No ... that's the delete." She roared. "You've deleted it?! You've fucking deleted it."

Diane looked up at Kat and smiled. "It's gone."

Chianne kicked the door and added another dent to the collection. "Are you having some sort of fucking threesome? This fucking school!" She clomped out into the corridor and thumped the plastic notice board. "I fucking hate this fucking school! Bunch of fucking lesbo weirdos!"

Kat stepped forwards. "Diane?"

Diane fingered her bleach blonde hair. "I was thinking about how to repay you for your kindness with my work." She pushed out her chest and spun to leave. "I think we'll call that quits."

CHAPTER TWENTY SIX

Two Years Later:

Lucy, Ben, Jess and Gary huddled on the modern sofa in Kat and Freya's equally modern home, hushing each other as the phone finally rang.

Benny bent down to Daisy who had been clomping around like a noisy toddler and lifted a quiet finger to her lips. "Daisy needs to be a good girl. Aunty Freya needs quiet for the telephone call."

Lucy gave him the thumbs up.

Benny gave a thumbs up back. "Don't worry, Mummy ... Daisy will be a good girl for Big Benny."

Ben smiled. "Good lad. Now let's all be very quiet."

Benny nodded. "Okay, Daddy."

Freya clicked the loud speaker button. "Hello?"

Kat's voice sounded out loud and clear. "Hello, is that Freya Elton?"

"It is."

"Hi Freya. It's Kat Spicer, Head of History at Coldfield Comprehensive."

"Hi!"

Jess and Lucy tried desperately not to giggle.

"Thank you for coming in to interview for the post of full time history teacher today. I would like you to know that both the Head Teacher and the Governors from the panel this afternoon think that you would be a perfect addition to the history department here at Coldfield."

"Okay."

Kat continued. "On that basis, we would like to offer you the job."

The room burst into cheers and rapturous applause.

"Okay, thank you!"

"Are you able to accept the position?"

Freya screeched into the receiver. "Too bloody right I am, lover girl! Now get yourself and your fit arse back home. This is going to be one hell of a party!"

Kat turned to the Chair of Governors. "Miss Elton has politely accepted the position."

The End

About the author:

Lambda Literary Award finalist and Polari First Book Prize judge, Kiki Archer is the UK-based author of ten best-selling, award-winning novels. Kiki ranked highly on the Guardian newspaper's Pride Power List and the Diva Pride Power List in 2017, 2018 and 2019.

Her debut novel *But She Is My Student* won the UK's 2012 SoSoGay Best Book Award. Its sequel *Instigations* took just 12 hours from its release to reach the top of the Amazon lesbian fiction chart.

Binding Devotion was a finalist in the 2013 Rainbow Awards.

One Foot Onto The Ice broke into the American Amazon contemporary fiction top 100 as well as achieving the lesbian fiction number ones. The sequel *When You Know* went straight to number one on the Amazon UK, Amazon America, and Amazon Australia lesbian fiction charts, as well as number one on the iTunes, Smashwords, and Lulu Gay and Lesbian chart.

Too Late... I Love You won the National Indie Excellence Award for Best LGBTQ Book, the Gold Global eBook Award for Best LGBT Fiction. It was a Rainbow Awards Finalist and received an Honourable Mention.

Lost In The Starlight was a finalist in the 2017 Lambda Literary Awards' Best Lesbian Romance category and was named a Distinguished Favourite in the Independent Press Awards.

A Fairytale Of Possibilities won Best Romance Novel at the 2017 Diva Literary Awards and was awarded a Distinguished Favourite in the New York Big Book Awards.

The Way You Smile was a finalist in the National Indie Excellence Awards for Best LGBTQ Book.

Kiki was crowned the Ultimate Planet's Independent Author of the Year in 2013 and she received an Honourable Mention in the 2014 Author of the Year category.

She won Best Independent Author and Best Book for *Too Late... I Love You* in the 2015 Lesbian Oscars and was a Finalist in the 2017 Diva250 Awards for Best Author.

In 2018 Kiki won Best Author at the Waldorf's star-studded Diva Awards.

Say You'll Love Me Again is Kiki's 10th and final novel.

Novels by Kiki Archer:

BUT SHE IS MY STUDENT - March 2012

INSTIGATIONS - August 2012

BINDING DEVOTION - February 2013

ONE FOOT ONTO THE ICE - September 2013

WHEN YOU KNOW - April 2014

TOO LATE… I LOVE YOU - June 2015

LOST IN THE STARLIGHT - September 2016

A FAIRYTALE OF POSSIBILITIES - June 2017

THE WAY YOU SMILE - November 2018

SAY YOU'LL LOVE ME AGAIN - June 2019

Connect with Kiki:

www.kikiarcherbooks.com
Twitter: @kikiarcherbooks
www.youtube.com/kikiarcherbooks
www.instagram.com/kikiarcherbooks

Printed in Great Britain
by Amazon